# IMPROVING THE SILENCE

# IMPROVING
# THE SILENCE

Peter Turnbull

severn House

This first world edition published 2009
in Great Britain and 2010 in the USA by
SEVERN HOUSE PUBLISHERS LTD of
9–15 High Street, Sutton, Surrey, England, SM1 1DF.
Trade paperback edition published
in Great Britain and the USA 2010 by
SEVERN HOUSE PUBLISHERS LTD

British Library Cataloguing in Publication Data

Turnbull, Peter, 1950–
    Improving the Silence.
    1. Police murders–Fiction. 2. Police corruption–Fiction.
    3. Detective and mystery stories.
    I. Title
    823.9'14-dc22


ISBN-13: 978-0-7278-6841-1     (cased)
ISBN-13: 978-1-84751-184-3     (trade paper)

*All Severn House titles are printed on acid-free paper.*


Typeset by Palimpsest Book Production Ltd.,
Grangemouth, Stirlingshire, Scotland.
Printed and bound in Great Britain by
MPG Books Ltd., Bodmin, Cornwall.

'Do not speak unless, by doing so,
you improve upon the silence.'

Spanish proverb

# ONE

The man who stopped to pick up acorns, pot them and nurture them into oak saplings prior to planting in a permanent location, found himself once again drawn back to the location. It was a constant tug, and a powerful pull, akin to a magnetic force which cannot be resisted and therefore must, eventually, be responded to, as if summoned by a Deity. It was akin, he felt, to the force which once pulled him, for that was the only word he could think of to use to describe the sensation, into a church he happened to be walking past at the time and which he had no prior intention of entering. That selfsame force had then compelled him to kneel in the pews as his mind seemed to lift from his body, although he could not get 'there', wherever 'there' was, but he had experienced the sensation of his mind rising. He had eventually stood and walked back to the door of the church to find that the verger and guardian had been patiently and silently waiting for him so that they could close and lock the building for the remainder of the day. He had never again felt such a tug into a church but the memory stayed with him. He doubted even that he could ever find that particular church again, for the incident had taken place in Leicester on the day that he visited the city to attend the civil wedding of a friend, never having been there before, and thus far, never having returned.

On this particular day, the pull, the tug, the magnetic draw, was once again similarly irresistible to the force which had once guided him into the church in Leicester, but far from being an experience of spiritual uplift, it had a darker, much, much darker resonance. So far as he knew, he was the only one of them who visited the scene, though he went seldom, once every few months perhaps, and always went alone, but whenever he felt the urge, or heard the call to return, he would always answer it, and do so as soon as was practical. Often it was the same day, and no matter what the weather, either in the uncomfortable heat of high summer, or the cold and the damp of deep midwinter. He had never fought to resist the urge, he had never wanted to resist it, and so whenever the call came to visit that particular corner of the forest he would respond. Always.

The route he took to reach the location never varied, and it was in fact the most convenient, and the most direct. Leaving his car at the pub he walked the half mile along the narrow path beside the campsite, making, and enjoying, observations of flora and fauna. The only building in the area was the brick-built blockhouse of toilets and washing facilities for the people using the campsite. Caravans were in one field, and tents in another, but both caravanners and hardier campers accessed the same facilities, with its twin entrances, left-hand entrance for men, right-hand entrance for women. The two fields were separated by a line of shrubs and the occasional tree which followed the route of a brook. The man noted that the field used by the campers was pitted with small holes excavated in the turf by the more experienced, permitting them to lay and sleep on their side more comfortably, their hips being accommodated by the cavity.

The man tended to feel the tug to the location midweek, for no reason that he could determine, but because of this he was usually able to avoid making the journey when the site was well populated with weekend campers and caravanners. Occasionally there were both few tents and few caravans, for over the years the man had observed that while caravans were drier and more comfortable and spacious than tents, it still takes good weather to make the majority of owners tow their vans to the site. If he felt the command to visit the location in the depths of winter he would trek beside empty fields with neither tent nor caravan in view. Just him alone, often in all-enveloping silence and no movement save for a dark line of geese against a grey sky uncoiling like a whip, as if also drawn by some invisible force.

But on this day it was summer, the June of the year. It had thus far been a wet June with more, much more rainfall than was normal and it had also been chilly, noticeably cooler than the month was wont to be. When he approached the location he saw that the site was thinly occupied by 'mid-weekers', retired folk in the main, so it seemed to him, content to sit on canvas chairs outside their vans, wearing a woollen pullover, reading thick novels with glossy covers, often accompanied by very small dogs who sat patiently at their feet. The man walked on the tenting side of the brook and noticed there to be fewer than usual tents, and of those that were there, most had their doors tied shut, the owners presumably away hiking in the forest. One or two larger tents had awnings which, as with the caravans, housed men and women in their silver years sitting on camp chairs reading, playing chess or slumbering. As he passed, those that were awake nodded and smiled at him perhaps, he thought, because he was taken for one of them with his casual but durable clothing. It is not like the southern English to smile at, or even acknowledge, a stranger unless seen as a kindred spirit. He was also like many of the campers, obviously at early retirement age and that, he felt, further explained the occasional smile or brief nod: another survivor, another one who had made it through. Well done you, matey.

Beyond the tents was the wood, which was part of Epping Forest to the north-east of London, once a vast forest reaching towards Cambridge but now reduced in the greater part to a narrow strip of woodland between Chingford in the south to Epping itself, some seven miles to the north. It was still large enough to lose oneself in, large enough for lovers to hide away, but a shadow, a fraction of its former vastness. It was surrounded by other smaller stands of woodland, but all were once part of the great forest which was previously known as Waltham Forest. The forest being renamed, so far as the man understood, in the mid-seventeenth century. He stepped from the open tenting area into the shade of the foliage canopy of the trees, appearing to be just another camper, just another man enjoying a day in the country, just a day out of London and the hurly-burly.

He walked as he always did, to *the* tree, that tree, with a wide stubbly trunk and a root system which he always felt were more like horizontal trunks half hidden in the soil than they were like roots, before plunging down into the thin gravelly soil that had helped preserve the wood from agriculture. That selfsame tree he had once come across as a youth when in the company of a spirited Australian girl, and she not seeming to notice the rising and diving roots which angled up from the base of the tree said, 'Wow, yes, wow', as he had pointed it out to her. She had then confessed that she would have needed 'a shot of mescaline' to appreciate so striking an image that that particular plant afforded. Sparing a thought for the girl of his youth and wondering whatever became of her, he walked on, deeper into the woodland and then noticed how unusually full of people the wood seemed to be. People stood silently amid the trees here and there in ones and twos and sometimes a small group huddled as if in fear. It was then that he more than sensed, he realized, that they knew something he did not, as if the people had come from the campsite as news of an incident had spread by word of mouth.

Then he saw the blue and white police tape strung from tree to tree, and the white inflatable tent beyond the tape.

The man's steady heart seemed to miss a beat as it thumped within his chest. His stomach seemed to sink sharply as he stopped walking. A police constable in a short-sleeved white shirt and dark serge trousers stood firmly holding his ground in front of the tape, with arms folded in front of him and a humourless 'they-shall-not-pass' countenance. The man did not go any nearer the tape but moved to a couple who stood a few feet away and asked them what had happened.

'Found a body,' the man said.

'Really?'

'Yes, skeleton though, so not a recent burial . . . just by chance.'

'Just by chance?' the man repeated.

'Yes, putting a pipe through the forest.' The woman spoke for the first time. She had a high-pitched voice, almost a whine, thought the man, a voice which he would find very difficult to live with, although, at that point, it was the least of his concerns.

'So we're told,' the man continued, 'the navvies came running out of the trees asking to borrow a mobile phone. Two feet to one side or the other and they would have missed it, so they said. The body was laid in such a way that it was parallel to the trench.'

'Could be anyone,' the woman sniffed. 'I mean, any age. Dick Turpin used to rob folk around these parts.'

'Yes,' the man, her husband, added, 'the old stand and deliver number . . . your money or your life, but he never rode that old horse of his . . . what was her name?'

'Black Bess,' the woman said absent-mindedly, 'she was called Black Bess.'

'Yes . . . huge mare . . . but she never did Epping to York in a day and a night, that's a right old myth. I saw a programme on the tele; they reckoned that the strongest horse couldn't do the journey in under three days, nearer four. So you can scratch that myth.'

But then the man was walking away, utterly unconcerned about the story of Dick Turpin and Black Bess. He walked out of the trees to a remote part of the tenting field and as soon as he was certain that he was not able to be overheard, he took his mobile from his jacket pocket and jabbed a series of numbers with fumbling fingers. When his call was answered he said, 'It's me, Tom, they've found the body. They've found him.'

Silence. There was no response from the person on the other end of the line. Just silence.

A very, very loud silence.

John Ernest Archibald Shaftoe called himself by the plain name of John Shaftoe and an observer might see him as being of plain appearance. He was broad shouldered, barrel-chested, squat and balding. He had a stubby nose set in a round face which, of late, had taken to reddening rapidly when he exerted himself. He had a thick neck and short but powerful legs. He would perhaps be assumed, by his image, to be a deep-seam, pigeon-fancying Yorkshire miner, which his late father had in fact been. John Shaftoe blended perfectly on the top deck of a bus anywhere east of Aldgate, south of Walthamstow and west of Dagenham. He was a man who was most at home in the tap room of The World Turned Upside Down on the Old Kent Road, or indeed any similar pub in the East End of London. John Shaftoe stepped into the inflatable tent, heavy with the aroma of freshly tilled soil, and turned warmly to the white-shirted constable within, 'One day they'll install air conditioning in these things.'

'Yes, sir,' the young constable replied with a broad grin,

as a bead of perspiration ran down the side of his head. 'It would be more than welcome, sir.'

Shaftoe considered the hole and the contents therein. He saw a neatly excavated pit and a skeleton lying at the bottom of it. 'Male,' he announced, 'adult male. This is a deep grave, it must be about five feet . . . or a metre and a half in new-speak.'

'We measured one metre and forty centimetres,' the plain-clothed officer who was also in the tent offered. 'But yes, we thought it was a deep burial as burials go, Epping Forest being the burial ground for London villainy for the last hundred years or so.'

'One forty,' John Shaftoe smiled a self-congratulatory smile. 'I can call that an outer bull. My eye is still good when it comes to assessing distance, but yes, this is a very deep shallow grave, as shallow graves are wont to go. Someone did not want this man found . . . and half on his side, one arm wrapped under the body, the other folded over his spine, one leg bent, the other straight.' Shaftoe placed his Gladstone bag on the ground and unzipped the front of his white, lightweight coverall tunic. 'Can hardly breathe in here,' he muttered. 'Damn good idea these tents. Like all good ideas it is simple and efficient, but air conditioning would be useful at times, at times like days like this. Well, unceremoniously buried, fully on their front or fully on their back would indicate ceremony and care, possibly in obser-vance of ancient customs and or beliefs, but he, poor soul, looks like he was rolled into his grave and then covered up. So first impressions are that of a suspicious death.'

'When, sir?' The plain-clothed officer pressed. 'As you know, any more than seventy years ago and we can wrap it up now, less than seventy years ago is the beginning of some-thing else.'

'Yes, as you say, Sergeant Vicary, I am aware of the seventy year cut-off point, but let's not be hasty, let's not rush our fences. You see, the depth of the grave suggests a recent burial, possibly in excess of seventy years, but historically speaking, still quite recent. You see, once I took part in an archaeological dig in mid-Wales. There were two bodies, male and female, buried just two or three feet below the

surface, and both had been buried face down. The historian
at the dig, fella called Mountjoy of the University of Wales,
he told us that the face down burial was probably because
of the Druid belief that if an evil person was buried face
down, then their spirit would not rise and walk the earth. So
what we had there was an Iron Age Hindley and Brady, or
a Bonnie and Clyde, who had been brought to justice and
laid in their graves in the manner prescribed by contempo-
rary law. But here, here, no indication of any such ritual, so
it is unlikely to be an ancient grave and the pit itself is more
than could be dug by flint axes. I think you'd need pretty
good kit to get this far down in the hours of darkness. So I
am afraid it's looking like work for you, Sergeant Vicary.'

'Don't mind that at all, sir.' Vicary brushed a fly away
from his face. 'There's just not enough hours in the day
anyway, so one more case won't make a dent and if it does
not amount to be a murder of interest to us, then we have
more than enough work to be getting on with.'

'Imagine you do, in fact you and me both. Well, as you
see, there's nothing around the skeleton to suggest a recent
corpse, no plastic buttons, no metal zip fasteners, no trace of
footwear or any other form of clothing, all rotted away or he
was naked when he was buried. Summer burial though . . .'

'You think so, sir?'

'Well, I find it difficult to envisage this hole; I mean a hole
of this magnitude, being dug one night in midwinter when
the ground would be frozen solid. Sorry, just me ruminating,
just ruminating aloud. Well there is nothing I can do now . .
. not here. So, if you have taken all the photographs you need,
you can have the skeleton lifted. Do try to get it all out in
one piece if you can, though the stronger sinews will hold
the long bones together. The more recent the skeleton is, the
stronger the sinews will be, but I'll leave that to you.' John
Shaftoe walked out of the inflatable tent and breathed deeply,
savouring the clean forest air, the birdsong, the blue sky
glimpsed through the green and gently swaying leaf canopy.
He had read once that a dying man can find beauty in a blade
of grass and he felt a sudden alarm that he too now could,
at his relatively early age, detect said beauty from said selfsame source. It was also quite true, he thought, so, so true

that a little learning can be a dangerous thing. The reddening of his complexion when exerting himself, the sharp twinges in his chest which he experienced from time to time were symptoms he would prefer not to be noticing in himself, especially when he was still shy of the half century.

He glanced to his left and saw the navvies who had found the skeleton and the small yellow excavating machine that they had used to dig the trench. The navvies stood next to the machine smoking cigarettes. Stripped to the waist, each man, it seemed to John Shaftoe, was possessed of a huge beer belly that hung grossly over a thick leather belt which held up their mud-caked denims. They were excited, and it seemed, quite happy to be paid for standing in a group chatting and smoking cigarettes, there evidently being no other job that their foreman could set them to do. John Shaftoe turned to his right and saw a crowd of people standing behind the blue and white police tape which, in turn, was guarded by a lone constable in a white shirt and serge trousers. The onlookers seemed to Shaftoe to be mainly middle-aged. Curious youth, he observed, was noticeably absent, and so they behaved in a sombre-minded and deferential manner. He then noticed one man, beyond the onlookers, but similarly middle-aged, walking away, across an open area beyond the treeline talking into his mobile phone, doubtless, thought Shaftoe, telling the news of what he had seen. It was, conceded Shaftoe, the sort of news which had legs: it would travel far and do so rapidly.

Rosalind Parsloe watered the plants which in small terracotta pots lined the windowsills of all the downstairs rooms, placed there, and in such numbers upon her husband's insistence, because after a big dog and a gravel drive, both of which they had, a line of potted plants along the windowsill of the downstairs windows is the best burglar deterrent that can be had. As she watered she glanced up as her eye was caught by the sight of her husband striding in what she thought was an agitated manner across the lawn which, recently cut, was a clear pattern of alternating dark and light shaded strips. Just as he liked it. Just as he insisted it should be. He walked from the lawn into the green painted gazebo that stood at the bottom left-hand corner of the rear garden, nestling upon a rockery, snug in the right angle created by the tall privet hedge at the side of the garden and the equally tall privet hedge at the bottom of their garden.

It was the phone call.

It could, she knew, only be because of the phone call.

She had known that there was something about that phone call. It had come at a strange time of day, just at 11.00 a.m., and while it sounded like any other phone call to the house, it had also, somehow, an insistent quality about it. A personal phone call itself was strange, most messages from friends being received by electronic mail, but yet it had been an acquaintance, not a telesales cold call, because her husband had listened to the content of the call and he had then quickly put the phone down without saying anything and had done so clumsily, as if angered, for she had heard the handset clatter against the phone. A few seconds later, he had marched out of the house; his gait strong, purposeful, heavy and sure-footed, directly to the gazebo where he had opened the door, entered, and had shut the door behind him. In this heat, she thought the air inside the glass and wood building must be close to unbreathable but yet he had still shut the door behind him.

Rosalind Parsloe put the small brown interior watering can down on the floor beneath the windowsill and looked at the gazebo into which her husband had retreated, dressed as he always was, immaculate, even when 'dressed down' in casual clothes as he was on that day, as if modelling the clothes for a mail order catalogue. Her husband had always kept himself well groomed and he and she in their youth had made such a handsome pair, both tall and slender, so much so that people would instinctively step out of their way when they walked along the pavement. Both had 'worn well' so their friends told them, even despite her bearing three children. She too was well dressed but more upon her husband's insistence rather than her taste, and in a light-weight summer dress, not being in possession of slacks or jeans. It had been a stricture upon the commencement of her married life that, 'you will not see me in a skirt, and I will not see you in trousers'. The purchase and wearing of a pair of Levi's 501's had thus become an ambition for her expected widowhood.

Her mother had told her that upon marriage she must prepare herself for widowhood and so Rosalind Parsloe had made plans, which she kept to herself, for that time. She would have money, an excellent pension that her husband had worked for and for which, in order to support him, she had abandoned her own career. Her plans included a pair of jeans and a holiday in Scotland, which her husband had steadfastly refused to visit because, 'I've locked up enough of those drunks to know what it's like up there. Even their vomit smells different,' and so in the meantime all she could do was to read about places with mystical names and which are steeped in history, places like Bannockburn, Glencoe, the Great Glen, Loch Ness, the Black Isle, which is not an island, and, of course, the Isle of Skye with which she had been fascinated since learning the 'Skye Boat Song' when in primary school. She would carry out those plans over a period of a few summers when she was on her own and when, if she retained her figure, she would wear jeans every day.

She believed that she could not fault her husband, after accepting the fact that all men are difficult to live with, because he had been an excellent provider and her house had always been a peaceful house because rules had been set and had been enforced. Her husband was a man who just liked to have his own way and her reward for accepting the rule that if two people ride a horse then one has to ride behind, was her lovely house in St John's Wood and their chateau in France, just on the other side of the Channel, and so not a prestigious part of France but still France and still a second home, and still theirs. She felt that she had much by means of compensation for never having any say in where they would holiday, being limited in the clothes she could wear and the diet they ate. She had been a wife of thirty years and she knew her husband, and that midsummer's morning she knew her husband was a troubled man, and she knew the trouble had come suddenly, unexpectedly, via the content of a very brief phone call.

Rosalind Parsloe walked out of the lounge of her house and into the hallway which at that moment was heavy with the smell of furniture polish liberally applied by Nancy, their Afro-Caribbean 'daily', who knelt as she worked, often humming softly to herself. Rosalind Parsloe exited the house via the scullery beyond the kitchen and stepped into the dazzling sunlight on to the patio which already baked in the sun. Half closing her eyes against the glare of the sun she stepped out on to the lawn, crossing it silently in her sandals. She slowed as she approached the gazebo noticing that her husband had fully shut the door as if cocooning himself, as if shutting the world out of his den.

She walked softly up to the door and tapped on the pane of glass. He didn't respond. Rosalind Parsloe decided then to open the door even though she risked being barked at for disturbing him. Her movement was slow and sensitive and when the anticipated snarl didn't come, she entered the hut, finding it difficult to breathe inside as she had expected it would be. She stood for a moment in the doorway. Still he did not respond. She looked at her husband and remarked silently that the years had also been good to him, a face slightly fuller than when they had first met but still handsome, still tall, still muscular, with a physique that would be the envy of many a twenty-year-old. 'Piers?' She probed softly, 'Piers, is there anything wrong? Who was that on the phone just now?'

'Nobody. It wasn't anybody.' He spoke quietly, as if deep in thought. She thought it was the reply of a man who was preoccupied, but more than that, it was, she felt, an evasive reply, transparently evasive. He had picked up the phone, listened, not made any reply, replaced the handset heavily, then had stormed across the rear lawn and had shut himself in the gazebo, but it was 'nobody' on the phone.

Rosalind Parsloe knew that in this case 'nobody' meant 'someone very significant' and it probably also meant 'somebody I didn't want to hear from – at least not with news like that'. His reply also meant 'don't ask any questions'.

'Well,' she turned to go, 'I am going to do lunch now . . . fish salad . . . it'll be ready in quarter of an hour. If you wish I can put yours in the fridge.'

'Yes,' Piers Parsloe replied softly, 'do that. Put mine in the fridge, I'll collect it later . . . I'll come in later.'

\* \* \*

Gaylord Midnight did what his Auntie Blossom told him to
do. He wrote to his mother in Montego Bay. He told her
about school. He told her about the weather in London. He
said he hoped he would see her soon. He bought the stamps
from the money he had and posted the letter at the post office
so it would get there quicker. About five days to get there
said the Post Mistress, same time for the reply to return. Ten
days later an envelope came addressed to him from Jamaica.
Inside was his letter returned unopened. That same day he
went out and bought the sharpest blade he could and went
looking for a victim. He found one, a white baby in a pram
which had been left outside a shop. He slashed the infant
across the face many times and ran, flinging the blade away
as he did so.

John Shaftoe rested his fleshy hands with their short, stubby
nail-bitten fingers on the edge of the stainless-steel table that
had a one inch 'lip' round the edge and was supported by a
single hollow upright leg, which served the secondary purpose
of a drain so as to permit any blood that might spill from a
recently deceased corpse to be easily disposed of. He paused
as he surveyed the skeleton excavated from Epping Forest
earlier that day. He then adjusted the angle poise arm which
hung above the table, fixed to the ceiling, so that the microphone attached to it was level with his mouth. He was obliged
to pull the arm downwards to do so, and knew by that action
that the previous post-mortem had been performed by
Professor Dykk, also of the London Hospital. Dykk often
complained loudly to John Shaftoe that when he performed
a p.m. he always had to put the microphone 'up', but Shaftoe,
not having the status of Dykk could not, in terms of hospital
protocol, make any form of counter complaint about having
to pull the microphone down. Shaftoe was a lowly pathologist, the third division of the medical profession, below
surgeons who could command five times the salary of a
pathologist, and also behind family doctors whose salary was
often twice that of Shaftoe's. Dykk, too, was a pathologist,
but he held a chair, he was a professor and the holder of a
chair in any branch of medicine was a person with clout.
Shaftoe knew his place and his form of protest was to leave

the microphone in the lower position upon completing each p.m. and holding his tongue when Dykk complained. Shaftoe might be middle-aged, he might be established and settled in his chosen field but he was still also the son of a Yorkshire pit man and the prejudice he encountered when at medical school created a resentment towards the senior members of the profession which he, by then, had accepted would never leave him.

'Well,' Shaftoe turned to Detective Inspector Dew who was observing the post-mortem for the police. 'It's male, as I informed DS Vicary this morning.'

Dew nodded in response.

'A young adult, approximately twenty-five years of age, the skull hasn't fully knitted, so a young adult male.' Shaftoe paused. 'Well, the first thing to do is to determine how old the skeleton is. There were indications that it is less than seventy years old as I said this morning, now we have to determine it, there being little point in wasting both our time if he trod the boards when Queen Victoria was upon the throne.'

'That would be sensible,' Dew growled. Dew was a powerfully built man, tall, serious, a man who John Shaftoe always thought had an aura which said, 'police officer'. He was, Shaftoe also thought, the sort of man who could silence a busy pub by just walking into it and do so with commanding respect, rather than telegraphing hostility. Much could, Shaftoe believed, be heard in a silence, and silence has differing sounds. The silence of peace and tranquillity, he would argue, was, for example, quite different from the sound of stress or fear. Pleasingly Shaftoe had found that Dew was not wholly without a sense of humour, essential for police work as much as it was for a successful pathology department. Dew, Shaftoe had found, was quite unlike Button, the fumbling, nervous pathology laboratory assistant who Shaftoe believed was utterly mismatched to a job, the stock-in-trade of which was the human corpse.

Billy Button, who at that moment was laying the instruments on the instrument trolley with trembling hands, was a man whose nervous disposition Shaftoe thought should have led him to the therapeutic world of tending parks and gardens of whatever London borough in which he lived. He should not be working with the dissecting of human remains, often accompanied by pathologist and observing police officers sharing a joke of dark humour, so John Shaftoe felt, especially since Button was by then approaching retirement. So fearful was Button of his death, that he had once confessed to Shaftoe that he would not venture out of his home at night and further, when he had had a particularly violent attack of 'the shakes', had wept as he said that he knew where his body would be taken, to which drawer, where the label would be tied round his big toe would be obtained, on to which table his body would be wheeled and lifted, which scalpel would be used to make an incision into his clammy, cardboard-stiff flesh, and from that knowledge had grown an obsessive fear and that fear had developed into a terror of the certainty of what would soon happen to his body.

All Shaftoe could say was, 'It won't necessarily be like that, Billy, not at all. If it's clean-cut natural causes no one will open your body up. No need for a p.m. in such cases. You know the rules and requirements same as me. I mean most deaths do not require a post-mortem,' but the weepy Button would only whimper that there was, 'No guarantee, Mr Shaftoe, no guarantee, and I know I am going to be on that shiny metal table with a towel over my middle. I just know it, sir,' and was said by the sixty-three-year-old with fists clenched so tightly that his knuckles whitened. On that particular afternoon, as Dew looked on, Button seemed to be holding his nerves together and containing any expression of terror he felt to only the occasional clatter of one stainless-steel instrument against another. Not dissimilar, Shaftoe thought, to an attention-seeking child who clatters plates together when doing the washing-up under protest after a family meal.

'So, first things first.' Shaftoe took a long stainless-steel rod and pushed it between the teeth of the skeleton and gently prized the mouth open. The lower jaw gave easily, all muscle and hence all rigour having rotted away, but nonetheless, Billy Button still made an audible gasp of distress. Shaftoe glanced at Button and then glanced at Dew and raised his eyes as if to say, 'Sorry about him', and Archibald Dew replied with a slight nod of his head which said, 'No worries, it happens'.

'The body in question is completely skeletal,' John Shaftoe spoke for the benefit of the audio typist who would soon be listening to the tape and typing as she listened, 'and is that of a young male of approximately twenty-five years when he died.' Shaftoe examined the teeth of the skeleton. 'Ah . . . post-war . . . late twentieth-century dentistry is observed.' Shaftoe stood and turned to Archibald Dew. 'Definitely one for you, chum,' and Dew nodded in recognition of the information. 'The deceased looked after his teeth. They are quite heavily filled. In fact, there isn't a molar which is not filled but he has all his teeth. No build-up of plaque so he flossed thoroughly and cleaned daily. There are no rotten teeth.'

'So he'll be missed,' Dew commented.

'I would think so. I observe British dentistry, so if he was not a Briton he was a long-time resident of these islands. So it's a near certainty that someone will have filed a missing persons report.'

'So what did kill him?' Dew said, a little testily for Shaftoe's liking.

'All in good time, Detective Inspector,' Shaftoe replied calmly, authoritatively, 'all in good time. Let's remain with the identification issue for a while, if you don't mind.'

Dew mumbled an apology and then fell silent.

'Well, as to racial extraction, he seems to have been Northern European or Caucasian. The teeth indicate that, as does the absence of a domed forehead and prognathism of the jaw which would both indicate Afro-Caribbean extraction. Caucasian and Indian-Asian skeletons look very similar but the Indian-Asian skeletons are more finely made. So I come to a definite identification that the skeleton is that of a white European.'

'White European,' Dew repeated.

'Yes, and very well built. Mr Button, the tape measure if you will.'

Button reached for a metal retractable tape measure and held it at the foot of the skeleton whilst John Shaftoe pulled the tape to the head. 'Six feet tall, as he is or one hundred and eighty-three centimetres in Europe speak. Add up to two inches on to that to allow for cartilage shrinkage and the absence of flesh from the soles of the feet and he could have been six foot two in life or one hundred and eighty-eight centimetres. He was large boned . . . a tall, well-built man. In fact your skeleton will look something like this, Mr Dew, were you to be filleted.' John Shaftoe grinned.

'Pleasant thought is that,' Dew scowled at Shaftoe, 'that is a very pleasant thought.'

'Mind you, you'll be past caring if you ever end up in this state.'

Button replaced the tape measure in its place on the bench at the side of the laboratory, looking very ill as he did so.

'It's unlikely to happen anyway,' Dew added defensively. 'I've made arrangements to be cremated. I don't want to make a meal for the worms.'

'So many people say that, so many people have a genuine fear of worms eating their remains. I always tell them that worms just don't go that far down, they are just subsurface creatures . . . but me, I want a pine box and a stone and a little piece of England to call my own.' Again Shaftoe paused and drummed his stubby fingers on the lip of the table. 'So, to turn to your question, what did kill him? Well, we can eliminate trauma, there is no damage at all to the skeleton, it's fully intact, no fractures at all. So we are left with causes such as poisoning or suffocation. Poisoning is very uncommon these days but the cause of death is one which didn't harm the skeleton . . . and . . . and I may not be able to identify it . . . no guarantee there, I make that plain now.'

'Understood, sir.'

'But I can extract the marrow samples from the long bones and send it to toxicology and I will also look at the marrow myself. I'll extract a tooth, that will allow me to determine how old he was when he died plus or minus one year. An examination of the cross-section of the tooth is all I need. So a six foot two inch tall, well-built male who disappeared within the last thirty years going by the dental work. I have a colleague who is a forensic dentist. I'll ask him to look at the dental work; he will be able to state with no small degree of accuracy which was the period during which this type of dentistry was practised.'

'It changes that rapidly?' Dew was genuinely surprised.

'Oh, yes, fillings used to be metal, made of a mercury

compound a long time ago; it was highly dangerous, gave folk metal poisoning. Now fillings are made of agar derived from seaweed. So, yes, dentistry progresses as do all branches of medical science. It's a continuous process of shoving back the frontiers of knowledge. So, brief as it is, that will be the content of my report which I'll fax to you at the Yard.'

'Thanks. It's something for us to be going on. I'll look over the mis per reports for twenty/thirty years ago.'

'I'll forward the results of the toxicology examination of the marrow and also my colleague's opinion about the era of the dentistry to you as soon as I have them, possibly tomorrow. I'll also have a look at the marrow in the long bones myself. I'll do that today.'

Archibald Dew took a taxi from the London hospital to New Scotland Yard. He alighted the cab next to the revolving triangle 'working together for a safer London' below the larger letters of 'New Scotland Yard' on each side of the triangle. He entered the building and took the lift to the 'Murder Squad' room and sat at his desk. He opened a file on the case of the unknown male who was found in a deeply dug shallow grave in Epping Forest. He phoned the collator and obtained a number for the file and then registered the number on the computer file of current cases.

Soon the file would also have the name of the deceased.

Soon a family will be weeping.

Piers Parsloe picked and poked indifferently at his lunch, sitting alone at the varnished pine table in the kitchen of his house, having retrieved the meal from the refrigerator where his wife had left it, as promised. Try as he might his appetite and taste for food evaded him and so he stood and scraped the meal into the waste bin which stood in the corner of the room hoping that the daily help would find it before his wife did. Rosalind Parsloe had grown up on the edge of the Essex marshes and had survived without experiencing excessive deprivation but had, in lean times, experienced her mother using the last six eggs in the house, which was all that remained of the food supply, to feed her husband so that he could go out and do a day's work for cash in hand. She and her mother had then waited in the house, without eating, until her father came home with money to buy food from the 'late' shop.

The small shop had charged excessively but it opened late and so food could be obtained. Waste of food still upset Rosalind Parsloe, even when living in Swiss Cottage, with two cars in the garage, and a chateau in France, and her children having benefited from private education. Piers Parsloe cared little for his wife's feelings and when she complained he would silence her with a glare, but that day her annoyance would be just one more issue to contend with, one more issue that he did not need, even if it was just another, 'Oh, Piers, I wish you wouldn't', and so he covered the wasted food with previously disposed-of refuse that was already in the bin. That and the likelihood that Nancy would empty the bin before leaving for the day ought to be sufficient to hide the waste from his wife.

Parsloe left the house and, choosing the Jaguar over the larger and heavier Mercedes, drove off the estate northwards, away from London cursing mobile phones which had since their coming made phone boxes obsolete and consequently few and far between. Eventually he saw a large pub with a small number of cars in the car park and pulled up to it, parking close to the door. Inside, the pub was, he thought, very north London; smug, well appointed, carpeted, polished wood and very quiet. He ordered a gin and tonic from the bar and asked if the pub had a payphone. The youthful, eager barman, 'Tony' by his name badge, directed him to a wood-panelled phone booth in an adjacent bar. He gave the barman ten pounds when he ordered the gin and asked for some fifty pence pieces in the change for the phone. He then carried the gin to the phone booth and dialled a number noticing his fingers to be trembling as he did so. He drank the gin in a single mouthful. He needed a stiffener.

'It's Piers,' he said simply when his call was answered.

'Yes, Piers.'

'We need to meet.'

'Yes, Piers.'

'You phone Neve.'

'Yes, Piers.'

'I'll phone Tom Last.'

'Yes, Piers. Piers, I did the right thing to phone you?'

'Yes, Freddie, you did the right thing.'

'Thank you, Piers.'

'But use the landline from now on.'

'Yes, Piers.'

'Calls from mobiles can be traced. You know that. Tell Neve to do the same. I'll say the same thing to Last.

'Yes, Piers, landlines all the time.'

'And use payphones in pubs or on the street, if and when you can find them.'

'Yes, Piers.'

'We'll meet tonight. Seven p.m.'

'Where?'

'At the Feathers, that seems appropriate.'

'If you say so, Piers.'

'I do say so. Seven p.m. in the Four Feathers.' Piers Parsloe put the phone down without waiting for the man's reply.

'He drowned,' John Shaftoe permitted a certain smugness to enter his voice, 'or he was drowned and then his body was buried. So "was drowned" is probably more the case, in fact certainly the case as near as certain as we can get in the absence of an eyewitness or other, further evidence. I mean, there being little or no need to bury the body of a victim of accidental drowning, but then that's your department, not mine . . . thine, not mine.'

'Drowned.' Archibald Dew wrote the word carefully on his notepad and then circled it, slowly, thoughtfully, twice. 'Well, so we have cause of death.'

'We have indeed. The diatoms are still in the long bone, marrow of same. I mean in the marrow of the long bones.'

'Diatoms?'

'Beasts. In large numbers. Microscopic, but beasts nonetheless. They live happily in the bodies of water and when a person drowns they are ingested by said drowning victim and then make their way into the long bones, or rather the marrow thereof, there to remain. Further tests will be able to determine whether he was drowned in fresh water or in salt, but I am prepared to lay my pound to your penny that he will have been drowned in fresh water.'

'That's a bet I wouldn't take, even if I only stood to lose a penny.' Dew allowed his smile to head down the phone. 'I just cannot see him, poor fellow, being drowned at sea and his body then being ferried back to land, in great secrecy, to be buried in Epping Forest.'

'Nor can I, nor can I. If they didn't want his body to be found they would have weighted it.' Shaftoe paused. 'Unfortunately, after this length of time . . . we agree we could be talking up to thirty years here, after this length of time I won't be able to determine the body or indeed even the type of fresh water he was drowned in.'

'You could do that if it was a more recent drowning?'

'Oh, yes, if the body was very recently recovered, within say a few weeks, but after twenty to thirty years, if the body of water in which he was drowned still exists the chemistry within will have changed so much and the diatoms in the bone marrow degraded so much that we couldn't get a match that would be regarded as an acceptable level of proof in the eyes of the law. I should, though, be able to determine whether it was relatively clean bath water or swimming pool water, or pond or river water, but beyond that, I'm afraid I cannot say or will not be able to say.'

'I see. Well, that's something to go on.'

'And it's early days.' Shaftoe paused as a helicopter approached and landed on the roof of the hospital, above the office in which he sat. 'Sorry,' he shouted into the phone, 'customers for Accident and Emergency.'

'Yes,' Dew also raised his voice, 'I can hear.'

'Laboratory in the basement and an office under the roof,' Shaftoe continued to raise his voice, 'but such is the logic of the Greater London Health Service.'

Dew grinned. 'It sounds as well organized as the Metropolitan Police.'

'Ah . . . peace . . .' Shaftoe said as the 'woof, woof, woof' of the rotor blades died down and the helicopter's engine sound faded. 'Silence is a lovely sound.'

'And peace is a lovely state.'

'So,' Shaftoe continued in his normal voice, 'seems to me you are looking for a multiplicity of suspects.'

'Oh?'

'Well, I was thinking logically rather than learnedly. The depth of the grave . . . I suppose one man could have done that, but in the hours of darkness? If he had time he could have done it but we assume he was constrained by the hours of darkness, two or three taking turns would be more efficient, much speedier. One man working for thirty minutes, the others resting, each do three half-hour stints.' Shaftoe leaned back in his chair. 'You see, once I was employed as an attendant in a crematorium when I was an undergraduate, it was a summer vacation job.'

'Were you?' Dew sounded intrigued.

'Yes, nominally employed as a gardener but from the start I was pressed into service pushing the coffins around, played dodgems with them, they were on wheeled trolleys . . . lining them up to get pushed into the furnace, looking through the peephole as the body sits up as the spine contracts and the tongue sticks out. I only saw that once and that was once too often. Even after gravitating to a working life which involves cutting up bodies that image stays with me.'

'It would.'

'But the ghouls who worked there would queue up at the peephole, shoving the guy at the hole away once he'd had his ten seconds of eye feast, then he'd join the back of the queue. What was eye opening for a twenty-year-old wasn't seeing the way a crematorium operated but the insight into human nature it afforded. Well, the nature of those humans attracted to such work.'

'Ghouls, as you say, Mr Shaftoe.'

'John, please.'

'John.'

'But I digress. The point I make is that at the crematorium there was also a cemetery and one man employed there, solely employed as a gravedigger. He was the only person who had anything approaching a skilled job and he would take a full working day to dig a single grave and do that whilst working steadily at a reasonable pace. He would carry his spade and grave template out from the hut at 8.30 in the forenoon, cut away the grass turf and roll it up and place it on one side and then, keeping the sides perfectly vertical, and the bottom perfectly horizontal, he'd inch the grave into the ground until he was six feet down. He'd come in with sweat pouring off his brow for his lunch break and then go back out again and he would finish the job at five p.m. One grave was a day's work for one man, and that man was skilled and experienced. He once explained to me the care needed to keep the sides vertical and the bottom level. Lose either, he said, and you've lost the grave. Have to fill it in and start another one somewhere else.'

'Yes,' Dew growled, 'I see where you are going with this, John. This is interesting, very interesting.'

'Well, to continue, I would have thought that the grave would have to have been dug in the hours of darkness and in some silence, though perhaps the campsite wasn't there then and no one would be close by.'

'We can find that out easily enough.'

'Yes. So I would think a team of men and a summertime burial.'

'Yes, I can understand your thinking there.'

'In addition there is the size of the victim, a young man, six feet tall, muscular – a rugby fullback sort of man, or a guardsman outside Buckingham Palace. Again, a man of that sort, not easily overpowered, not a lightweight corpse to lift and drop in a hole . . .'

'He'd have to be immobilized before he was drowned,' Dew added, 'he could otherwise have successfully fought for his life.'

'Yes, it would have required an unexpected blow to the head, or the combined force of many men to subdue him.'

'Yes.' Dew absent-mindedly inscribed a third circle round the word 'drowned' on his notepad and then equally absent-mindedly underlined it, three times. 'I do take your point. So, a team . . .'

'I would think so. Your box and my box are not non-co-terminus boxes; we do overlap lest anything should slip between the crack.'

'Agreed, so please overlap all you like.'

'Well, that's my tuppence worth of overlap, a team of felons, a summer burial. I'll write this up and fax it to you a.s.a.p.' John Shaftoe glanced at his watch. 'Just on four p.m. I'll put this in for typing. You won't get it before tomorrow now, but that's the nuts and bolts of it.'

John Shaftoe wrote his report on the post-mortem of the still-to-be-identified remains of the body exhumed that morning in Epping Forest and marked it for the attention of DCI Archibald Dew of New Scotland Yard, using plain, simple English where he could, using scientific and medical phrases only where he was obliged to. He took the report to the typing pool and it being after 5.00 p.m. when he arrived there and there being no one present, he placed his report under all other typing in the 'in' tray, knowing that the practice of the secretaries was to select the bottom-most item from the tray when a fresh piece of work was to be commenced. Shaftoe had found that by taking work to the typing pool when the secretaries were at their coffee or lunch break, or, as then, had left for the day, and placing his work at the bottom of the tray he would get it back sometimes fully a day earlier than would otherwise be the case.

John Shaftoe returned to his office and put on his light-weight summer jacket and light golfers' flat cap and left the imposing nineteenth-century building and walked into Whitechapel, it being a pleasant, mellow evening and the need having come upon him not to want to return directly home. He crossed Whitechapel Road and entered Jack the Ripper territory of Hanbury Street and Bucks Row, and other streets in a small locality made famous by the 1888 Jack the Ripper murders. The area he found had, by the twenty-first century, been much redeveloped and the artists and writers were moving into recently 'gentrified' houses which once housed London's poor. Initially the slaughterhouses were replaced by clothing manufacturing sweatshops, they in turn were replaced by Asian garment traders' warehouses and now the area, once described as having 'no meaner streets in London' is now 'trendy' prior to becoming 'fashionable' and then 'much sought after'.

The original street pattern though remains as do many of the original nineteenth-century buildings, with the names of the streets where a Ripper murder took place being solidly attached to the buildings, the originals and subsequent replacement street names having over the years been spirited away by so-called 'Ripperologists'. That the area was Jack the Ripper territory was of no concern to John Shaftoe (he had long formed the opinion that Jack the Ripper was not one man but several, each acting independently of each other, committing copycat crimes in a much publicised spree). Rather, what drew him magnetically to the area was its still-remaining working-class ethos and atmosphere, which was to be found most strongly in the public houses of the area. That mild, early evening, as the stresses of the day fell from his shoulders, he fetched up quite by chance in the Queen's Head where he stood at the bar, one foot resting on the foot rail, leaning cross arms on the bar in front of a pint of IPA. He would, on such occasions, be left alone, just a man and his pint. On other occasions he would be vetted by the locals; either the publican himself or one of the regulars would sidle up and engage him in conversation, just to get the measure of him, a stranger. On such occasions he would tell his new companion that he was 'down from Thurnscoe', pronouncing the town 'Thurns-kuh', as any native of the town would, 'near Barnsley', he would add. Sometimes he'd be asked what he did for a living and John Shaftoe, speaking like his father spoke, speaking like he spoke in the rough school he attended would say, 'bit of this, bit of that, best that's going tha' knows', and what was he doing in London? 'Visiting my sister and brother-in-law for a couple of days,' was John Shaftoe's stock reply. It would be sufficient to satisfy the locals and Shaftoe would often hear said new companion return to his mates and say, 'He's OK. He's down from the north', and he would then be left alone.

John Shaftoe found the Queen's Head to be loudly decorated in bright colours, with no less than six television sets high up on the wall, showing music videos and horse racing. There was a cash dispensing machine charging a high service charge but if a punter is drunk enough such things are of little concern, so John Shaftoe had observed. Outside the pub, the red double-decker London buses could be seen through the frosted glass, as could the hurrying black taxis, though the latter were slowing noticeably as the strangely misnamed, thought John Shaftoe, rush hour set in, there being very little rush about traffic inching homeward. On that evening he wasn't vetted by the locals and so he supped his wet in a very enjoyable privacy.

\*     \*     \*

'Never thought we'd be back here.' Frederic Wolfe glanced round the open-plan layout of The Four Feathers, a vast maroon carpet, dark wood-stained tables and chairs, sepia and black and white photographs on the wall, all to age a revamped public house. 'Changed a bit, can't hardly make the old pub out any more.'

'Ruined it.' Idris Neve sipped his beer. 'Open-plan doesn't work, open-plan never works in a pub. A pub needs rooms, but at least it's quiet . . . don't like piped music.'

'All right,' Piers Parsloe growled and put his beer glass down heavily, gavel-like, on the surface of the circular table. 'We might have a problem. Freddie?'

Freddie Wolfe leaned forward and spoke in a hushed tone, glancing at the nearest occupied table some fifteen feet away, where two elderly men were hunched over a game of chess and the young barmaid beyond them in a white blouse and black skirt polished the tabletops, as if satisfying himself that all three persons were comfortably out of earshot. 'OK, there's no easy way of saying this so I'll just say it,' he glanced at Neve and then at Last, 'but they've found him.'

Last and Neve sat back and groaned loudly.

'You said it might be a bit of a problem, Piers.' Neve glanced at Parsloe. 'There is no "might", it is an "is" and it's not "a bit", it's huge. Mammoth.'

Piers shrugged. 'I am an Englishman. We are given to understatement. It's a national trait. Or haven't you noticed?'

'So what happened?' Last addressed Wolfe.

'I go back there. Often.'

'Often!' Parsloe glanced at Wolfe.

'Three, four times a year.'

'Stupid,' Last hissed. 'Stupid. Stupid.'

Wolfe shook his head. 'Not so, middle of the day, middle-aged, retired man, used to take the dog when we had her. So what is strange about a man walking his dog in Epping Forest? I'd often stop and have a chat with other dog walkers, but I go there. I am drawn to the place. I go and look at the villa as well.'

Piers Parsloe groaned.

'It's an old persons' home now. I just walk past it, a dog

walker, on the pavement. You can see the pool from the road
except it's a flowerbed now . . . four or five times a year.'
'Three or four has now become four or five.' Last spoke
with a note of dismay.

'All right, about once every two months, to both places,'
Wolfe took a sip of his beer, 'but only lately has it been that
often, but I don't loiter, I don't stand there staring. I am not
that stupid.'

'I do the same.' Idris Neve spoke calmly; he looked at the
tabletop. He was a tall, thin-faced man and like the others
in the company he was in his mid to late fifties, casually
dressed but expensively so. An observer might take the four
men for a group of successful businessmen relaxing after an
early morning round of golf. The Jaguars, Audis and
Mercedes Benz in which they arrived, and which did not
look out of place in the car park of 'The Feathers', would
aid such an impression. 'Not as often as once a month,' Neve
continued in his soft but distinct Welsh accent, 'but I know
what Fred means. I too am drawn to the place. The forest.
Haven't been to the villa. Can't say I have been there. Dare
say me and Fred would have bumped into each other at some
point.'

'Blimey,' Parsloe groaned, 'halfwits.'

'It's not so bad. There's a campsite there now, plenty of
people walking about, children playing in the trees. It's like
a city-centre park, just missing swings and roundabouts. One
guy walking, especially with his dog, well . . . just doesn't
merit a second glance.' Idris Neve spoke defensively. 'And,
like I said, I don't loiter, don't stand over the grave looking
at the ground.'

'And maybe it's a good thing we . . . at least I, visited the
area,' Fred Wolfe added. 'We know that he's been found,
that's a card up our sleeves if they don't go public as they
don't know that we know that they know. We are one step
ahead.'

'How did they find him anyway? We put him in deep
enough.'

'Building on the green belt aren't they,' Wolfe shrugged.
'Just bad luck really. They were digging a trench for a main
drain and they came across him. Two feet either side and

they would have missed him. He's been down there twenty-five years, just another twenty and we would have been well out of it.'

'Twenty-seven,' Parsloe said softly. 'I worked it out last night. We put him down there twenty-seven years ago this month.'

'Do we know who's leading the inquiry?' Neve asked, displaying, thought Parsloe, an alarming level of nervousness.

'Not yet, but we can make enquiries. We still have wires in where wires need to be. We'll find out soon enough. It's early days yet but we'll keep our ears to the ground.' Parsloe paused. 'All right, let's have some gang rules.' Last, Neve and Wolfe sat forward. Attentively.

'First rule; don't use mobile phones to contact each other. Calls to and from mobiles can be logged. Places where the phones are used can be determined by triangulation from the satellite dishes. You can't make a phone call from the middle of London and claim to have been in Newcastle at the time because your mobile will put you in London. If you want to contact each other, if you want to meet up, use a postcard.'

'Postcards,' Neve gasped. 'They can be read.'

'Course they can, so keep it cryptic.' Parsloe gave Neve a pained look. 'Just write "How about a beer?" and we'll all know what it means and we'll meet here. If it's too crowded we can go outside to talk. But "a beer" means a rendezvous at "The Feathers" say, at midday the day after the card is received. Agreed?'

'Yes, boss.' Neve smiled.

'If you need to phone, use a landline public call box or payphone in a pub, but try to avoid pubs or public places where there is CCTV if you can.'

'OK,' Neve nodded.

'Apart from that, just act normally, keep your head down and act normally. I can't see how we can be linked. They'll identify him soon enough but that won't link us. We'll weather this . . . so, mum's the word. Keep schtum. Just keep schtum.'

John Shaftoe remained in the pub without being bothered by locals until 8.00 p.m. by which time, he reasoned, the 'rush hour' would have comfortably subsided and he stepped out of the building into a warm, mellow midsummer's evening. He took the Metropolitan Line from Whitechapel to King's Cross and then boarded an overground train bound for Welwyn. He alighted the train at Brookman's Park, exited the station via the footbridge, turned right on to the road bridge and strolled casually into the leafy suburb. Walking up Brookman's Lane he once again found himself thinking 'aren't we self-satisfied' as he cast his eyes from left to right at the large, detached, interwar development houses, many with 'U' shaped 'in and out' driveways and which he knew to have vast gardens in the rear. The houses to his left on the north side of the lane being particularly fortunate to back on to the golf course, which offered even more open space to look out upon. But, eventually, he turned into the driveway of one such house with a large and a small car parked in just such an 'in and out' driveway and he let himself in through the front door.

'Touching base?' The slender, finely built lady greeted him with a smile as she enfolded her arms about him.

'Aye, pet,' John Shaftoe replied, equally warmly.

'Shepherd's pie all right?' the woman asked. 'A bit of a winter dish I know, but I thought you'd be hungry. You didn't come home on time, gave me chance to make one, thought you'd be at your beer.'

'Lovely.' John Shaftoe peeled off his summer jacket and knelt to tug at his shoelaces. 'Champion, pet, just champion.'

Tom Last glanced at the youth beside him. 'You'll have to do time.'

'I know. I want to get some prison time in.'

'Sure?'

'Yes. There's nothing for me on that side of the fence. Thanks for the start, Mr Last.'

'Just watching for the most part.'

'Watching?'

'Following. Nothing bad there, won't do time for that, following folk, but that's all I want right now. Later there'll be proper jobs.'

'Good.' Roderick Himes stared out of the car windscreen,

his eyes unmoving as if fixed upon some object only he could see. He was tall, muscular; his hair was cut short, very short. 'I don't want to be a gofer, got more about me than that.' 'I know, Roddy.' Last handed him an envelope. 'Five hundred for you and your expenses.' Roderick Himes snatched the envelope greedily. 'I'll be telling you who to follow. You tell me where they go and who they talk to. Bigger jobs will come soon.'

# TWO

Archibald Dew and Harry Vicary drove out to Epping Forest in silence with Dew, as both the older and senior man, at the wheel. It was, both men found, a relaxed and a comfortable silence of the type that is engendered when two men know, trust, like and respect each other, can relax in each other's company, but just don't have anything interesting, useful or of note to say. Later Vicary would recall with some poignancy a bright sunny day, with little cloud, sufficiently warm for him and Dew to remove their jackets and roll up their shirtsleeves as both men enjoyed the drive out of the city into the country. It was a rare treat for Metropolitan Police Officers and both officers savoured it with no little relish. Dew drove to the campsite which at that moment in midweek was occupied by just five caravans, and the further field, separated by the line of shrubs which followed the stream, had similarly few tents. Both men alighted from the car and walked to the edge of the field and glanced about them.

'Isn't there supposed to be a site hut in these sorts of places?' Dew asked, letting his eyes run along the treeline beyond the field.

'You'd think so, sir.' Vicary, for his turn, let his eyes rest upon two magpies in the field in the middle distance and thought 'two for joy'. 'Someone to collect the ground rent. Mind you, I confess I have never seen the attraction in caravanning and my tenting days are behind me, thankfully so.'

Dew smiled. 'Same here on both counts, also thankfully so.' Dew turned and looked at the pub they had driven past to reach the campsite. It was, he saw, a red brick building, definitely interwar, and it seemed to be well positioned to serve both the campsite and the small collection of houses which stood beyond it, and whose roofs could be seen above a stand of shrubs and trees. 'Pub or door to door at the houses, which do you think? Either suits me.'

'Pub's nearer, sir, and they're usually a good source of information.'

The two officers strolled casually towards the pub, alongside the narrow lane on which they had driven, which was bordered by generous grass kerbs that were baked hard and were concrete-like to walk upon. They turned into the asphalt-covered car park of the pub which they noted was called, not surprisingly, The Woodman. The car park at that time of day, mid-morning, was quite empty and the curtains of the pub were shut on both the ground and the upper level. Dew and Vicary walked up to the red-painted double outer doors of The Woodman, and Vicary banged upon them with his fleshy open palm. Both officers heard the satisfyingly loud sound of the banging echo within the building. They waited, allowing time for the clearly slumbering occupants to respond to the knocking, but no such response was forthcoming. Again, Vicary smote the door, in the midst of which action an upstairs window opened with a mechanical sound and a woman looked out and down upon them. She was, thought the officers, in her forties, wide, round face, a mop of black hair and seemed to be wearing a nightdress. She smiled warmly and both Dew and Vicary felt some relief that she did not appear angry at being woken.

'Yes?' she smiled.

'Police, madam.' Dew held up his ID. 'No trouble, nothing to worry about, we need some information about the locality.'

The woman said she'd get her husband and withdrew from sight, leaving the window open. Moments later the officers heard the rattle of keys from within the pub, locks being turned and bolts being drawn. The left-hand door of the double doors was pushed open, and a well-built man in his fifties filled the frame. He seemed to have pulled on a pair of jeans and an old tee shirt in order to meet the officers. He was barefoot, his hair was uncombed and whiskers adorned his chin and neck. 'Police?' he smiled.

'Yes.' Again Dew showed his ID. Vicary did likewise.

'So how can I help you, gents?' The man brushed his fingers through his hair. 'It'll be about the body that was dug up yesterday, I'll be bound.' The man had a jovial manner which Dew and Vicary had found to be common among publicans, both also fancied that he would have a short temper, which was also, they believed, a common trait among those who work in the licensed retail trade.

'Yes, we are,' Dew answered. 'You've heard about it?'

'Of course, a few campers and vanners were in here last night, it was the talk of the pub. A body had been dug up by the navvies who were laying a main drain, much police activity and the corpse removed in a black van.'

'The navvies didn't come in?'

'Not a chance! No industrial clothing and unwashed bodies in my establishment, wouldn't allow it.'

The publican stood squarely in the doorway. He clearly had no intention of inviting the officers inside The Woodman, though equally he did not give either Dew or Vicary the impression that he had anything to hide. It was his pub and if he was going to do the police a favour, he was going to do it on his terms and that evidently meant doing it on the threshold and nowhere else.

'Yes,' Dew nodded, 'it is about the body, as you correctly believe. What we really want to know is how long has the camping and caravanning site been here?'

The man pursed his lips. 'Now you're asking. What can I tell you? Hang on . . .' He turned and went inside the gloom of the still-shuttered public house and then reappeared two minutes later looking pleased with himself. 'Nineteen years,' he said with a note of pride in his voice, as if pleased to have been able to provide the answer. 'Nineteen years last March.'

'Sure?'

'Positive. We were new in the pub then, me and Rita. That's the wife, she who opened the window when you banged on the door just now. We were in the pub just a few weeks when her sister got married, and we had the reception here; an Easter wedding it was and most of the reception was held in the beer garden, that's round the back,' he raised a thumb indicating the area behind him, 'and as we were having the reception the first caravans began to arrive for the Easter break. The first vans ever to use the field. I just asked Rita how long her sister Helen had been wed and she said nineteen years and three months and that was nineteen years and three months too long. She never did take to her brother-in-law didn't her indoors, but I always got along with the geezer.'

'Nineteen years and three months,' Dew repeated, and Vicary wrote the information in his notepad.

'Yes . . . it was part of Tillings Farm before that. Harry Tilling sold off two fields to raise capital and the new owner rents out space to campers and caravanners for a maximum of three weeks per tent or van so as to prevent it becoming a travellers' site, though such folk don't do a lot of travelling these days; if that happened it would destroy the community hereabouts. So three weeks is the maximum stay.'

'Is there a site office?'

'No. The owner, a geezer called Ball, comes with his fifteen cwt and then walks from tent to tent and van to van collecting the ground rent.'

'I see,' Dew murmured. 'We wondered about that. I assume it's empty in the winter months?'

'Emptier. I've come to know that some folk like the challenge of tenting or vanning in the winter. Rain is a real turn-off for folk but not the cold. They will come in here for a beer in the evening and tell you that with a four season sleeping bag and other such kit that they are fully equipped for anything short of a flood and that never happens round here, rain drains very quickly round here; it's just that type of soil and there isn't a river near here. Anyway, they tell that there's nothing like standing outside on a chilly December or January morning, well wrapped-up and drinking tea while the bacon cooks over a wood fire. They say it makes them feel more alive. I say I'll take their word for it. We get the regulars, one couple who spend the Christmas period in a tent, walking in the woods on Christmas Day. They say the woods have a special peace about them then. It's not just that no one else is there, but it's the knowing that it's Christmas Day that makes it very special. And another come for the New Year, just to escape the silliness of it all but "silliness" as they call it means money for me, but they escape the drunken revellers and the powerful fireworks going off over the road from their house.'

'I can see their reason for doing that.' Rita pushed the

second door open and stood next to her husband, holding a tray on which were three mugs of tea, and a small bowl of sugar and three teaspoons. The mugs were of the same style, Dew noted, dark blue with a sign of the zodiac embossed upon each in gold. Dew selected Leo with mumbled thanks, and after the publican had removed Capricorn, Vicary was left with the Hobson's choice of Gemini. All three men declined sugar. 'See,' the woman continued, 'my sister's house, nice area, but they have got a joint cricket and rugby club a few hundred yards away on one side and on the other a whole bunch of young persons' pubs, and all of them get a late bar licence each New Year's Eve and they all let off fireworks, starting at midnight . . . and keep letting them off for an hour. She says it's like being in the middle of no man's land in the First World War. It terrifies the pets in the area. They have a Dobermann. Have you ever seen a terri- fied Dobermann?'

'Can't say I have.' Dew sipped his tea.

'Anyway, I can see why Neil and Frances pitch their tent on New Year's Eve and stay until the second of January. I really can.' And with that, she retired into the pub carrying the tray and the declined sugar with her.

'So you'll know that the body was buried?' Dew asked.

'Yes.'

'Deeply?'

'Yes.' The man's name was Aaron Wainwright, by the plate screwed into the doorframe above his head. 'They said it was a proper grave, no coffin, but the full six-feet number, so a proper grave all right.'

'Well, probably not quite as deep as that but it was deep, as shallow graves go. So of interest to us is whether there is often a caravan or a tent on the fields?'

'Often . . . I would say three hundred and sixty-five. Like I said, we've been here for damn near twenty years and in that time I have never seen either field empty, even if it is just one tent and one van.'

'I see. Just trying to ascertain how old the grave is.' Dew drew a deep breath.

'Yes, I know.' Wainwright smiled. 'I could see where you were going. The grave couldn't have been dug if the fields were used as camping sites, not if it is as deep as they say it is. So over nineteen years old?'

'Seems so.'

'I can tell you that the wood, that part of the forest is popular with dog walkers.' He glanced to his left, indicating the cluster of houses some few hundred yards along. 'But it may be that turning the fields into a campsite opened up the route for dog walkers. If the fields were full of cattle or covered in wheat then that might have been a barrier to them. So, just don't know whether that was something a digger of a shallow grave would have to contend with and I can't put you in the direction of anyone who might help there. It's also too close to the built-up area to be of interest to poachers, they hunt deeper in the forest. Access would have been difficult, you'd need a four-by-four to carry a body up to that bit and this road here . . .' he nodded to the road on which the pub stood, '. . . this is the only road in or out.'

'So.' Dew tapped the warm roof of their car after they had taken leave of Aaron Wainwright and The Woodman and had done so with thanks. 'We need to look at the mis per files from nineteen years ago and beyond.'

'Seems so, sir.' Vicary opened the car door. 'Want to see the grave, sir, while we are here?'

Dew nodded. 'Yes, yes . . . I had better. Won't tell me anything but it might help to "visualize" it as they say; to see the damn thing would have been good enough when I was a constable, now we have to "visualize" scenes. All right, lead on, please.'

Vicary shut and locked the door of their car. 'We dug down below the body, sir,' he said as he and Dew walked towards the forest, 'until we were sure we were digging consolidated soil. There was nothing below the skeleton. We left the tape in place but vacated the scene, no need to keep a presence there.'

'I see.' Dew nodded as he cast an eye over the campsite. He and Vicary were attracting many glances from many people. 'Let's see the thing.'

\*　　\*　　\*

Freddie Wolfe and Idris Neve strolled along the path that led from Millfield Lane towards Spaniards Road under the shadow of Parliament Hill. They had cleared the trees, rich in birdsong, and entered an area of open ground where the path upon which they strolled was joined by a second path which drove up the heath from the lakes and beyond.

'Piers is bloody reckless,' Wolfe complained. Neve thought Wolfe to be irritated, nervous, fearful. 'We just can't meet in The Feathers again, even if that barmaid didn't hear anything we'll be recognized as regulars . . . they'll have us on CCTV.'

'They don't keep the tapes,' Neve offered soothingly, 'only if there's trouble in the pub.'

'You never know, do you?' Wolfe glanced about him anxiously. 'I get like this, paranoid. I can't go on like this; it's why I phoned you. Of us all, I thought you thought like me, that's why you went to the forest isn't it? It's why you go there?'

'Went.' Idris Neve allowed his eyes to follow a young female jogger, slender, long legs, tight, very tight, scarlet jogging shorts covering a pert bottom, blonde hair done in a bun. 'I went there. I won't be going back.'

'Yes, but you went there, and I went there . . . not often, but I went there.' Wolfe also savoured the image presented by the jogger.

'But Piers "living on the edge" Parsloe . . . What's Tom like? How's he taking it? What's his attitude?'

'Tom? Holding up, he's quiet, nerves of steel. You know Tom Last.'

'Yes, but I can't do the same. Wolfe by name, rabbit-like by nature.' Wolfe paused and then said, 'Look, Idris, I don't like saying this. I don't suggest it easily . . .'

'Spit it out.'

'Well, supposing we turn Queen's evidence, you and me, what do you think?'

Neve glared at him. 'Don't even dream about it.'

'Look, Idris, it's coming out; finding the boy's body is just the beginning of it all and it's the end for us. I mean, do you want to go down for life at your age, late fifties, pushing sixties? If you do, I don't. I wouldn't make it out the other side. I'll die in there, we all will. Look, we turn Queen's, collect ten years, out in five, that's survivable.'

'And poverty, is that survivable?' Neve stopped and turned to face Wolfe. 'Is that survivable? Loss of your pension, seizure of your assets because you won't be able to prove you came by them lawfully? Will your wife stay loyal? Mine won't if she finds out the cop she married and stayed married to is a murderer . . . among other things. Is that survivable? Ponder the loss of your standing in the eyes of your family.'

'I never wanted this.' Wolfe's hand went up to his head. 'I never wanted this at all, not in the first place. I knew we shouldn't have gone along with Piers.'

'We can't turn the clock back and you're up to your neck in it but Piers is right; they have a long way to go before we are even suspected, then they can suspect all they like, they can only act on proof.'

'Or admission of guilt!' Wolfe raised his voice. 'Look at this, all around you, all this green here in the centre of London . . . green . . . clean air . . . blue sky, not just a little bit that you might, just might, be able to see from your cell window but the whole welkin, from skyline to skyline. Up here on the Heath and this evening we can each go for a pint, or stay at home with the family, decide which DVD to hire and where to go for a curry if we decide to go for a meal.'

'So what's your point, Freddie?'

'The point is that this is liberty, this is freedom. You might take it for granted. I did, until yesterday when I realized I could lose it all and lose it forever, which is what happens at our time of life, Idris . . . forever . . . and we're ex-cops, they'll put us in the vulnerable prisoners' unit. Do you want to share a cell with a guy who likes talking about all the eight-year-olds they've bedded . . . the girls and the boys?'

'They won't put us anywhere . . .'

'And that girl that went by just now, that jogger? OK, so we can't touch but we can look. How often do you get eye candy like that in the slammer?'

'Look!' Idris Neve took hold of Wolfe's forearm. 'Just get a grip, Freddie, get a grip. So they have found the body and OK, so they'll ID it quickly enough but then what? It'll end there. They won't link it to us. So schtum, like Piers said. Schtum. Schtum. Schtum. Keep it zipped.' Neve walked on carrying Wolfe a reluctant half-step behind him. He felt like he was walking an old dog. He turned and smiled. 'Spaniards Road,' he pointed to the road ahead, 'right for Spaniard's Inn. It's long enough since I have had a drink in Spaniard's Inn and I think you could use a stiffener.'

Archibald Dew relaxed in the chair at his desk and calmly and unhurriedly read the report of the post-mortem on the skeleton that had been faxed to him by John Shaftoe esquire of the London Hospital. Dew's office in New Scotland Yard was bright and airy, smelled gently of disinfectant and afforded pleasant views of the rooftops of Westminster. The decoration of his office was confined to a Police Mutual Calendar, although he was permitted a small plant, a cactus, which he kept on top of the grey steel Home Office issue filing cabinet. He also had a photograph of his wife and daughter and himself, which was taken by an obliging stranger when they were enjoying happier years, on holiday in France.

The report told Dew nothing new. The toxicology tests for heavy poisons, arsenic, for example, had proved negative, and lighter toxins like alcohol, would, Shaftoe advised in the report, have been untraceable after such a length of time between burial and exhumation. John Shaftoe, having extracted a tooth and cut it widthways, was able to determine the age at death of the deceased as being twenty-six years, plus or minus one year. Death was confirmed as by drowning in fresh water. Dew attached the report to the file on the unknown person and then became aware of a sombre-looking and pale-faced Harry Vicary standing, leaning in fact, against the doorframe of his office. He had no idea how long Vicary had been standing there. Dew thought how unlike Vicary it was to stand so motionless at the entrance of his office. Usually the keen Detective Sergeant would breeze enthusiastically into Dew's office tapping the door as he did so. But, that morning, he stood, statue-like, and was holding a missing persons report in his right hand.

Dew held Vicary's stare, the eye contact with him for a few seconds and then leaned back in his chair and asked, 'What have you got there, Harry?'

'Something I wish I would rather not have, sir.' Vicary

advanced slowly towards Dew's desk. 'If it be he. I mean a
lot of people go missing in the smoke, but I have found mis
per reports of young men of the right height and age
numbering twenty . . . starting nineteen years ago.'

'Yes?' Dew extended an open palm indicating the chair
in front of his desk.

'And then I found this report,' Vicary slid on to the chair,
'and I wished I had not.'

'Oh?'

'A young male, twenty-seven years old when he was
reported missing . . . right height; it's him, sir . . . twenty-
seven years missing.' Vicary tapped the file.

'So why the long face?'

'Because this is very close to home, sir, it's in-house.'

'In-house?'

'He was a copper, a constable with the Met. Disappeared
whilst on duty.' Vicary's voice was shaking. His anger was,
Dew felt, palpable. He handed Dew the file. Dew took the
file and opened it.

The name of the missing person was Detective Constable
James Coventry, just a few weeks short of his twenty-eighth
birthday when he was reported missing by his colleagues.
The photograph of a dark-haired, confident-looking young
man with warm eyes and which women, thought Dew, would
find attractive, quite attractive indeed. Put this young man
in a uniform and the girls will stand in line, Dew thought,
and stand in a very long line. 'Still, have to be careful, Harry,
but I can see your reasoning.'

'It's the size of the damn grave that clinches it for me, sir.
I mean, all right, half the disappeared villainy in London is
beneath Epping Forest, the bodies of the other half are
working their way deeper and deeper into the mud in the
estuary, but there seems to be a pattern to the burials, in
respect of the depth of the grave. Sometimes the gofers are
not even buried, they're just dumped to be found sooner or
later, but the sergeants of the villains' crew got a deeper
grave, the captains, a still deeper grave, and the generals an
even deeper grave. The only person who would merit a grave
as deep as the one we're looking at, and as young as he is,
would be a copper. Someone who has some power, some

authority, did not want this body to be found and twenty-six years ago the campsite was a cow field or a wheat field, no campers to worry about when you are digging a deep grave. You could even take two nights over it . . . he disappeared in summer. I'll look at the climate records but if it was a wet summer, after a mild winter, the soil would be diggable, probably a bit heavy because of rain, but not rock hard like it would be now in this heat or in a cold winter.'

'I hope you are wrong,' Dew pondered the report, 'but I fear you are not.'

'Nothing on the body, sir, as you will have read, no clothing, so no zip fasteners or buttons. He was naked when he went in the ground. He wasn't to be identified if he was found. It's a very heavy number. It's a heavy team we are dealing with. Teeth will be able to be matched with dental records . . .'

'If his dentist still has them after twenty-seven years. Dentists are obliged to keep records for eleven years only, after that they can dispose of them but we still can identify him by his DNA. His parents are likely to be alive; we can use their DNA to match his. Got Dr Shaftoe's report by the way, he puts the age of the deceased at twenty-six years plus or minus one year.'

'So it fits.'

'Yes.' Dew read the report. 'Premium Road, Richmond; do you know it?'

'I know Richmond but not Premium Road. Pleasant area . . . trendy, Victorian houses in terraces, very nice . . . well out of a police officer's pocket.'

'All the desirable areas are.' Dew forced a smile and stood, reaching for his panama. 'Let's take a drive out to Kew, Richmond.'

Idris Neve excused himself from Wolfe's shaking-with-fear company and walked to the gentleman's lavatory. He entered a cubicle and sank back against the scrubbed clean wall. He was worried, very, very worried. He didn't want Freddie Wolfe to see and then realize just how worried he was. It was clear, he felt, very clear that something had to be done.

Fast. Very fast.

\*   \*   \*

'It was what we always wanted to hear and it was also what we had always dreaded to hear all rolled into one.' Unusually for householders who are receiving guests, in Dew's experience and observations, Philip and Phyllis Coventry sat side by side on the settee in the back room of their small but neatly kept terraced house on Premium Road, Richmond, having invited Dew and Vicary to each occupy an armchair. 'But after this length of time, it's more welcome than it's not welcome,' Phyllis Coventry turned to her husband, 'if you see what I mean?'

Philip Coventry nodded slightly but said nothing by means of reply.

'I never told you, Philip, but I didn't want to die without knowing what had happened to Jimmy.'

Philip Coventry held his silence but his eyes betrayed a welter of emotion. He was, noted Dew, a tall man of slender but muscular build, and clearly the same man who posed for a photograph when in military uniform in an earlier phase of life, and which photograph now stood on the mantelpiece. Beside the black and white photograph of a young Philip Coventry was a large colour photograph of James Coventry and clearly from the same negative as was the print in the missing persons file.

'It may not be him,' Dew spoke softly, 'but that photograph . . .'

'It will be him,' Philip Coventry said quietly, 'and I know I want it to be him. As Phyllis said, I also want to know before I die. After this length of time without contact, twenty-seven years, a boy like Jim who always kept in good touch . . . over a quarter of a century . . . and he used to phone two or three times a week and come over for Sunday lunch . . .'

'Yes,' Phyllis smiled, 'we'd do that, we'd have Sunday lunch each week. Most often we'd have it midweek because he'd be working on the actual Sunday but whatever day he had off, once a week we'd deem that day Sunday and we'd sit down to a roast; that was the sort of contact we had with him.'

'Then he went missing when he was on duty.' Philip Coventry glanced up at the ceiling and then down at the carpet. 'Of course something had happened. Now we are going to find out what, looks like.'

'Looks like,' parroted Phyllis Coventry.

Dew and Vicary had driven out to Richmond and had parked their car outside the Coventry house on Premier Road. Dew saw that it was exactly as Vicary had described, a road of neat late-Victorian terraced houses, each proudly upkept to a high standard of maintenance and it was, he thought, a lovely location to live, near the upper part of the river, near the famous Kew Gardens, fast connections to central London on the District Line, and a pleasant 'village' as its focus, but plagued by the noise from low-flying aircraft on their final approach to Heathrow Airport. The two officers had walked up the garden path past an array of bloom in the front garden to their right, and to their left, on the other side of a low brick wall, a similar array of bloom in their neighbour's front garden. Just six steps took them from the gate to the green-painted, heavy-looking solid-wood front door. Dew had tapped on the door as gently as he could although he unthinkingly used the classic police officer's knock, tap, tap . . . tap. The door had been opened rapidly upon his knock by a woman of medium height and slender build, a lean face, who upon seeing Dew and Vicary turned and called, 'Philip . . . Philip,' before Dew and Vicary had identified themselves or their reason for calling upon the house. Mrs Coventry then added, 'It's about Jimmy.' She then turned to Dew and asked, 'It is, isn't it? It's about Jimmy?'

'Yes,' Dew said solemnly, pausing to allow the sound of a low-flying aircraft to fade, 'yes, it is. I'm sorry.'

The officers had then been invited in and asked to sit in the back or 'living' room of the house which smelled of pine-scented furniture polish, the aroma being enriched by garden fragrance because the French windows, not, observed Dew, an original feature of the house, were fully opened on to a neatly cut lawn surrounded by flowerbeds thick with flowers and boarded by a wooden fence at either side and shrubs on the bottom of the garden. Dew was grateful for the open French windows, as the house was hot within, and he thought much benefited from the ventilation provided by the open windows. The officers had then been invited to sit, in the armchairs, as Mr and Mrs Coventry sat with no little humility upon the settee. Dew had then explained that a body had been found buried in Epping Forest. It was then that Phyllis Coventry had said that it was what they had always wanted to hear, and had always dreaded to hear.

'We can be certain it is Jimmy with a simple DNA test,' Dew said. 'Blood samples from you both will be needed but if you have something that will contain James's DNA . . .'

'Like his hair?' Phyllis Coventry offered. 'Will that be suitable?'

'Ideal,' Dew beamed. 'Do you have any?'

Phyllis Coventry smiled. 'In his comb. We kept his room for him in case he returned. Everything is just so. Nothing touched, nothing removed . . . nothing at all . . . everything just so.' She stood. 'I'll go and get it and his hairbrush too, excuse me.'

'Thank you,' Dew smiled.

The three men waited in a heavy, and for both Dew and Vicary, a very uncomfortable silence, until Phyllis Coventry returned to the room holding a comb and a man's hairbrush which she offered to Dew, then to Vicary, then to Dew.

'I'll take them.' Vicary extended his hand with a respectful smile. He took a production bag from his jacket pocket and placed the items within.

'We'd like them back, please.' Phyllis Coventry returned to sit beside her husband.

'Of course, I'll see to it personally,' Vicary replied, 'as soon as is practical. I'll return them personally.'

'Appreciated.' Phyllis Coventry forced a smile and took her husband's hand.

'So, tell us about his grave.' Philip Coventry addressed Dew.

'It was a fairly deep grave in Epping Forest,' Dew explained allowing his eye to sweep round the room and finding it all appropriate to the age and social class of the householders, then rested his gaze briefly on the multitude of colour that was the rear garden of the Coventrys' home, as seen through the open French windows. He then returned his gaze to Mr and Mrs Coventry. 'It was discovered quite by chance by a team of navvies who were digging a trench for a mains drain. A few feet either side and they would have missed it.'

'Lucky,' Philip Coventry whispered.

'Lucky indeed,' Phyllis Coventry said equally softly. 'Now we have a body to bury, we'll have a grave to visit. Is it possible to see where he had been buried . . . his body? His soul ascended, we know that.'

'He was one of those sorts of persons,' Philip Coventry said. 'When he was born someone in the world saw a comet in the sky and when he died someone else, somewhere else saw the same thing. He was that sort of man.'

'Special,' Phyllis Coventry said. 'Not just to us but to the world. But his grave . . .? I'd like to see it . . . we'd like to see it.'

'Yes,' Vicary glanced at Dew who nodded, 'yes, we could arrange that, take you there.'

'In a few days, we need to prepare ourselves and buy a wreath.'

'Of course.' Vicary took a card from his pocket and stood and placed it on the mantelpiece. 'My card, phone me anytime and we'll arrange a date.'

'Your son was a police officer,' Dew said.

'Yes, we were so proud of him . . . the passing-out parade at Hendon Police College, so smart, so handsome.'

'Were you told anything at all about the circumstances of his disappearance?'

'Don't you have records?' Coventry asked of Dew with a raised eyebrow. 'I would have thought you would know more than we do.'

'Yes, we've asked for all documentation to be sent up from the archives but anything you could tell us now would be very helpful.'

'I can tell you that he was frightened,' Coventry said. 'That won't be in the records.'

'Frightened?' Dew sat up. 'Of what? Of whom?'

'Of the job he was on.'

'Of being a police officer?'

'No . . . no . . . I mean he was frightened by the investigation he was part of.'

'Aah . . .'

'He was recently in the CID. Just out of uniform. He told me that things were not as he expected them to be and he had real reasons to be worried. We went for a beer a week before he disappeared and it was then he told me that he was frightened.'

'Interesting.'

'He told me that he was part of a surveillance team of a house. Then we were told that it was when he was on surveillance that he disappeared, one night-time.'

Dew held up his hand. 'Aah . . . I remember the case. I am sorry I didn't make the connection, the name just didn't ring any bells but the police officer who went missing whilst on surveillance of a house, it made a huge splash in the media.'

'Yes, that was Jim. We still have all the press cuttings, all of them in a shoebox under our bed.'

'We'll cross-check our investigation with the investigation he was part of.'

'The certainty,' said Philip Coventry, 'was that he was overpowered, but by who? The police raided the house they were watching, totally blew their cover looking for Jimmy. Years of work went out of the window but Jimmy was more important . . . pulled all the villains but none of them would talk. We do appreciate that getting Jim back became a priority, the loss of their investigation, years of work, was a price they were prepared to take, hundreds of hours, thousands of hours of police time . . .'

'Well, if it was the gang who kidnapped Jimmy they knew they'd been rumbled, so raiding the house probably wasn't so altruistic after all.' Phyllis Coventry spoke drily. 'Sorry, I get a little cynical at times, it's a failing with me. I inherited it from my parents and I have been fighting it all my life, usually successfully but sometimes it emerges.'

'That is a fair point,' Dew replied. 'Quite fair.'

'What is certain,' Philip Coventry continued, 'is that they put everything into looking for Jimmy but in the event, they just didn't get a result and that's it. Not any result at all. Didn't find Jimmy, didn't get a prosecution of the gang they were after.'

'Do you know anything of the criminals in question? Their identities? The nature of the crime?'

Philip Coventry shook his head. 'Nothing, nothing at all. Jimmy never said anything and the police never told us, probably didn't think that it was relevant for us to know.'

'Very unusual though,' Vicary commented. 'It's a very unusual thing for organized crime to do, and it sounds as though it was organized crime that was being investigated, night-time surveillance and all.'

A bee, a large and rare bumble bee, flew through the open windows and into the room. It turned round in the gloom of the room and back towards the light, but failing to find the open window, came up against a pane of glass upon which it buzzed in angry frustration. Philip Coventry stood and left the room and returned a few moments later with a glass tumbler and a sheet of paper. He strode up to the window and placed the tumbler over the bee, trapping it within against the pane of glass. He then slid the paper between the pane of glass, and holding the paper in place, lifted the tumbler and the bee away from the window. He held the tumbler up against his face and said, 'For you, Englishman, the war is over,' and then walked to the French windows and, extending his arms, removed the paper from over the tumbler and the bee flew away over the splendour of the back garden and was soon lost from sight.

'Good things, bees,' he said, sitting once again next to his wife, holding the tumbler in his hands.

'Very good things,' Phyllis Coventry echoed.

'So . . .' Philip Coventry turned to Vicary. 'Why unusual?'

'Well,' Dew sat back in the armchair, 'we mentioned this earlier, Harry Vicary and I . . . how to explain? Well . . .'

'The people who are involved in organized crime,' Vicary sat forward resting his elbows on his knees and clasped his hands together, 'they have a code of conduct, they police themselves, they control their own and for them the murder of a police officer or innocent bystander is considered by them to be well out of order, well outside the box. They don't want to rack up the game to the level of warfare and the wilful murder of a junior police officer is guaranteed to do just that.'

'Seems to have been a bit of a phoney war to me,' Phyllis Coventry growled. 'Casualties only on one side.'

'There will have been some questionable behaviour on the part of the police when they were questioning people in the gang after Jim was abducted. Maybe not fatalities, but blood would have been put on the walls of the cells . . . and the felons would have accepted it under the circumstances, so no complaints were made.'

Mrs Coventry grunted as if to say, 'Well, that's something at least'.

'These people are not fond of violence,' Archibald Dew added. 'They are not frightened of it, not frightened at all, and can be very violent if they have to be, but they are not fond of it either. You see, if they carry sawn-offs on a bank raid, they use them to fire into the ceiling so as to seize control of the premises, to frighten people into surrender. They do not carry them to shoot people. Armed robbers hire their guns or their "tools" as they are known, from people known as "gunsmiths" who hold a stock of illegal weapons. The agreement is that if not one person is injured in the raid, then the gunsmith will accept all the "tools" back and return half the rental money, but if one single person is injured then the "gunsmith" will not accept the return of the guns and keeps all the rental money. It's just an example of how far these people go to avoid violence.'

'I see . . . interesting,' Philip Coventry sighed, 'interesting. Didn't help Jimmy though.'

'No, which is why the murder of a police officer who was just watching a home is very out of character, unless they're foreign "Yardies" from the West Indies or Russian Mafia who are more vicious but they were not on the scene twenty-seven years ago . . . so . . . strange indeed. Did Jimmy have a girl?'

'Florence.' Phyllis Coventry's face brightened as she mentioned the name. 'Florence Reilly. They were engaged. She was a lovely girl. We were so happy for them both. To think what could have been. She'd be a woman in her late forties now; our grandchildren would be university students. We had our family when we were young, you see. I was eighteen when our daughter was born, a year later I had Jimmy, then a year after that we had Anthony. We're in our early seventies now, we two.'

'You look very fit for your ages,' Dew smiled, 'if you don't mind me commenting.' He was genuinely surprised to hear their age, he had thought them a good ten years younger but that, he had found, was the nature of life; some people just age rapidly and others just don't fully lose that bloom of youth.

'Aye . . . we'll get our telegram from the Queen yet.' Philip Coventry smiled. 'Our other son and daughter did well, it was just Jimmy's death that has caused sadness in our family.'

'And such sadness.' Phyllis Coventry again took hold of her husband's hand.

'I am sorry,' Dew said softly. 'But Florence Reilly?'

'We lost contact,' Philip Coventry explained. 'She was a good lass, kept in touch for a year or two, then she called round on us to tell us that she had a new man in her life and wanted to move on. We could understand that. So then it was just a card at Christmas and then those eventually stopped. So we don't know where she is now. She was such a bonny girl . . . a real gem. She wouldn't be short of offers of marriage, so when she called round that day, I wasn't surprised.'

'No, me neither,' Phyllis Coventry added. 'She was a teacher of mentally handicapped children. She was devoted to her job.'

'Where did she teach?'

'At the Ian Freemantle School. It's still there, still for mentally handicapped children. It's in Isleworth, near the hospital. What is the name of the road it's on . . . now?' Philip Coventry looked up at the ceiling.

'No matter, we can find it, that's all we need, Ian Freemantle School, Isleworth, near the hospital.'

'Name of another hospital . . .' Philip Coventry continued to search his memory.

'What is it?'

'The school . . . the road the school is on, I mean, has the name of a famous hospital. Got it! Stoke Mandeville Hospital, and the school is on Mandeville Road, right opposite the West Middlesex Hospital. Can't miss it.'

'About half an hour ago . . .' Neve hissed into his mobile phone. 'Didn't want to use the payphone in the pub so left him buying whisky for himself, walked out to look for another payphone, but this is Hampstead, it's like looking for a penguin in the desert.'

'OK . . .'

'Anyway, he's talking about turning Queen's, Piers, so whatever you decide to do, it had better be quick.'

Archibald Dew's heart sank. 'Australia?' he groaned.

'Yes, sorry.' The head teacher of the Ian Freemantle School smiled and shrugged her shoulders. 'And strangely enough, of all the places in the vastness of the world's largest island or the world's smallest continent, where do you think she settled?'

'Freemantle,' Vicary offered. He shared Dew's disappointment but rapidly reminded himself that there was such an organization as Interpol and he was sure that The Man in Blue in Freemantle would readily agree to interview Miss Reilly, or whatever she was now called.

'She met her young man here in London, he was an Australian working here as an exchange teacher but sadly the marriage didn't last and Florence returned to England. Fortunately they broke up before the children arrived, otherwise things would have been much more difficult for her . . . well, for both of them really. Children complicate a divorce, believe me, I know.'

Mrs Darragh by her introduction and by the nameplate upon her desk glanced out of the window at the neat semi-detached houses on the other side of Mandeville Road. She seemed to the officers to be in her early fifties, wore her hair short and had large-lensed spectacles and was dressed that day in a lightweight yellow dress with vertical white stripes. 'Believe me, I know.'

'Miss Reilly returned to the UK, you say?'

'Oh, yes, she's back and settled. In Palmers Green, I believe.'

'Do you have her address?' Dew struggled to contain his sense of relief.

Mrs Darragh turned to consult the timetable which was attached to the wall behind her. 'You only need her address?'

'Yes, that's all.'

'Well, the member of staff who has retained contact with Florence Reilly is teaching at the moment but I dare say she can step out of her class for a second or two, but if you wish to interview her, I will have to ask you to wait until she is free.'

Dew smiled, 'Just as long as it takes to obtain Miss Reilly's present address.'

Florence Reilly had, it transpired, remained Florence Reilly and Dew and Vicary called on her at her home on Old Park Road, N13. The road transpired to be lined with gracious late-Victorian or Edwardian semi-detached houses with small front gardens. Interestingly, the line of buildings was interrupted near the junction with Alderman Hill by a modern building, indicating as so often in London and other cities in the UK, where a bomb fell during the Hitler war.

'You've been dashing all over London,' she smiled meekly after inviting the officers to sit down in the vacant chairs in her living room, which overlooked the rear gardens that were more generously proportioned than the front gardens. She was a slender woman, auburn haired, wearing jeans and a white tee shirt.

'Goes with the territory,' Dew explained warmly, though he did feel tired: driving in London he had found takes its toll.

'James,' she said softly. 'I never really got . . .' She was interrupted by a thump on the ceiling. She smiled apologetically. 'That's the old lady who lives in the upstairs flat, quite harmless but she does bang about, dreadfully so. This is quiet for her. The property has been divided into three separate flats . . . heavens, what teacher of special needs children do you know who can afford a whole house in Palmers Green?'

'Special needs?'

'New speak . . . political correctness for what used to be called mentally handicapped.'

'Ah . . .'

'But Jimmy . . . it made my marriage fail. I do feel guilty, it wasn't Nigel's fault. He was devastated when I left him but he just wasn't James. They say that if you can't be with the one you love, then love the one you're with . . . but I just couldn't. I found out early on that I couldn't go on with the rest of my life lying next to a man and resenting him for not being Detective Constable James Coventry of the Metropolitan Police. I would also resent any children we would have had for not being Jimmy's children. That is no frame of mind with which to enter motherhood but that would have been my frame of mind.' She paused as the sound of furniture being scraped across the floor in the room above was heard. 'Ah, so that's what she's doing, rearranging the furniture. Again. Could be worse, could be a young person playing loud music and at least she sleeps when other mortals also sleep.'

'Indeed,' Dew smiled. 'It could be a lot worse.'

'It seemed the correct thing to do at the time, a new man, a new life in a new country, but it was a disaster. As soon as I stepped off the plane at Perth . . . Australia has such sweet-smelling air . . . but I knew I'd made a mistake. I loved Jim, I love London and I love England and I had lost all three by marrying an Australian and going to live on the other side of the planet. I felt I had lost Jim because his presence is in London. Sorry if that sounds a bit silly but it's how I feel. I would walk down Paddy Troy Mall in downtown Freemantle, or along our road, Blinco Street, and I would think Jimmy just isn't here.'

'No, I quite understand,' Dew smiled sympathetically.

'Well . . . so I returned. Nigel remarried a local girl so I don't worry about him. I am pleased for him . . . and me. I returned to where I need to be. I have had lovers over the years but I have always avoided marriage. The first cut is the deepest . . . he was also the first man who "knew" me.'

'I'm very sorry,' Dew said softly.

'Thank you, but . . . well, that's it. I have a small part-time job, mornings only, with special needs pupils. Soon be the summer holidays, six weeks of peace and that will be me until I retire. I could go at fifty-five but I wouldn't know what to do with my time so I'll soldier on until they throw me out at sixty.'

Vicary read the room – large, neatly kept, smelling of furniture polish. It said, 'single, middle-aged school teacher', it said 'nothing for the police to be suspicious about'. The framed photograph of the handsome young James Coventry on the sideboard said to the officers that love ran deeply within this woman.

'This is very quiet . . . I mean . . .' Florence Reilly clasped her hands together, 'I mean, I have not seen nor heard anything of this mentioned in the media.'

'We're keeping it quiet,' Dew explained. 'Informing next of kin of course and interviewing associates, but clearly Jimmy was murdered. We don't want to tip off the culprits; it isn't as though it happened yesterday and we need witnesses to step forward. The first twenty-four hours of any murder investigation are the most important and . . . well, they are long gone.'

'Indeed,' she responded with a smile.

'So,' Vicary added, 'we're playing our cards close to our chest. Need to know basis only.'

'At least Phyllis and Philip know, better than not knowing. Are they well?'

'Yes. Very. Holding their ages very successfully.'

'I will write to them and visit also.'

'They spoke highly of you. I am sure they would appreciate contact from you.'

'I will then . . . today. So how can I help you?'

'Jimmy disappeared whist on duty and so we assume that his abduction and murder were related to the investigation he was part of. We'll be looking at the case file, of course, but did he perhaps mention anything to you?'

'His parents told us he seemed frightened,' Vicary probed, 'did you get the same impression?'

'Yes, definitely, something worried him. There was a fear for his own safety and he said that CID work wasn't what he had expected it to be. I did think his fear was strange, a policeman being afraid of a gangster, whoever heard of that?'

'Did he give you any explanation?'

'No, he was very cagey. To use the expression you just used, sir, he played his cards close to his chest. He said it was safer for me if I didn't know too much.'

'Interesting. Can you remember for how long before he disappeared did he seem frightened?'

Florence Reilly pursed her lips and exhaled. 'So long ago now . . . Initially he loved CID, happy as a sandboy for the first year and a half, then he was made part of a big operation. Up to then things had been low grade, burglars and car thieves, fairly petty stuff. I mean burglary isn't petty if you are a victim of it but on the scale of things . . .'

'Yes, yes . . . we know what you mean.'

'Anyway he was drafted, if that is the right word, drafted into a big operation which he was thrilled about because it meant a step closer to the Serious Crime Squad which is where he was aiming. He always said he wanted to shut down some real villains, not the petty criminals.'

Dew smiled. 'It's like that. The pay is the same but there's more prestige in specialist police work.'

'Are you gentlemen Serious Crime Squad?'

'No. We are Murder Squad.'

'Serious enough,' Florence Reilly smiled.

'So . . . Jimmy became frightened when he became part of a big investigation?'

'Yes, but not initially. Initially he was bursting with pride and enthusiasm . . . he seemed to get disillusioned and then became frightened. He once told me that he didn't know what to do. I didn't press him, I thought he'd tell me if he wanted to and by then he'd already told me that it was best if I didn't know too much. Then he grew a beard and told me he'd be away for days at a time. The beard didn't suit him but he told me he had to grow it for the job.'

Dew nodded. 'Deep cover.'

'That can be risky,' Vicary said. 'Not a favourite job . . . volunteers only. It appeals to some . . . never appealed to me; you can lose your sense of identity. We had deep-cover officers attempting to infiltrate the football "casuals" some years ago, stayed under for months at a time. It got to the point where undercover officers found themselves helping "casuals" commit serious assaults, even assaulting police officers.'

'Heavens, but that's exactly the sort of thing Jimmy would volunteer for. I don't mean to assault people but what you call deep-cover work, that was Jim Coventry.' She paused. 'I remember now, he said that if it could happen to Jacky footwear, it could happen to me . . . don't want to end up like that.'

'Jacky footwear?'

'Yes, the surname was an item of footwear, shoe . . . sandal . . . something like that.'

'Slipper?' Vicary suggested.

'No. What was it now? What was it? Heel . . .?'

'Boot?' Vicary tried again.

'Yes,' Florence Reilly smiled at him, 'that was it, Jacky Boot. I thought at the time how thoughtless of his parents to call their son "John", he was bound to get called "Jack Boot". So his colleagues showed respect for him by calling him Jacky but something happened to him that really scared Jim. Apart from that . . . oh!' She raised a finger.

'Something else?'

'Someone. He had a very good friend, another constable . . . stayed in uniform when Jim went plain clothes in the CID. They used to go for a beer together. He might have told him things that he wouldn't have told me, I mean, him being a fellow police officer. Chambers was his name, I remember because that was my mother's maiden name and his initial was "L" same as my mother. She was Lillian, he was Lawrence. That's it, I remember now, Lawrence "Larry" Chambers. He was more or less the same age as Jim.'

'Thank you.' Dew smiled and stood, as did Vicary. 'This has been very helpful. Should anything else occur to you . . .' Dew took a card from his pocket and handed it to her, 'please contact us.'

'Yes, of course.' Florence Reilly also stood, took the card from Dew and placed it on the mantelpiece next to the photograph of Jim Coventry. 'I'll come out with you. I want to go to St Urban's . . . light a candle for Jim.'

In the room above, something large and heavy was dragged across the floor.

Harry Vicary sat in the meeting and again found himself despairing and thinking, 'I do not need this. Whatever I might need, it is not this.' He was once again surrounded by mild-mannered, harmless, psychiatrically ill people who he felt had a big hole in their personality where self-confidence should be. The more confident ones over-embellished their problem, boasting at the degree to which they had succumbed. He glanced out of the window at the sun setting over London. The sunset, he thought, could fairly be described as 'spectacular'. That night, there was a newcomer to the group, a raven-haired woman in her thirties, conservatively dressed, clean looking, someone who seemed not to have sunk as low as others, someone who seemed to be in employment and had retained her self-respect and her self-confidence. When the facilitator asked her to introduce herself she stood and said in a clear soft voice with distinct Received Pronunciation, 'Hello, my name is Kathleen and I am an alcoholic.'

The group responded by saying, 'Hello, Kathleen,' except for Vicary who said to himself, 'Kathleen, must remember that name. Kathleen, Kathleen.'

That warm evening Archibald and Miriam Dew drove from their modest house in Pembroke Road, Seven Kings, to Friern Barnet in Hertfordshire. They passed the journey in an awkward silence as Dew drove across the northern edge of London, west to Chingford and then, leaving the built-up areas, they drove north, passing through Enfield and Barnet, finally arriving at the Psychiatric Hospital in Friern Barnet. Dew parked their car in the visitors' car park and then he and Miriam walked arm in arm but still in silence along the echoing corridors of the nineteenth-century building, evoking, Dew thought, as he walked, the era when lunatics were placed in asylums on the very edge of the cities. They halted and turned into a ward and were met warmly by a genuine-seeming male nurse in his twenties. Miriam Dew went straight to sit with her daughter; Archibald Dew remained by the nursing station.

'Haven't met you before, Daniel.' Dew extended his hand, reading the nurse's name badge.

'No, sir, just completed my training, this is my first post.'

'Good for you. We are Olivia Dew's parents.'

'Olivia, yes . . . I am still just getting to know the patients, but Olivia, I have gotten to know Olivia a little better than the other patients. She is very poorly, I am sorry . . . very bright too.'

'She was,' Archibald Dew sighed, finding the smell of disinfectant and formaldehyde overpowering. The ward was brightly coloured and softly furnished. One or two patients lay on their beds in the Nightingale-style ward, though the majority sat close to the television set, all dressed in dressing gowns. 'She was very bright.'

'It's still in there, sir. That bit hasn't deserted her. It isn't as though she has suffered brain damage, that would be different, but the clever cells are still there, we have to access them, somehow. Frankly the medication isn't helping.'

'You think not?' Dew was surprised to hear a nurse make such a statement.

'Yes, sir, it makes her very docile. She doesn't self-harm any more, but the price paid is that it shuts down most other functions. It's the psychiatric equivalent of radical surgery, removing the tumour and all the healthy tissue around it to ensure you have caught all the malignant cells.'

'Interesting to hear you say that. Do the doctors know of your disapproval?'

'Oh, yes,' Daniel smiled, 'and they all agree with me that it's a desperate treatment but it's the best anyone can do. They try new drug regimes each week, it's wholly hit and miss, like shooting arrows into the pitch darkness hoping you'll hit something but I am afraid that's how it works, even in the twenty-first century but eventually we'll hit the right medication, then we can start considering her discharge home.'

'Even I could do that,' Dew growled. 'I didn't know that was the way of it. I thought she was being treated, not experimented on.'

'It would be the way of it in any other hospital, sir, and believe me, Olivia is very lucky to be here. I like working here, dedicated staff, very high quality of care. If I fell ill, psychiatrically speaking, I'd want to be here,' he pointed to the polished floor of the nursing station, 'in this hospital.'

Dew nodded. 'Well, that's comforting. Thank you.'

'She was at Cambridge University, I believe?'

'Yes, we were so proud of her. I left school at sixteen, her mother grew up in a children's home and she also stacked shelves when she was sixteen. Olivia is our only child and we never thought she'd amount to anything special but she turned out to have a real powerhouse between her ears. She went up to Cambridge on a scholarship when she was just seventeen. Murray Edwards College.'

'Yes, I know it,' Daniel smiled, 'used to be known as New Hall, on the Huntingdon Road.'

'That's the one,' Dew returned the smile. He found himself

warming to Daniel and would not be worrying about his daughter's welfare in the hands of staff like this youth. 'She was studying for a science degree. We had no inkling anything was wrong until she threw out all her *Scientific American*s and copies of *Nature*, learned publications, and started to read children's comics. The first suicide attempt took place a few days later.'

'An overdose?'

'Yes, you've read the case notes.'

'Yes, sir, I have to. But fortunately she is female.'

'What do you mean?'

'Well the pattern of suicide method is different for men and women.'

'Really?'

'Yes, sir, with exceptions to prove the rule of course, but generally men will go towards death, women will bring death unto them. Men will keep control, women will surrender control.'

'I see . . . so?'

'So a man will step in front of an express train, keeping control right up until the last second, a woman will lie on a bed having taken an overdose, surrendering herself anything up to an hour before actual death. So, fortunately, Olivia, being female, brought death upon her, she was found in time, stomach pumped, and she's still with us.'

'I see what you mean, had she been a man we would likely be visiting a grave right now.'

'That's about it, sir.'

'That's something to be thankful for,' Dew pondered, 'she never gave us a reason for doing what she did. She just told us that she had come to realize that doing the Hokey Cokey really was what it's all about. We assumed that meant she felt that life had neither meaning nor purpose.'

'It's a tragedy, sir, no mistake, but we are working as best we can and she is still a lot nearer the beginning than the end. She's still a young woman and, like I said, once we find the correct cocktail of drugs for her, then she can be discharged into the community seeing us on an outpatient basis, but it's a serious diagnosis, "paranoid schizophrenia with complications", you'll have read the file?'

'Yes . . . all I can understand, which basically means the social background reports. The nursing notes might as well be in Mandarin for all the sense I can make of them.'

Daniel grinned. 'Hospital speak, sir. Is there anything you'd like explaining?'

'No, no . . . the background reports will suffice, thank you. Well, nice to meet you, Daniel. I'll go and say hello.'

Archibald Dew walked the length of the ward to where his wife and daughter were sitting, just outside the television viewing area.

'Hello, dad.' Olivia Dew looked up at her father and smiled a weak smile. She was a slender woman but she had inherited her father's height and was, records showed, just under six feet tall. She was dressed in a blue dressing gown; her feet were enclosed in matching blue slippers.

'How are you, Olivia?' Dew sat in the vacant chair next to his wife. 'It's a lovely evening. Have you been out today for some sun?'

'I'm well, thank you. Yes, it's a lovely evening. Yes, I had a little walk today to get some sun.'

That same flatness of effect, that same encapsulating of his questions in her answers, Dew could not detect any improvement in his daughter's condition. No deterioration but also no improvement. It was hard for him and his wife to accept that just a few years ago it was this selfsame girl of whom her delighted headmistress said, 'There's nothing we *can't* teach her, she grasps everything at once . . . the world's at her feet.'

The leaving, as always, was easy. No tears, no pleas for them to stay a little longer, in fact no display of emotion at all. Just a 'Goodbye, yes, I'll see you again soon,' and then staring straight ahead as if lost somewhere, someplace, known only to herself.

The Dews' journey home was, similarly, completed largely in an uncomfortable silence, each feeling that it was somehow their fault that Olivia's glittering future had been taken from her. Their once-beautiful daughter with her beautiful mind, now zombie-like in a blue for a boy dressing gown, sitting contentedly among other zombies staring straight ahead except for an occasional glance at any visitor who spoke to her.

Upon returning home, Archibald and Miriam Dew did what they always seemed to do upon their return from their weekly visit to their daughter. They went away from each other. Archibald sat on the low wall outside the front of the house which separated his house from his neighbour's. Both properties, like the majority of properties on Pembroke Road, had their small front gardens concreted over to provide off-the-road parking and were separated by brick walls rather than small privet hedges. Miriam Dew on the other hand, as was her wont, went to the rear of the house and sat on the patio. Both he and she observed the vast scarlet sunset settling over the rooftops to the west and both came indoors only when night had fully fallen. That night, also as usual, they retired to the bed which had served them throughout their marriage, without a word passing between them. The following morning, however, Archibald Dew brought his wife a cup of tea while she was in bed. She smiled and said, 'You're so good to me, Archie. Have a good day, love. I'll make a good supper for you to come home to. Take care.'

# THREE

Lawrence 'Larry' Chambers, Archibald Dew and Harry Vicary strolled side by side along the promenade at Bournemouth. The line of white painted buildings on the skyline dazzled in the sun, under a clear blue sky, and the beach to their right and below them was bedecked with sunbathing youth.

'Students mostly, from Brighton University, just along the coast from here,' Chambers explained, 'displaying great intelligence by spending a day like this on the beach rather than inside stuffy lecture theatres,' he grinned, 'and . . . well, for a woman to go topless is still a public order offence but as you see, it is so widely honoured in the breach than the observance . . . that we'd be wasting our time trying to enforce it.'

'Well, if you've got the equipment then display it,' Vicary grinned, 'while it lasts anyway . . . it won't always be there, age takes its toll on all of us.'

'Indeed . . . and we get few complaints. Mind you we did draw the line at a game of naked volleyball played by mixed doubles. We didn't prosecute, just pointed them in the direction of the designated naturist beach a few miles down the coast.'

The three men walked on, shirtsleeves folded up, jackets slung over forearms. Dew wore a panama, Vicary and Chambers, having hair, were bareheaded.

'Did you train down?' Chambers asked.

'Drove,' Dew replied, watching a leggy blonde, naked save for a black thong, run from her friends to the surf.

'Nice drive,' Chambers said. 'I prefer the train, there is something soothing and civilized about a rail journey and I always think that a railway line links a town to the rest of the world in a way that a road does not.'

'I know what you mean,' Dew nodded. 'It has a permanency about it, does a railway line.'

'Safer.' Lawrence Chambers' eyes lighted upon a second young woman who caught a Frisbee skimmed to her by a third young woman, both wearing only bikini bottoms.

'Rail travel you mean?'

'No . . . out here . . . it is safer from prying eyes and ears.'

'Interesting you should say that.'

'Well you wanted information about Jim Coventry. Confess I have found myself thinking about him more and more often in recent years, just getting old I suppose. I once heard that as you get older you tend to think more and more about people you once knew and who died young. In his final years of life my father couldn't stop thinking about four young lads who soldiered with him in the Second World War and who didn't make it. After the war when he was getting on with the peace and starting his family he barely gave them a thought but in his final years . . . each day they came to his mind. Suppose it means I'm getting on now, thinking about Jim Coventry as often as I do. So, who gave you my name?'

'His fiancée, Florence Reilly.'

'Flo!' Chambers' face beamed with a broad smile. 'How is she? I heard she married an Australian and went to live in Perth.'

'Freemantle, but that's basically a suburb of Perth. Yes she did, but the marriage didn't work . . . she blamed herself. Anyway she returned, she lives in north London, didn't remarry.'

'It would be lovely to see her again.'

'I'll let her have your workplace number.'

'Please do.' Chambers shook his head. 'Jim Coventry, Florence Reilly, names from yesteryear. Well, Jim didn't tell me a great deal once he was seconded to the Serious Crime Squad, he was part of Operation Fennel . . . then he disappeared.'

'Fennel?' Dew and Vicary glanced at each other.

'Yes, why? You sound surprised.' Chambers had a soft voice which Dew, particularly, found difficult to hear above the screech of the herring gulls, the murmur of conversation and laughter from the beach and the rhythmic crashing of the surf at high tide.

'Interested rather than surprised, the detail of the operation he was on seems to have been extracted from the missing
persons report.'

'That doesn't surprise me. I'll bet the file on Operation
Fennel has disappeared completely. It was the climate at the
time.'

Again Dew and Vicary glanced at each other. Dew asked,
'Do we need A-Ten on this?'

'Possibly . . . in fact probably, but you'll need something
for them to work on, some start.'

'You've been sitting on this for twenty-seven years!'

Chambers turned sharply and angrily to Dew. 'I have been
sitting on nothing! Jim and I were friends. He was a beautiful person, just a beautiful person . . . very handsome but
modest. He could have been so arrogant and cruel with his
looks but he wasn't, he was sensitive and modest and had a
strong sense of justice and thought people mattered, just a
lovely man who was clearly earmarked as a high-flyer. I
mean, the early secondment to SCS not a transfer, more of
a let's-see-how-you-get-on-and-fit-in sort of move, but definitely a vote of confidence in him from the top floor and me,
by contrast, I have reached the lofty heights of Detective
Sergeant, still nicking car thieves and low-level drug dealers.
I won't be going any higher. I left the Met shortly after Jim
disappeared, moved down here. I was pretty rootless and
happy to pick up my wife's roots. She's a good Hampshire
lass . . . and look,' he extended his arms and took a deep
breath, 'sea air, you don't get air to breathe like this in the
smoke.'

'So what do you know about Operation Fennel? It is
Fennel, as in the herb?'

'Yes, as in the herb. Nothing, I know nothing about it
which is why I haven't been sitting on anything for twenty-
seven years. Jim and I would meet for a beer occasionally.
He told me a few things but no details. It was as if he was
protecting me, as if he thought the less I knew, the safer I'd
be, that was Jim, always caring, always considerate. If he
was in danger, he did not make himself safer by spreading
the danger, spreading the load, as a lesser man would have
done.'

'What was he frightened of?'

Chambers shrugged as a cream and red open-topped bus whirred slowly along the esplanade. 'He talked about a climate of fear in the team.'

'Fear?'

'Yes.'

'Of?'

'The top guys . . .'

'The senior officers?'

'Yes . . . perhaps not the very top but the middle rankers.'

'I see.' Dew breathed deeply. 'Did he mention any names?'

'No, none, keeping the danger to himself you see.'

'What about a bloke, a fellow officer called John or "Jack" Boot? Unfortunate name, but anyway . . . we can't find any record of him.'

'You won't,' Chambers smiled.

'Why not?'

'Because he's a she, Jacqueline Boot. Jackie Boot with an "i e" not a "y". She drowned. Sadly.'

'Drowned?'

'That's interesting.'

'It is?'

'Yes . . . Jim Coventry also drowned. We are not making this public by the way . . . so, discretion, please.'

'Oh, mum's the word. But thank you for telling me . . . but you said he was buried? Poor Jim.' Chambers bit his upper lip. 'What could have been . . . but Jackie drowned in the Thames when she was off duty, so I heard, right at the mouth of the estuary, off Sheerness, at least that's where they fished her body out of the water. No telling where she went in, one cold night in February or March, I think, but cold water anyway, very cold.'

'Suspicious.'

'I'll say but the enquiry came to nought. She was a long way from where she worked and lived . . . found in city clothes like she'd come from work, or from a pub. It was as if she'd allowed herself to be invited on to a boat and then pitched over the side in the night. No sign of violence at all, again, so I heard. She was also in her mid-twenties, also part of Operation Fennel, so I believe.'

'So you're talking murder?'

'Yes,' Chambers spoke flatly. 'Two young police officers, both part of Operation Fennel, both murdered. Her death and Jim's disappearance didn't seem to have been connected, largely because she was off duty when she drowned, as if she'd been partying but she was too close to Jim for her death to be coincidental, or so I thought later. Both part of the same operation and Jim was in fear of the senior officers. You can smell the whiff. At least I can.'

The three men continued to walk on in silence. Dew then asked if Chambers knew what Jim Coventry was doing in Operation Fennel.

'As I said, he told me nothing. He was in deep cover though, I can tell you that. Grew a beard which didn't suit him, he would only be doing that if he was trying to infiltrate a gang of high-level criminals, as you know.'

'Or observe them without looking like a copper, but that is just as dangerous.'

'Twenty-five, thirty, thirty-five years ago, a lot of investigations into corrupt officers then.'

'I recall.'

'A lot got away with it . . . insufficient evidence . . . not in the public interest to prosecute, a few token prosecutions, tip of the iceberg stuff, a different lifetime.'

'Again, as I recall.'

'Not as much corruption about these days because crime and criminals have changed. In those days the police and the East End blaggers grew up together, same council school, same manor, they understood each other and a cop would accept a wedge to make an inquiry go away if the only person hurt was the insurance company, even after a big bullion snatch . . .' Chambers reflected. 'But today if a copper is bent he has to get into bed with the Russian Mafia who are into people smuggling and what police officer would do that? Damn few, if any, if you ask me.'

'Yes . . . agree there.'

'If I were you, I'd do two things, sir.'

'Yes?'

'Firstly I'd find out who else was a junior officer on Operation Fennel, they'll be close to retirement now, if not wholly retired, not in fear any more . . . they'll feel safe to talk. Safer anyway. And if they were part of the corruption they'll sing like canaries in return for an immunity deal which will allow them to keep their pensions.'

'OK . . . and the second?'

'I'd be careful, gentlemen, I'd be very careful. These people appear to have killed twice and killed coppers. They'll kill again and kill coppers again.'

Commander Horace Gentle sat back in his chair in his spartan room. He was a man whom Dew had known for many years and had come to know him as a man who would not tolerate any form of softening or decoration within his office. Gentle eyed Dew coldly with a penetrating gaze. 'Are you sure about this, Archie?'

'No, sir,' Dew tried to relax beneath Gentle's raptor-like stare, 'I am not sure about anything, not sure about anything at all. It's all getting too much though, which is why I came to you, sir. I decided to come straight to the top rather than pass it up through the hierarchy.'

'Yes, pleased you did that, Archie, very pleased.' Gentle was a tall, thin man, immaculately dressed, a pencil-line moustache and eyes of steel. 'So what do we know?'

'It seems, sir, that a PC was murdered whilst on duty.'

'He was, I remember the incident.'

'So we're looking at very heavy-duty criminals. We know PC Coventry had been seconded to the Serious Crime Squad because he seemed to be thought of as being made of the right stuff and he was part of an operation called Operation Fennel.'

'Fennel?'

'Yes, sir, as in the herb.'

'Go on . . .'

'We don't know anything about Operation Fennel.'

'We must!'

'We don't. The collator has no record of it.'

Gentle's eyes knitted. 'No record? There must be a record.'

'I know, sir, but there isn't. No trace at all.'

Gentle breathed deeply and let out a long, deep sigh. 'Carry on . . .'

'We also found out that, shortly before PC Coventry was abducted and murdered, a WPC named Jacqueline Boot was drowned.'

'And that has a link to Operation Fennel and the murder of PC Coventry?'

'Possibly, even probably. She was found drowned, no witness to the incident. Her body was found floating in the estuary, cold water, dressed in city clothes. It was recorded as an accidental death but our information is that her death was suspicious.'

'From whom?'

'PC Coventry's fiancée, sir. She remembers Jim Coventry as being frightened, saying something like he didn't want to end up like Jackie Boot, who was also part of Operation Fennel but she was off duty when she died.'

'I see . . .'

'The second informant is a DS with the Hampshire Constabulary, a personal friend of Jim Coventry's back in the day and he also remembers Jim Coventry making reference to "a climate of fear" in the team that comprised Operation Fennel; that is fear amongst the junior officers, of the middle-ranking officers.'

'I like not the sound of this.'

'Me neither, sir, which is why I brought it to you, straight to you, it smells like Billingsgate Fish Market at the end of a long summer's day.'

'Have you contacted A-Ten?'

'Not yet, sir.'

'I suggest a courtesy call. Jim Coventry was not frightened of the felons he was investigating. He was frightened of his senior officers when he was murdered and a second officer connected to the mysterious Operation Fennel drowned in the Thames and no one saw her fall in the water. She wasn't suicidal or anything?'

'We don't believe so, sir.'

'Very iffy. Tell A-Ten you're sniffing the air and so far the smell indicates corruption within the police but you have no evidence yet. It might be twenty-seven years ago but it's still police corruption, still their box.'

'Yes, sir.'

'And find out what Fennel was about, files do go missing
. . . nearly three decades now, but there must be some trace . . .'

'The computer files appear to have been wiped also. No
manilla folder, no reference on the relevant disk of an operation involving the Serious Crime Squad wherein one and
possibly two junior officers were murdered.'

There followed a long and an uncomfortable silence broken
by Gentle who said, 'Definitely contact A-Ten. After that,
keep it on a "need to know" basis.'

'Yes, sir.'

'Who's working with you on this one?'

'Detective Sergeant Vicary, sir.'

'I don't know him. Is he as up to speed with this as
yourself?'

'Yes, sir, the three of us now are equally informed.'

'Right, liaise with A-Ten and work with them jointly . . .'
Gentle paused. 'No . . . no, let me contact them, I will insist
on joint working with you and A-Ten. They won't like it but
I have the rank.'

'Very good, sir.' Dew stood. 'How shall I keep you
informed, sir? Daily or weekly reports?'

'Significant developments, as they occur.'

'Understood, sir.'

'What is your next step? Have you decided?'

'To find out all I can about Jackie Boot, sir.'


'She did well to get out of Bermondsey, did our Jackie.'
Gerald Boot sat in an armchair in his small living room
where clever use had been made of all the available space.
By pursuing a policy of neatness and everything in its proper
place he had, in Dew's view, made cramped living bearable.
His home was a flat in a medium-rise block built during the
1920s and 1930s of which many similar developments remain
in London, all doing sterling work attesting, Dew felt, to the
high quality of their construction. Boot himself was frail and
elderly and had a slight trace of the smell of an old person
about him, faint, but there. A yellow canary hopped and
flitted in a cage above and behind his chair.

'Yes,' Dew nodded.

'High, high anti-police feeling on the estate, in the whole

of Bermondsey in fact, not just on these streets, and there's
the Queen's jewellery box just across the river, just a river's
width away from hard times. We're an old Bermondsey
family, my grandparents talked about their grandparents
talking about Jacob's Well. It was a stream used as a sewer
and also a source of drinking water. Can you imagine that?
No wonder they had those cholera epidemics, blimey, no
wonder at all. It was buried beneath the southern approach
road to Tower Bridge when the bridge was built. Those
sorts of stories get handed down . . . they don't half do.
Anyway, our Jackie, that's her.' Boot nodded to a framed
photograph on his cluttered but swept-clean mantelpiece,
of a young, thin-faced girl with dark hair and what appeared
to be a ready smile. There was, thought Dew, a genuine
warmth caught by the camera in her eyes. 'She set her
heart on being a copper, not easy around here and at the
time all her girlfriends had boyfriends who were getting
criminal records . . . and . . . and being proud of them for
it. She wanted in the Old Bill, lost all her friends, the
neighbours stopped talking to her, but she made it. Took
her two applications to get in but later she found out that
was normal practice, it tests a person's determination. It
also lets the Bill see how the person spends the year before
the next application.'

'It is and it does,' Vicary smiled. 'It's the normal practice,
as you say.'

'Well, Jackie got a job in a day centre for blind people
*and* kept out of trouble, so that was good enough and she
got accepted on her second application. So why the interest
now? Pushing thirty years since she died. Me, I always
thought her death was iffy, killed Annie, her mother.' Boot
again nodded in the direction of the mantelpiece. Beside the
photograph of Jackie Boot was a photograph, black and
white, of another young woman. The two women did indeed
look similar. 'Twenty-one,' Boot added.

'Sorry?'

'That one of Jackie is when she was twenty-one and the
other is of her mother Annie when she was twenty-one. Me,
I was behind a Bren gun in Malaya when I was twenty-one,'
he grinned, 'they don't allow cameras there. But Annie just

pined. Jackie was our only one and when she died Annie just seemed to lose the will to live . . .'

He fell silent as the room was swamped by the sound of a train on the network of railway lines near the house which fed into Charing Cross and Cannon Street.

'I like the sound of the trains,' Boot said. 'All day and all night . . . a bit less at night, but still there rattling away, it means that all's right with the world, especially at night. They help me sleep at night.'

'Talked to a gentleman just yesterday who also sang the praises of railway lines,' Vicary said. 'He said a railway line links a town more strongly to the outside world than does a road. Confess I have never thought about railways much but two men in as many days singing the praises for reasons other than a means of transport. It's got me thinking.'

'I love living by a railway line,' Boot replied warmly. 'Love it.'

'But Jackie,' Dew said, 'she drowned.'

'See, that's why it's iffy. At the inquest they said she had salt water in her lungs. Think about that,' he held eye contact with Dew and then Vicary, 'she was washed back from the sea into the estuary. She didn't fall off Southend Pier or anything, she went over the side of a boat in the middle of the English Channel but the people that pushed her didn't know the river, least ways they didn't check the tides, and her body was brought back on the flood to where it was fished out. The ebb would have taken her back out to sea but someone saw her floating and called the River Police, otherwise she'd be a missing person . . . even today, a missing person. But she was dead, she wasn't telling no tales, except to St Peter.'

'You believe she was murdered to silence her?'

'What else? No sign of violence they said, all her clothes were on her body, even her shoulder bag was still around her neck with her purse inside it. That's how she was identified so quickly . . . but no witnesses.' Boot glanced up at the canary. 'Not right that, is it, darlin'?' He paused and looked at Dew. 'Coroner said misadventure. Dare say that is all he could do. You can always reopen an inquest if new evidence comes to light, I understand?'

'Yes, that is the case.'

'She was off duty when she drowned, so we believe.'

'Yes, she was on sick leave . . . just a few days.'

'Sick leave?'

'Nothing serious, a chest infection, her doctor signed her off for three days. So . . . see, that's another thing, who goes out on the river with a chest infection in winter?'

'Winter?'

'Well, spring, March, April . . . but still cold, especially so on the water and in the water. Still get easterlies at that time of the year and your east wind can be a real biter coming across the channel.'

'Do you know what she was working on at the time she drowned?'

'No . . . but I would have thought you would have records about that bit.'

'Her file told us little,' Dew replied, not wishing to give anything away in respect of missing documentation and erased computer discs.

'I see . . . well I can't tell you because she didn't tell me . . . sort of "mum's the word" it seemed like.'

'What was her manner like . . . her behaviour . . . her attitude at the time?'

'Well, she rented a drum so we didn't see her often just before she died. She was a young person making her way in the world. She did seem a little quiet the last time she visited as if something was preying her mind. You should ask Mary Street.'

'Who is she? Where is she?'

'Jackie's childhood friend, used to be Mary Little. She was about the only school chum of Jackie's that didn't turn her back on her when Jackie joined the Old Bill, but even then they couldn't be seen together in Bermondsey, they had to arrange to meet each other off the manor if they wanted a natter, otherwise things would be difficult for Mary, her husband being a blagger.'

'Really?' Dew smiled.

'Yes, long-time petty crook but has grown to be a major villain. Anyway, they would grab an afternoon and go for a drink somewhere but if our Jackie said anything to anyone it'd be to Mary Street.'

'Where does she live?'

'Dunno, but you'll have her husband on your books. Ricky Street, geezer in his fifties now, and I hear he's in Wormwood Scrubs at the moment so you can visit her and folk will think you're the Bill calling on her, which you will be, but not like the neighbours will think.' Boot smiled. 'I like the thought of that.'

'So do we.' Dew also smiled. He stood. 'So do we.'

'We like it a lot.' Vicary also stood.

'You'll let us know if you find out anything?'

'Yes,' Dew nodded and held eye contact with Gerald Boot, 'we'll let you know. Don't get up, we'll see ourselves out. Thanks.'

Mary Street flung the door open with undisguised rage. 'He's inside, you know he's inside. What more do you want?'

'How do you know we're the police?' Dew asked with a gentle smile.

'Because "Old Bill" is stamped on your forehead.'

'Well, we'd still like a word,' Dew spoke softly, 'and it's not about your husband.'

Mary Street looked questioningly at Dew. Dew turned and raised his panama to the group of summer-clothed women who had gathered on the far side of the narrow road, which was lined with a new-build council development of pale-cream brick, PVC window frames and doors so small that, Dew thought, they would scarce admit an infant. 'Good afternoon, ladies,' he called jovially. The women scowled at him.

Vicary whispered, 'It's about Jackie Boot.'

'Jaqu . . .' Mary gasped. 'You'd better come in.' She turned and stormed into the house with a display of indignation which was clearly for the benefit of the audience at the other side of the road. Dew followed her and Vicary, after turning to smile at the women, also stepped into the house of Street and closed the door behind him.

Mary Street walked into the kitchen at the rear of her house and then turned, peacefully, to the officers. 'Sorry about the act,' she smiled, displaying a gentleness of manner.

'Not to worry, we're used to it.'

'It was for the benefit of those cows across the road. One

of them, the one with horns, she's my sister-in-law, her brother is my husband, Ricky. He's doing seventeen for armed robbery.'

'Yes, we know.' Richard 'Ricky' Street had transpired to be a lot more 'grown' than Gerald Boot had led the officers to believe. 'We have just come from Jackie's father. He told us Ricky was inside.'

'Gerald? How is he?'

'Seems to be all right, bit frail and elderly as you'd expect, but he's wearing well.'

'He's a lovely old geezer.' Mary Street seemed burdened with worry, older looking than her actual years, in Dew's eyes, overweight, face lined with anxiety, a mop of unkempt hair. Her kitchen was decorated and furnished with the cheapest of equipment; the table with thin metal legs and a yellow Formica surface, the four matching chairs, each equally flimsy. The rear door, which had been opened to allow fresh air into the house, led on to a small paved area across which a short washing line had been hung. Beyond the wooden fence at the bottom of the yard were the roofs of similar houses and beyond them a multi-storey block of flats. A fly buzzed on the window pane. The kitchen smelled of recently fried food. 'He took Jackie's death hard, they both did . . . she, Annie, she just lost all her will to live, but the old boy, he found it in himself to soldier on. So well done him but he has ploughed a lonely furrow. So how can I help you?'

'Jackie's father told us that you knew Jackie before and around the time she died? You remained a good friend to her when the rest of the manor turned their backs on her after she joined the police force.'

'Well, that's Bermondsey for you. But, yes, we used to meet up. We had to be discreet but that was part of the fun, like playing secret agents. It was about once a month we would meet up. We met just for a good natter, two girls together, we were like two non-stop talking machines . . . golden days . . . twenty years ago, must be.'

'Twenty-seven in March. Jackie died twenty-seven years and three months ago.'

Mary Street gasped, 'That long ago? Where did my life go?'

'We all feel like that,' Dew offered reassuringly, 'suddenly you are old.'

Mary Street groaned and shook her head. 'You know I heard my youngest telling his mate that he was selling his motor because "the suspension has sagged and the clutch is gone", I felt he could have been talking about me.'

'So, the golden days?'

'Yes, me and Jackie, playing secret agents, her a cop and me a blagger's girl but I never grassed anybody up.'

'I'm sure.'

'Ricky never told me anything anyway and when he got seventeen that came as a shock. He's had a few fives, cut to three, but seventeen, I didn't know he'd moved so far up the ladder. He won't get considered for parole for at least another seven years . . . that suits me.'

'Not a happy marriage?'

'Well, look around you; this is the sort of house you get to live in if you're a blagger's trouble and strife. For every blagger's wife with a villa in Spain and a little red Alfa Romeo to use on her own, there's fifty who live like this, scratching pennies on Income Support and shored up with Valium and Librium and all the other "ums" that the doctor can throw at you.' She turned and sank into one of the metal chairs by the table. It creaked slightly as it accepted her weight. 'My eldest is "known" now, wants to be like his dad, got to get some prison time under your belt he says, so he got himself caught and got sent down . . . six months in Brixton . . . a rite of passage number but that's what he wants. I've got two younger than him and they're wanting to go the same way, already thieving they are. You can't help worry but it changes nothing. So here I am. You know, when I was about nineteen, me and my mates went camping in the Lake District, right up north because we'd heard that you get quality people on campsites like doctors and lawyers. We went all the way up there to try and pull a doctor or a lawyer . . . it rained all the time. We didn't meet any quality people and it was the only time in my life I've been out of London, and if that's the north, you can keep it, but sometimes I wonder, I just wonder, supposing I had met a young doctor . . . and in those days I could make heads turn . . . men looked at me, I mean, really gave me the "once over". I wouldn't have aged so much as a doctor's wife and I would have worked hard to keep my figure. Now men ignore me.'

She glanced out of the window and up at the tower block beyond her neighbour's roof line. 'But me and Jackie in the golden time . . . we'd meet when we could, when her rota allowed it. We'd walk separately to London Bridge Railway Station about an hour apart, take a train to Greenwich and meet in a pub by the covered market. I could get the time off if I told Ricky I was going shopping. We weren't married then and I lived with me mum, so we'd meet up and have a good natter then fix up a date to meet in about a month's time, then get the train back separately. I always went before her; she poked round the market for an hour before returning. We couldn't afford to be seen together but you know what London is like, on the manor everybody knows your business, move off the manor and, well, you might as well be in the middle of Australia for all the chance there is of being clocked by someone you know. But then she drowned, still a young woman; it was all before her . . . poor Jackie. I was thinking of her only last week . . . now you two gents call . . . it's like I had a premonition.'

'Yes, but what we want to know, Mary . . . I can call you, Mary?'

'Yes, please do.'

'What we want to know, Mary, is what was she like in herself just before she died?'

'She was frightened; I can tell you that, very frightened.'

'Can you tell us why?'

'Don't particularly want to but, twenty-seven years . . . What were you doing twenty-seven years ago, sir?' She addressed Dew.

'I was a constable in the Dog Branch.'

'You?' She looked at Vicary.

'Still at school in Hastings.'

'One in uniform, the other still at school, I suppose it's safe. She probably told me more than she should have done but we were like sisters. She was undercover, that's dangerous for any copper but it's very dangerous for a woman. They were really heavy-duty blaggers she was infiltrating; they had a huge cannabis-growing operation.'

'Growing! Twenty-seven years ago? Growing?' Dew gasped.

'Yes, I told you she told me more than she should have done.'

'But growing?'

'Yes, growing. Ninety per cent of cannabis is grown in "farms" over here these days, I am sure you know that.'

'Yes,' Dew nodded, 'we know the score. We are able to identify such "farms", ordinary houses in suburbia but with the heat turned up so high it melts the snow on the roof and causes the wallpaper to peel off the walls of the adjoining house, shines like a beacon in infrared imaging, looked after by a "gardener" who keeps the plants watered. They say a greenhouse in summer is cool in comparison. The "gardener" is almost always an illegal who is scared of being sent home and so lives there in return for a bit of food. Each "farm" can produce four harvests a year.'

'Yes, but twenty years, thirty years ago, did you know it started as long ago as that? When the Old Bill and the Customs was looking for it being smuggled in from Africa and India, it was being grown in Britain, on housing estates. So that's what Jackie was investigating, a home-grown cannabis racket, one of the first in Britain but twenty-seven years ago, neither of you could have been part of it, so now you've been told.'

'Part of it?' Dew sighed. 'You mean the police were part of it?'

'That's what Jackie . . . well, that's what she suggested. She didn't say so, not in so many words but she did say that she didn't know who she could trust.'

'That's very interesting.' Dew spoke with a heavy heart.

'Do you know any details?'

'I can tell you that she dressed up.'

Dew raised his eyebrows.

'I mean, I've got to know the Old Bill, like all the blaggers' wives, like any other gangster's moll, it's often the talk down the boozer, how to spot an undercover cop . . . always look uncomfortable in cheap clothes, eyes always darting about, always tall and muscular . . . just better looking and in better shape than your average East End blagger . . . but I thought it was a bit funny that Jackie should get dressed up to go undercover. She'd go to wine bars, particularly up the West End, really posh pubs like she was passing herself off as a Sloane Ranger.'

'She went undercover as a Sloane Ranger?'

'Yes,' Mary Street replied flatly, 'she went undercover as a Sloane Ranger. She had the looks for it, high cheek bones, slender long legs, really looked like she was the product of fifteen generations of selective breeding she did. Looking at her in her finery you'd never guess she came out of South East One and had left the local council school at sixteen. But the last few times we met up in Greenwich she was just "our Jackie". It was like she just needed to touch base with her own kind, so she could be Jackie Boot from Bermondsey again for a while, just stop the game playing, just to be an honest working-class girl again. Our meet-ups did get a bit irregular towards the end. She said that being undercover was a twenty-four seven thing, just couldn't work shifts. She could grab a bit of free time now and again, so towards the end we'd meet when she could get away. I was seeing a lot of Ricky then but he was a daytime drinker, so she could phone without much risk of him answering and if she did phone and he answered, she was to say she was "Ruth" but she always got me and we'd make a date to go down to Greenwich.'

'Did she mention any names?'

'Couple . . . a man with a name of a Midlands town.'

'Coventry?'

'Yes, that was it. She said he and she had seen things and "they" knew we'd seen them and also she said, "Fillet doesn't seem to know what's going on."'

'Fillet?'

'Long time ago now but sometimes you can remember conversations like they were yesterday.'

'Yes, that is quite true . . . I have the same perfect recollections of conversations.'

'So it sounded like Fillet, but could have been Fillot, or Fillit, or Fillat, or Fillut.'

'Fill . . . at . . . et . . . it . . . ot . . . ut . . .' Dew repeated, committing the alternatives to memory.

'I don't think I can tell you any more.'

'I'll leave my card.' Dew reached into his jacket pocket.

'Oh, don't do that,' Mary Street smiled. 'That will make things difficult for me if I have a copper's calling card on my shelf, me a blagger's wife. Do me a favour, duck . . .'

Dew smiled. 'Sorry, I wasn't thinking. The name's Dew, like the stuff you get on grass at dawn, Archie Dew, New Scotland Yard.'

'I can remember that . . . the stuff what you get on grass at dawn . . . and Archie, well, I had an Uncle Archie, so I can remember that.' She stood with difficulty. She did not, observed Dew, cope well with her weight. 'I'd better put on a show for the herd of prize Jerseys across the road. I'll scream but don't take it personally.'

'We won't, but what will you tell them?'

'You were questioning me about a job but I could prove I had an alibi . . . like I'm a suspect.'

'You'll be all right?'

'Oh, yes, the Bill is always knocking on doors round here.'

Dew and Vicary walked down the narrow corridor to the door. Dew opened it and walked out into the sunlight with Vicary close behind him. Mary Street screamed, 'Satisfied!' and slammed the door shut behind the officers.

'More curious than satisfied,' Dew whispered as he and Vicary walked to where they had parked their car, and as the group of women advanced as one body across the road to Mary Street's door, 'but yes . . . some satisfaction as well.'

'It's ten times worse than the worst hangover you can imagine. I mean think of the worst damn hangover you can remember and double it . . . triple it.' The thin-drawn, white-haired man sat beside Parsloe in Parsloe's car. 'They said they'd improved it. If this is improvement, what could it have been like before?'

'You said you got the last one next week?'

'Yes.' The frail man looked to one side and let his gaze rest on the starling which had alighted upon a short concrete upright post beside the car. 'Seeing details now,' he murmured. 'That bird . . . before I wouldn't have given it a second glance, its eyes, its beak, the way it looks around and it'll still be alive when I won't be. I've got a month, five, six weeks and for the first time in my life, I give a bird a second look. I might finish it after . . . you know, after I have done it.'

'But you'll go through with it?'

The man nodded. 'Oh, yes . . . guaranteed.' The man looked further afield. The supermarket car park had a few cars and none in the corner where Parsloe had parked his car. That Parsloe drove into the supermarket car park had surprised him given the presence of CCTV cameras, but he noted that Parsloe had parked facing away from the camera and so whatever happened inside the car would not be able to be photographed. And since nothing of interest was likely to happen anyway, the CCTV tape would be wiped clean in twenty-four hours.

'We can't do this twice,' Parsloe said. 'It has to be done right first time.'

'I'll do it.' The man gazed at the roof line and then at the blue sky with wispy white clouds above the roof line. 'I won't be here much longer and when you think that London will be under water soon, global warming and all that, probably a good time to go. I love this city, wouldn't want to live to see it drowned.'

'We all go at some point, Ernie. The ferryman has room for all of us.'

'Yeah, we all go sometime. I thought it would be a bit later though, seems a bit early. It feels like I am being cheated out of the last bit, like I get the soup then the main course but I have to do without the spotted dick and custard. Mind you there's a bloke at the clinic, I see him and we've got to know each other, who is still in his thirties, early thirties, school teacher, that's really early but most are older than me, most have had their pudding. Me and the teacher go for a drink after the session, whichever one goes in first, he waits for the other.'

'You can do that?'

'Oh . . . yes, the after-effects don't kick in until the next day and we only have one pint each. I tell him I was an odd-job man all my days.'

'Which you were.'

The thin man grinned. 'Odd bank here . . . odd post office there . . . odd smash and grab . . . odd bit of ringing . . . suppose it's not too far from the truth.'

Parsloe opened an ex-army canvas knapsack and took out a .22 automatic. He handed it to the thin man, who, like Parsloe, wore gloves.

'Shooter,' the man said, accepting the gun into his hands, 'never used a shooter before . . . sawn-offs, yes, but never a shooter.'

'It's not loaded, you can test the action.'

The thin man turned off the safety catch and pulled the trigger twice. He found it to have a smooth, well-lubricated action.

'You can hold it with both hands, easier that way.' Parsloe turned and smiled graciously at the woman who had parked her car a few feet away. He turned to the thin man. 'Keep it out of sight.'

The man put the gun down between his knees. 'Yes, I'll do that, two hands. I am not as strong as I used to be.'

Parsloe took an empty plastic bottle and a roll of masking tape from the bag and asked for the gun. He inserted the barrel of the gun into the plastic bottle and wound the masking tape around the top and then to the neck of the bottle and continued winding the tape until it had captured the barrel of the gun as far back as the trigger guard. The bottle was thus fastened at an odd and awkward-looking angle to the barrel.

'You have to remember to point the gun barrel.' Parsloe handed the gun back to the man. 'Don't point the bottle but that, Ernie, is known as the "pauper's silencer". The plastic won't stop the bullet, but it will contain the sound of the explosion. It's a twenty-two, small calibre, and fairly thick plastic as plastic bottles go. With luck, you'll get three fairly quiet rounds off before the bottle gives way, so phut . . . phut . . . phut . . . bang.'

'Got it.'

'Avoid the bang and you'll make your escape.'

'Savvy, chief. Savvy.' The man held the silenced gun, pointing it down towards the footwell. 'When do we do the biz?'

'Tonight.'

'So soon?'

'Yes.'

'Who is the mark?'

'I'll point him out to you. You needn't know anything about him. Safer that way.'

'Yes. When do I get the money?'

'Half now.' Parsloe handed an envelope to the man. 'Fifty thousand of your English pounds.'

'And the rest?' he asked, putting the money in his pocket. 'How soon do I get the rest?'

'Immediately. I'll be parked close by, in this car, this old thing . . . I bought it this morning. Usually drive a Jaguar but sometimes a ten-year-old VW does very nicely indeed.'

'Doesn't do to stand out at times,' the frail man nodded. 'I can see that.' He handed the silenced weapon back to Parsloe who slid it inside the knapsack. 'So, see you later.' He opened the car door.

'You don't want a lift? It's a long way back to your manor from here.'

'No,' the man forced a smile, 'I want to walk as far as I can, then I'll jump on a bus. Saying goodbye to the old town. See you in a few hours. Thanks for this.' He patted his jacket pocket.

Archie Dew took his tray of tea and toast from the counter and walked across the floor of the canteen of New Scotland Yard to where an elderly sergeant sat by the window, taking his own rest and refreshment. The canteen was, estimated Dew, about one quarter occupied with few totally vacant tables so sitting at a table which was already occupied did not, he hoped, seem unusual. He put the tray down on the table and smiled at the sergeant. 'Mind if I join you?'

'Please do.' The sergeant returned the smile.

Dew glanced out of the window at the small backyards of the buildings and narrow service roads at the rear of New Scotland Yard. 'Can't wait to finish.' Dew nibbled at his slice of toast.

'The day? Been a bad one? It happens.'

'The job,' Dew grinned. 'The day hasn't been a bad day, but I meant the job. Retirement beckons.'

'I know what you mean. I don't have long to go myself. I never got as far as I should have done. I should have gone further, but sergeant, could be worse. What are you?'

'Detective Chief Inspector.'

'Not bad, sir, nice little package awaits you, sir. I have seen you about the building, of course, never spoken.'

'Yes, same here . . . and it's Archie by the way, please . . . police canteen.'

'Archie,' the sergeant nodded. 'I'm Robert May, as in the merry month.'

'Robert. Been in long, Robert?'

'Thirty years.'

'Not bad . . . full pension then?'

'Yes, guaranteed, enough to live on.'

There was the sound of breaking plates and a woman's scream from behind the counter. Dew and May smiled at each other.

'We used to cheer when someone dropped plates in the school canteen,' Dew commented.

'So did we, same in all schools, I think.'

'Any plans, Robert?'

'Extended holiday in Ireland, that will be the first thing . . . round Galway area. Know it?'

'Can't say I do, Robert, my wife and I have always gone to France.'

'I see. Any family, Archie?'

'One daughter.'

'Nice. I have two sons, both in the force.'

'Really?' Dew raised his eyebrows and inclined his head in a gesture of approval. 'Excellent.'

'Well, if they make the sort of rank you have made, it will be very excellent . . .' May paused. 'Personally I would have wanted them to go to university but they were all for joining as soon as they could.'

'So,' Dew sipped his tea, 'thirty years, you must remember Fillet.'

'Fillet?' Robert May looked puzzled.

'Fillot,' Dew tried again, 'senior officer a long time ago, be when you started.'

'Oh, you mean Phil Ott,' May grinned. 'That is going back a long time. He would have retired about ten or twelve years ago now, same rank as you are now, if I recall correctly, young for his rank, a real blue-eyed boy.'

'Yes, Phil . . . I mean, talking about retirement as we were.'

'Yes, I often think of the ones who have retired, wonder what they got up to, if they're still with us. Phil will be in his late sixties now. Yes, he went at fifty-five, so he'll be sixty-seven now. Not old, not these days. But really, he was more of a name I knew rather than a man I knew.'

'Yes, met him briefly,' Dew nodded. 'Good man. Blue-eyed boy, as you say.'

Not wanting the good Robert May to think that he had sought out his company merely to obtain the intelligence that 'Fillat' or 'Fillett', or 'Fillit' or 'Fillet' or 'Fillot' was in fact Philip 'Phil' Ott, Dew remained with Sergeant May for a further thirty minutes discussing retirement plans and the good fortune they both had in soon being able to retire at fifty-five years with an inflation-proof police pension after thirty years' exemplary service.

Liverpool Road, Canning Town, London E16, was an area of post-Second World War new-build council development, with trees planted as saplings during the area's renewal now approaching maturity. It was a wide road, near where the Lea joined the Old Father, with green space at either end. A person could breathe in Liverpool Road. In one house on Liverpool Road, near the southern end, the Malmerbury Road end, Ernie Spicer sat at the kitchen table with his family, his wife and three sons. An ice cream van drove slowly by, loudly playing Greensleeves and drowning the sound of children playing in the street. In contrast to the noise outside their home, Mrs Spicer and the three Spicer boys looked at the table in stunned silence.

'It's good money,' Ernie Spicer said reassuringly.

'Good money,' Sadie Spicer repeated. 'What does that mean?'

'Genuine. Kosher, not counterfeit and not stolen either.'

'OK.'

Ernie Spicer picked up a bundle of the money. 'It's still in sequence, we have to break that up,' and then began to peel off one twenty-pound note at a time and placed each note in front of first his wife and then his sons in descending order of age. 'I haven't done much for you,' he said as he divided the money, 'but I can do this at the end of it all.' And he continued dividing the money as a child might be saying 'one for you, and one for you, and one for you, and one for you' until his wife and his three sons each had an equal share of fifty thousand pounds. 'You know the sketch,' he leaned back in his chair, 'that's why I have been on at you all your lives to open as many bank accounts and building society and post office accounts as you can and you've all got five or six accounts, that is good.' He breathed deeply as if fighting for breath. 'So you know what to do.'

'Yes, dad,' Ernest Spicer's youngest son spoke for the family, 'a little bit into each, a little bit at a time.'

'Good boy,' Spicer smiled, 'you remember that, don't get impatient and bung it all into one account all at once. Remember, the banks are obliged to report any unusually large deposits to the law and the Bill will be round here wanting to know where you got it from and if you don't give a good answer, they can freeze it. Who wants that? That's just over ten big ones each. So it will need patience, no flashing it around. Keep quiet when you're in the boozer, there's five people know about this dosh and we want to keep it that way. It's you I'm worried about,' Spicer pointed to his eldest son, 'always was hasty you was, no patience, not ever. So, if the Bill does come round it'll be down to you. So rest of you,' he addressed his wife and two youngest sons, 'you watch him . . . right?'

'Yes, Ernie,' his wife replied, eyeing her first born coldly, 'we'll watch him. We'll watch him good.'

'And hide your bank books.'

'Yes, dad.'

'So pay in about two hundred pounds to each account on a different day of the week – so post office Monday, building society Tuesday, bank Wednesday, the other building society on Thursday, the other banks on Friday. Paying in two hundred a week won't get noticed, not even round here. Remember the plain-clothed cops are on the street corners. If they see you walk out of one bank and into another they'll smell a rat. So one day, one bank.'

'Yes, dad.'

'And do it separately, not all together.'

'Yes, dad.'

'So, you'll pay in one large a week. All told it'll take twenty weeks to get it all in because I am going to post the same amount to you tomorrow, registered post, so make sure you're here to receive it from the postie.'

'OK.' His wife nodded and for the first time she smelled the unpleasant aroma of death about her husband, much, much more than his malodorous breath from corrupted lungs, something else, as if the smell was seeping from the pores of his skin. It was the end.

'So be canny. It'll take twenty weeks all told and it just needs one careless word, one bit of flash spending and the world will come through the front door. So one of you be in the house at all times. If there's a whiff of hard cash inside this house the windows will get turned, so keep it occupied twenty-four seven, even if you have to organize it so one of you stays up all night, until all the dosh is in the bank accounts.'

'Yes, dad.'

'And when you get the next fifty thousand, divide it up like I did this lot, break the sequence.' He fell silent a moment. 'This is going to be my last job, it pays one hundred large, so that will be twenty-five large each . . . it's something . . . use it wisely. I squandered my money, I should have been more sensible. If it wasn't for this job, I wouldn't have left you nothing. So be sensible with it. Don't end up like me.'

'Yes, dad.'

Ernest Spicer stood. 'I'm going now.' He put on his lightweight summer jacket and walked out of the door, leaving his family seated in silence and with downcast eyes. He had always said that he wanted it this way, just to walk out of his house, to take his own life before it was taken from him, go on his terms. He just did not want to die in bed, either at home or in a hospital. He wanted no words, no tears, no emotion, no last-time embraces. He just wanted to be allowed to walk out of his house and make his own arrangements.

Archibald Dew returned from the canteen to his office, picked up the phone as he turned to sit in his chair and jabbed a four figure internal number.

'Personnel.' The voice was female. Crisp. Efficient.

'DCI Dew, Murder Squad.'

'Yes, sir. Fiona Beals speaking.'

'I'd like the file on a retired police officer sent up to me, please.'

'I'll need a memo for that, please, sir, confidentiality issue.'

'I see. All right, just tell me his present address.'

Fiona Beals gasped, 'I'm sorry, sir, I can't.'

'Just tell me by phone, better this way, no paper trail. Just tell me where Phil Ott lives.'

'Sir, this is most irregular.'

'I know. Look, clear it with Commander Gentle, then phone me back. Thank you.' He replaced the phone without waiting for the reply from the clearly aghast Fiona Beals, and became aware of Harry Vicary standing in the doorframe of his office.'

'Harry . . .' Dew reclined in his seat. 'Come in, do.'

'Sir.' Vicary entered Dew's office. A second man walked behind him. The second man was tall, even for a police officer he was tall. He was dressed in what Dew would describe as an impeccable light-brown summer suit, highly polished brown shoes, tie fastened with a gold tiepin, pencil-line moustache, very closely trimmed hair. 'This is DS Garrick Forbes. He is with A-Ten.'

'I see.' Dew stood. He and Forbes shook hands. 'How do we address you? As you see I use DS Vicary's first name.'

'DS Forbes, if you don't mind. I find it helps to keep things formal when you are joint working, doesn't blur the boundaries.'

'As you wish, DS Forbes. Please take a seat . . . please.' Dew indicated the chairs in front of his desk.

'I am here on the orders of Commander Gentle. Any suggestion of police corruption becomes a matter for A-Ten. But I must tell you I dislike joint working.'

'Thank you.' Dew leaned forward as Forbes and Vicary sat down in the chairs. 'I appreciate your honesty but this is still the murder of a police officer and a possible murder of a second officer.'

'Two officers?' Forbes raised his eyebrows.

'Possibly. One certainly, two is a possibility. I'll bring you up to speed of course and let you read the file, but it seems that twenty-seven years ago two officers were part of a team investigating a large-scale cannabis-growing operation.'

'Growing?'

'Yes.'

'Farms, you mean?'

'Yes.'

'But twenty-seven years ago? I thought "farms" were a recent development.'

'Came as a surprise to us, confess, but anyway, the two officers, James Coventry and Jacqueline Boot, both Detective Constables, were in deep cover as part of an operation called Operation Fennel, all records of which are missing from the archives, both hard and soft copy.'

Forbes smiled. 'Now that I find interesting, very interesting indeed, it is just such developments that whet my appetite. It is just such revelations which caused me to apply to A-Ten.'

'Yes,' Dew replied drily.

'We have just now ascertained that the officer in charge of Operation Fennel was one Philip Ott, now retired. We'll have to talk to him, pick his brains. That is the next step once personnel . . .' The phone on Dew's desk warbled softly. He let it ring twice before picking up the handset. '. . . Dew.' He listened and wrote on his notepad as he did so. 'Thank you.' He replaced the handset gently.

'We are going to Norfolk,' he said.

'We are, sir?' Vicary smiled.

'Yes, Philip Ott retired there, to a place called Burnham Market, wherever that is.'

'Norfolk – on the coast.' Forbes grinned. 'My wife grew up in Fakenham. When we were engaged we would visit her parents and borrow their old tandem and cycle to Burnham

Market. Lovely ride across flat Norfolk countryside. You see
I have already proved useful.'

'A good start, thank you, DS Forbes.'

'Pleasure. I'll need office accommodation; no one should
know I am with A-Ten.'

'Yes.' Dew and Vicary looked at each other and nodded.
'Yes, we'll keep it under our hats.'

'There's a spare desk in the office by mine,' Vicary offered.

'That is good,' Forbes said. 'Near you but not in your
office is good.'

'We'll drive up tomorrow,' Dew said. 'I'll phone him, make
sure he's going to be there to receive us.'

'They call this area "Moneyhill".' Parsloe drove his car along
tree-lined avenues of detached houses. 'Appropriate, don't
you think?'

Spicer grunted. He had lost all interest in money and property values. Now he saw only lush vegetation and what he
thought was a splendid sunset.

'We'll park up when it gets dark,' Parsloe said. 'They call
the police round here if they see there are guys sitting in a
car. Looks a bit iffy but the mark is a man of habit. We've
been watching him. I know when he'll be where it is you'll
do the business.'

Ernest Spicer grunted. 'Never been here before,' he said.
'Looks nice.'

'Well . . . so I've done you a favour, Ernie, see
Rickmansworth and die.' Parsloe grinned.

Spicer glared at him. 'You got the money?'

'Yes, I've brought the money, new notes so you'll have to
launder it. It's the only way I could get it, no time to launder
it myself.'

'That's taken care of,' Spicer growled. 'It's in both our
interests to wash it.'

'Good.' Parsloe glanced at his watch. 'OK, we can make
our way to the drop zone.'

'The drop zone?'

'Yes, where you're going to do the biz, Ernie, where you are
going to drop the mark. The drop zone.'

Moments later, when the sky was more black than it was

scarlet, Parsloe halted his VW at the corner of the meeting of one leafy suburban street with another, and switched off the lights and the engine. 'He'll be here in five minutes,' he said. 'If he's coming at all, he'll be here in five minutes.' He settled back in the driver's seat and adjusted the rear-view mirror, keeping his eyes on the pavement behind the car. 'He's pushing the boat out lately,' Parsloe commented, 'hitting it hard but it should make it easier for you.'

'Yes.' Spicer wound down the window. 'Glad it's summer.'

'To do the job?'

'No, just glad it's summer. What will it feel like?'

'Just a slight kick in your hand, it's only a twenty-two.'

'No . . . I mean . . . in here.' Ernest Spicer tapped his chest. 'What will it feel like in here? When you kill someone, what does it feel like?'

'It feels good.' Parsloe kept his eye on the pavement behind him. 'It feels very, very good. If you don't like your target it feels very good indeed. If you don't know your target it feels . . . it feels powerful. You feel power and life seems more real. You know you should look at it this way, once, a long time ago I talked to a geezer who had been an infantry-man in the Second World War, Middlesex Regiment.'

'Had to be good, then.'

'Best in the line, the Middlesex boys. Anyway, he went thinking he had to kill two Germans. If he got killed without killing a single Jerry, he'd lost the game, if he killed one then he was killed, then that was a drawn game, kill two, then it's a won game, which he did and a few more he reck-oned and he came home. So you're going to draw your game Ernie, at least it's a drawn game for you.'

'And for you?'

'Won game for me,' Parsloe said smugly, 'already a won game for little me. You see the more victims you have . . . he's here. Got the shooter?'

Spicer patted the canvas knapsack.

'He's the guy coming up behind you, white coat, only one of him, no one else around. Wait until he's just at the back of the car . . . I'll tell you when.'

In the event Ernest Spicer had found it quite easy to kill. He had forced thought from his mind, just acted, just went through the motions like a ten-year-old playing cowboys and Indians. Parsloe had said, 'Now!' He had stepped from the car, turned round and found himself three or four feet from the mark who was a tall man, like Parsloe. He had raised the gun and had aimed the barrel, not the bottle, squeezed the trigger as the man's face drained of colour and a look of shock and realization crossed his eyes. He had squeezed the trigger and the gun had made a soft 'phutt' sound and had kicked in his hand. The man had fallen with a small hole in the middle of his forehead. Spicer had stepped forward, pushed the shattered bottom of the plastic bottle up against the man's head and pulled the trigger a second time, and for a second time the gun made a soft 'phutt' sound, distinctly louder than the first though still not loud enough to cause curtains to twitch in sleepy, leafy suburban Rickmansworth at ten thirty p.m. Even a nearby owl continued to hoot.

Spicer turned and knelt down so as to face Parsloe. 'Money,' he said, 'job done.' Spicer took the plastic bottle from the gun and tossed it away, utterly unconcerned about leaving his fingerprints on it and the masking tape. He sat in the passenger seat and put the gun in his pocket.

'You're keeping the gun?' Parsloe started the car and drove slowly away.

'Yes. I have use for it.'

'Suit yourself,' Parsloe growled, 'it would only go into the river. Where can I drop you?'

'Anywhere inside London.'

'OK. The rest of the money is on the back seat.'

Spicer twisted and retrieved it. The rest of the journey was passed in silence, until both men had bade each other a cursory farewell when Parsloe stopped the car in Willesden, enabling Spicer to leave it and walk away into the evening gloom.

Ernie Spicer walked until he found the suburbs, until he found what he was looking for, being a house with an over-grown front garden in which he hid until dawn. He thought about his life. He had no regrets, there was no time for regrets, he had lived his life as he had and that was it.

He waited until dawn came.

He waited until a milk float whined and rattled by.

He waited until the first car drove by and the first foot-steps of the earliest commuter passed him.

He waited until he heard an alarm clock ring from within the home of the garden in which he had concealed himself.

He emerged slowly, cautiously, and then began to walk out of the suburbs towards the centre of Willesden. He asked a postman in a blue shirt carrying a red high-definition Royal Mail shoulder bag the directions to the nearest post office. The post office was large and newly built. He was obliged to wait for an hour before it opened and so walked out for forty minutes observing Willesden waking, and then walked back, feeling totally detached and unconcerned, free of all worry. At the post office he joined the queue and then having addressed the envelope to his family in Liverpool Road, Canning Town, arranged for it to be sent by recorded delivery.

'Anything valuable inside, sir?' asked the cheery receptionist.

'No,' Spicer answered with a smile, 'nothing of value.'

Two hours and thirty-seven minutes later Ernest Spicer, sixty-two years of age, was deceased.

# FOUR

I t was, thought Dew, a most pleasing spectacle and he glanced at Vicary and Forbes. Vicary seemed as taken as he was taken, while Forbes smiled as if to say, 'I told you so, delightful isn't it?' The village formed a tight 'V' shape with an Anglican Church standing at the opening of the 'V'. The church was built of white flint and had a square tower with a flagpole mounted upon it. The clock face was painted a rich shade of blue, and the hands, painted gold, and pointing to gold painted Roman numerals showed the correct time. Turning to look towards the point of the 'V' Dew saw that the road through the village was bounded by greens on either side with a service road between the greens and the buildings. A dry stream bed ran the length of the northern green, terminating where an old pump stood together with a classic Gilbert Scott telephone box. Mature trees lined the northern green sheltering the stream.

The war memorial on the southern green was of a Celtic cross design and, Dew noticed, it had two distinct 'voices'. The sons of the village who fell in the 1914–18 War were remembered in a homely, affectionate manner; Arthur Pike, Robert Raven, John Raven, Reginald Rumbles, Frederick Rumbles, Arthur Hendy, Bertie Hendy. The war had clearly taken a heavy toll on the Ravens, Rumbles and the Hendys. By contrast, the fallen of the village in the 1939–45 conflict were remembered in a cold, detached manner; Bottomley, Robert, James, Scotes, Robert . . . The road sign beyond the war memorial fixed the place to the millimetre: Wells 6, Fakenham 10, Hunstanton 11, for this was the village Burnham Market, North Norfolk, 1°E, 53°N.

After enquiring at the post office which he found doubled as a newsagent and a general store, Dew returned to where Vicary and Forbes stood and said, 'It's directly opposite and is the nearest thing to a hill round here,' clearly reporting what he had been told in the post office. The entrance to Herring's Lane was a narrow gap between two lines of build-

ings, so narrow that a stranger could walk past without realizing it was the beginning of a thoroughfare that drove north
towards the coast. After the opening that Dew estimated
would perhaps admit a small car but nothing larger, the road
opened out as it inclined to the low summit. At either side
of the road were detached properties of perhaps nineteenth-
century, early twentieth-century vintage, many with trees in
their gardens which were considerably older than the building
and gave Dew the impression that a wood had been cleared
to make room for the houses, save for a few trees which had
been selectively spared. The houses had, he thought, as he
walked, jacket over his arm, pleasing names, 'Swansong',
'Easterly', 'Mittens Way', 'Orchard Ring'. The house they
sought, the equally pleasingly named, 'Jay's Nest', was well
marked and had, as had been promised, a red sports car
parked in the driveway, closer to the gates than to the house.

'I don't like to be early.' Dew glanced at his watch.

'Agreed,' Forbes mumbled, 'a few minutes after the agreed
time is politic.'

'Let's walk on a little,' Vicary offered, 'see what's at the
top of the hill.'

What was at the top of the hill was a landscape which Dew
thought quintessentially English. It was of a gently undulating
landscape of largely arable farming of ancient, enclosed fields,
lined with mature trees and shrubs. A windmill with a distinct
white crown and white sails and with a gloss black tower
stood proudly in the middle-distance and of sufficient height
to interrupt the skyline against the blue of the North Sea.
Beneath the windmill was a cluster of red-roofed cottages.
To the officers' right a bridleway led towards a derelict church
with a circular tower. A wood lay off to the left and heard,
but unseen, a man methodically chopped timber behind a
neatly clipped hedge. Wooden poles carried low-slung power
lines across the vista and, thought Dew, if they could be
ignored, he and his companions were looking at a landscape
that had probably not changed much in a hundred and fifty
years. The three men stood in silence absorbing the view,
none feeling inclined to comment. With some reluctance
Vicary glanced at his watch and said, 'Time's up.'

The three men turned and walked slowly back to 'Jay's

Nest' and turned left into the gateway forming a single file as they squeezed between the sports car and the gatepost. They entered a wide, neatly tended garden with a red gravel drive which fronted on to a black and white half-timbered house with a cluttered, rambling red-tiled roof line, and was, Dew thought, built some time between the homely inscriptions and the detached inscriptions. As they approached the house a tall, thin man with fawn-coloured slacks and a white short-sleeved shirt opened the front door. He smiled a ready smile and raised a hand in greeting. He had neatly trimmed silver hair, teeth of such perfection that for his age Dew assumed them to be false, and liver-spotted hands. 'Mr Dew?'

'Yes, sir.' Dew approached, extending his hand as he did so. 'Saw the car, thank you, it is an unmissable landmark.'

'Thank you. I am Philip Ott, as I assume you assumed.' The two men shook hands warmly. 'Yes, Triumph Spitfire, 1965, not a scratch on her, starts on the button and drives like a dream, my retirement present to myself and my passion in the summer months. I'll put it safely back in its little house later, but please, do come in, gentlemen. I think Mrs Ott has made us some tea and toasted teacakes.'

Dew, Vicary and Forbes were led through the darkly panelled, rich-carpeted hallway into a rear sitting room and through open French windows that led on to a patio, beyond which was a lawn which had a badminton court painted on it and a net strung across. It was surrounded by tall shrubs and the occasional tree. A round highly polished wooden table surrounded by matching chairs stood upon the patio.

'Shall we sit outside?' Philip Ott indicated the table and the four men sat down. Bees buzzed amid the flowers, birds sang and an elderly yellow dog lay unconcerned in the shade at the left side of the garden after casting a desultory eye at the visitors. She barked once and then ignored them.

'That's Tilly,' Ott said. 'Matilda to give her her full name. Fourteen years ago she was a yellow blur, but that's dogs, they age quickly. Dogs are like men, they live short lives, whilst cats, like women, live forever.' He turned and glanced at his garden. 'What was it that Shakespeare said about desire outliving performance? Our back garden can't be overlooked and I often think how me and Mrs Ott would have frolicked naked on a day like today if we were in our twenties, now we're too damned old to get the full benefit of privacy – seems so unfair,' he grinned.

'Well you still do all right, sir,' Dew returned the grin, 'sports car, badminton.' He had often seen men in their fifties who looked older than Philip Ott did in his late sixties.

'Yes, I have . . . we have both been blessed with the keeping of good health and having a marriage as blissful now as it was forty-odd years ago when it began has been a major contributor. Happiness makes for good health, I feel.'

Mrs Ott stepped on to the patio carrying a tray of tea and teacakes. The men stood as one upon her arrival and Dew noted that, as Philip Ott had claimed, she too had held her age remarkably well. She was in her sixties but wore a tee shirt and jeans capably well, had a fresh young woman's complexion and neatly cut black hair. 'Good morning, gentlemen.' She had a pleasant chirpy speaking voice with just a trace of a soft London accent. She placed the tray gently on the table. 'For a.m. it still is . . . just. It wants but half an hour to the meridian but it is still the forenoon. Will you be staying for lunch?'

Dew, Forbes and Vicary glanced at each other, but Ott answered for them. 'No, thank you,' he said, 'we'll be taking lunch in the village.'

'Very well,' she smiled and withdrew, gently closing the French windows behind her as she did so.

Philip Ott leaned forward and took the lid off the china teapot and stirred the contents with a silver teaspoon. He stood and poured the tea and invited the three officers to help themselves to milk, sugar and a teacake as they desired. He then sat down and said, 'So who's who? You are DCI Dew and . . .?'

'Vicary, sir, Detective Sergeant with Mr Dew in the Murder Squad.'

'Murder Squad?'

'I am Detective Sergeant Garrick Forbes, sir. I am with A-Ten.'

'A-Ten?' Philip Ott inclined his head slightly backwards. 'I see . . . Murder Squad. A-Ten. Serious.'

'We think so, sir.'

'So . . . how can I be of help? Confess your phone call yesterday took me by surprise.'

'Yes, sorry about the short notice but things are happening quickly.'

'No matter. So, again, how can I help?'

'Operation Fennel,' Dew spoke softly.

The mention of the name caused Ott's eyebrows to furrow. The name clearly had associations for him, possibly of a painful nature. 'You are going back a long way there.'

'Twenty-seven years,' Dew said.

'As long as that? Well, I don't think I can tell you anything that isn't in the file.'

'Well,' Dew helped himself to a teacake, 'there you have hit the nail on the head, sir. The file is missing.'

'That can't happen,' Ott gasped. 'The vault is as safe as houses.'

'It has happened, I'm afraid, sir.'

'Hence my interest,' Forbes added.

'Oh . . .' Ott put his cup and saucer down heavily on the tabletop.

'You will not know, sir, because we have not issued a press statement but the body of PC Coventry has been found.'

'Oh . . . Jim Coventry.' Ott leaned forward and squeezed his eyes together as if resisting tears. 'Jim,' he sighed. 'What happened? Where . . . when . . . tell me.'

'Shallow grave in Epping Forest, drowned. When? Don't know . . . but shortly after he was abducted. When found? A few days ago by navvies digging a trench.'

'Oh . . .' Again, Ott sighed.

'We are looking again at the death of Jacqueline Boot. She also drowned and was also part of Operation Fennel.'

'Yes, I remember her.' Ott rested his forehead in his palm. 'I shouldn't have used them so young but they were both made of the right stuff and using older officers in their thirties never worked because the criminals always used to be able to identify them and they were rumbled. So we . . . I tried younger officers . . . gave them flats to live in, whole new identities. It was a risk but we were after big game.'

'What was Operation Fennel, sir?' Dew asked.

'Targeting home-grown cannabis farms . . . very strong stuff. These days it's known as "skunk". In those days it had no name, just known as "strong stuff". Twenty, thirty years ago the majority of cannabis was smuggled into the UK, now I believe the figure is less than ten per cent. The majority is grown in so-called "farms". It all began about thirty years ago, and Fennel was an attempt to stop that method of production from establishing itself.'

'I see,' Dew said, 'interesting.'

'Failed totally, otherwise there wouldn't be so many "farms" in the UK. In our day it was London villains who were running it, now it's controlled by the Vietnamese, getting four, five, even six harvests a year and creating big money. I mean a multimillion pound per annum concern.'

'I have heard of such "farms", of course. I confess I didn't realize how old the practice is.'

'Its massive extent is quite recent but the practice itself stretches back thirty years. The early days were of course experimental but like the tiny mustard seed it has grown into a huge shrub, if not a tree. We were observing known farms, not bothered by the "farmer", we wanted the Mr Big. That was Operation Fennel.'

'Do you know who he was?'

'Geezer called Pirie.'

Vicary took the notebook from his pocket and wrote the name on the top of a fresh page.

'Maxwell "Mad Max" Pirie, believed to be connected to the deaths of many persons; he was our number one target. Now, he had a couple of lieutenants, Peabody and Powell. All the "P's" . . . Pirie, Peabody and Powell. It might sound like a respectable firm of solicitors but these guys were anything but lawful. Hard core criminals who came up through Borstal training but they made money and drank in upmarket wine bars in Chelsea; their favourite was The Stork. That was Jackie Boot's job, to get chatted up by Pirie's mob.'

'You asked her to do that!' Dew gasped.

'Yes,' Ott held eye contact with the pale-faced Dew, 'yes we did . . . yes I did. Volunteers only of course and they could excuse themselves if they felt they were in danger.'

Forbes glanced at Dew. 'That's true. Volunteers only but

you are right; it's risky to use females in deep cover, risky for them.'

'The important point is that we made it clear to them that they were not to be "honey traps".' Ott held up a finger. 'We never asked any female officer to offer sexual favours but we knew the risk was there. The female officers knew they could be chatted up but at some point they might have to decide to get out or get undressed . . . and if they chose the former, as they were encouraged to do, no ill would be thought of them.'

'But still . . .' Dew's words failed, and then he asked, 'Who else was part of Operation Fennel, the undercover officers?'

'The undercover officers, well . . . Julia Crabtree, she worked with Jackie, they went to the Stork Club together. She lives in Scotland now, so I heard.'

'Scotland!'

'Yes. Edinburgh, married a Scottish lawyer.'

'Any others?' Dew asked, noting Vicary to be writing in his notebook.

'Owen Davies. He was a young officer with a promising future; he left after Fennel went pear-shaped, took a farm in Wales. He had a rural background so he knew what he was taking on, no dewy-eyed notion about farming for him. Both Davies and Crabtree knew Jim Coventry and Jacqueline Boot.'

'We'll have to talk to them.' Dew paused to take a sip of his tea. 'Can I ask you, sir, what do you know about Jim Coventry's abduction?'

'Very little. He was on surveillance duty, watching a remote house one night.'

'Alone?'

'Alone at his station, yes, but he was one of half a dozen officers who were surrounding the house . . . it was on the Essex–Suffolk border. His relief went to the station and Jim just wasn't there. Massive damage to the foliage, signs of a struggle, but no Jim Coventry. So we knew that they knew they were being watched and that they had abducted a police officer.'

'Serious,' Vicary commented, brushing a fly from the plate of teacakes.

'Doesn't get more serious. So, of course we raided the house, arrested everything and everyone before we wanted to do so, really before we had any evidence linking the farm to the three "P's". So the operation went out of the window, nearly two years' work all told, though Jim Coventry and Jackie Boot were not part of Fennel for that length of time, and a quarter of a million pounds worth of public money – and that was a quarter of a million nearly thirty years ago . . . wasted . . . but we wanted our man back. We pulled everybody, sweated them . . . things were not done by the book, no PACE in those days. If Jim had been abducted he might still be alive and we wanted him. We wanted him bad. We tried everything from bribes to putting blood on the cell walls but nobody knew anything from Pirie and Peabody and Powell down to the poor "farmer" who could not speak English. We took the "farmer's" fingerprints and then handed them to the immigration people but nobody knew anything about Jim's abduction. They all pointed out that the abduction of a copper was so offside, so out of order, so left field that no villain would do it and they had a point there.'

'The same occurred to us.' Dew glanced at Vicary who nodded in agreement. 'It was just not a villains' thing to do.'

'Yes, I doubt even the Russian Mafia or the West Indian Yardies would abduct a police officer and they play a harder game than Pirie was playing thirty years ago.'

Ott paused as a hawk swooped fast and low across his neatly tended lawn.

'Marsh harrier,' Vicary announced.

'Well identified,' Ott smiled. 'Are you a bird watcher?'

'Was.' Vicary smiled. 'Lapsed boyhood interest but birds haven't changed much in the last quarter century.'

'Indeed. It's a recent interest of mine, something to fill up the leisure years. There is a bird sanctuary near here on the coast, a salt marsh; you can walk on it at low tide.'

'Risky.'

'Well, keep a check on the tides, but there's a good one hour window between the last of the ebb and the first of the flood, plus an hour either side of dead-low water. If you don't wander too far from dry land it is safe. We get a lot of seabirds in this area but it's really good for all bird life. We have a bird table in the garden . . . see?' He pointed to the right-hand edge of the garden where a wooden platform was raised to adult eye level. 'It's elevated to protect the birds from cats but there's no protecting the food from the squirrels, damned pests that they are but there's no doubting that they are highly acrobatic and ingenious creatures. It's as though if you give a squirrel an obstacle to get over he'll say, "Oh good" and find a way over it.' He smiled. 'One day Mrs Ott and I were standing either side of the table when a blue tit was feeding. At that point something flashed between us and just above us right out of the blue and wham! The tit had gone . . . a sparrowhawk flying at eighty, ninety miles an hour took the blue tit from right in front of us . . . outstanding.'

'Amazing,' commented Dew.

'Indeed, you don't have to go up the Amazon on a raft to see wildlife; it's here in your backyard. So where were we?'

'Operation Fennel,' Forbes assisted Ott's memory, 'the operation was blown when Jim Coventry was abducted, you broke cover to find him.'

'Yes, as I said, no holds barred, no punches pulled, nice cop, bad cop . . . bribes . . . but nobody under investigation claimed to know anything about Jim Coventry's disappearance and after a while we began to believe them and it occurred to us that his disappearance might be unconnected with Operation Fennel after all and indeed someone said, "He's been taken by aliens." No one gave that any credibility of course but the comment did catch the mood, although I have always believed there to have been a link . . . must have been. Must have been.'

'I feel the same,' Dew spoke quietly, 'otherwise it just does not make sense, it just does not add up and deliver.'

'So where are they now, sir?' Forbes asked.

'The three "P's"?'

'Yes, sir.'

'Well, Powell was convicted for a vicious gangland murder a few years later. He collected life with a minimum tariff of thirty summers. When we heard about that we thought, well we got one for something. So he'll still be tucked up some-where, nice and institutionalized now. He might be willing to help himself. Pirie and Peabody, his lieutenants? Can't help you there but they won't be difficult to find. Dead or alive, they will have left a spoor.'

'We'll pay a call on them, won't do them any harm to let 'em know we remember them, won't do any harm at all.'

'No harm at all,' Philip Ott smiled. 'Do remember old Phil Ott to them, won't you?'

'So . . . speaking of lieutenants, sir,' Forbes probed, 'what . . . who were your lieutenants on the operation, it might be useful to speak to them?'

'Oh, a good team of Detective Sergeants . . . they're all retired now, recently so . . . young men then, now they'll be mid to late fifties. Let's see . . . Piers Parsloe, he seemed to be the leader of the group although they were all of the same rank, Idris Neve . . . Welshman as you'd guess by his name, Tom Last and Freddie Wolfe . . . all seemed to look up to Piers Parsloe.'

'Another "P",' Dew commented as he saw Vicary committing the names to his notebook.

'Yes, but a good "P",' Philip Ott said. 'I was lucky to have them.'

'How did they take the disappearance of Jim Coventry?'

'Badly, well, we all did. Not only was he one of the team, he was one of the babies of the team, a young man; we felt we had failed to protect him. Freddie Wolfe seemed particularly shaken, if I recall, but we all took it badly.'

'Was Jim Coventry's abduction investigated separately?'

'No,' Ott leaned back, 'no, it wasn't, it was seen as part and parcel of Operation Fennel. The operation was abandoned after that, the officers assigned to other cases.'

'Jackie Boot's death?' Forbes pressed.

'Not seen as relevant.' Ott drew breath between his teeth. 'One hell of a tragedy but not seen as relevant at the time.'

'At the time,' Forbes echoed drily.

The three officers took their leave of Mrs Ott, thanking her for the tea and cakes and they and Philip Ott walked down Herring's Lane to the pub. The interior of the pub was pleasingly cool in the summer weather and was to Dew's taste: low beams, tiled floor, exposed wooden uprights in the wall with bookcases of hardbacked books to soften the interior and ancient brewing industry tools by the fireplace.

'It's just been refurbished,' Ott said after ordering four pints of Norfolk Wherry and asking to see the lunch menu. 'This used to be a forgotten corner of England then the wealthy London crowd discovered it. Once it was famous only as the locality of Horatio Nelson's birthplace, now it's known as "Chelsea North". I kid you not; the pile of *Financial Times* in the post office each Saturday morning must be six feet high . . . says everything about the area, all these weekend cottages owned by stockbrokers. The property values around here have sky rocketed because of it. Mrs Ott and I couldn't afford our house if we wanted to retire here now.'

Garrick Forbes smiled as he accepted his pint of Wherry. Philip Ott had just answered a question that was burning away inside his mind but he didn't know how to ask.

Colin Dover MD, MRCP, FRCPath, DMJ (Path) pulled the starched white sheet back over the body. 'Very straightforward.' He turned to the officer who attended the postmortem for the police. 'Two small-calibre bullets to the head at close range. The second entry wound had gunpowder residue round the side, first shot had a sliver of what appears to have been plastic embedded in the wound. One bullet would have been sufficient but the second made sure. Not sure about the plastic, possibly from a plastic bottle.'

'A bottle, sir?'

'Yes . . . I have come across it before, shoot a small-calibre weapon into a plastic bottle you have a very efficient silencer for the first two rounds at least.'

'I see.'

'Frederic Wolfe by name,' Colin Dover read the report sheet, 'fifty-seven years . . . police officer.'

'Retired,' said the officer, 'he had retired to Rickmansworth. We didn't know him, ex-Metropolitan Police.'

'And he retired to this part of the world . . . on a police officer's pension?' Dover raised his eyebrows.

'Dare say he had an eye for a good bet on the horses, sir.'

'He'd have to. For a police officer to retire amongst the stockbrokers, private means just isn't the word.'

\*   \*   \*

Trevor Liu Ko Haung Powell revealed himself to be a man of mixed race, not simply half Caucasian and half oriental. It seemed to Dew that he might be one quarter oriental. It wasn't immediately obvious but eventually the flat face, the narrow eyes and the gentle yellow pigmentation became apparent. His manner and accent, however, were wholly East End villain. He wore his striking blond hair in a pigtail which, to Dew's eyes, looked a little odd for a man in his fifties, but Powell seemed to carry it off. The man had scars on his neck and wrists which he did not attempt to disguise. He had cold eyes and what seemed to Dew to be a very suspicious attitude. He sat in the agent's room of Wormwood Scrubs prison wearing a blue and white shirt, denim jeans and inexpensive white sports shoes. 'So what,' he asked, 'does the law want with me now, after all this time?'

'Help,' Dew replied, offering Powell a cigarette.

Powell sneered but accepted the cigarette. 'You want *me* to help you?' He put the cigarette in his mouth and inhaled as Dew held the flame of his lighter to the tip.

'Yes, in a word.' Dew slipped the lighter back into his jacket pocket. 'In a word, yes.'

'I have a thirty-year tariff; I've done twenty-five. What can you offer me?'

'Reduced category,' Forbes replied, 'a very good word at your first parole hearing. The thirty-year tariff is the minimum you must serve; you could still be in here for another ten years.'

'No one can survive more than ten years in Cat A and I haven't. I saw what it did to the other lags and I tried to top myself.' Powell drew deeply and lovingly on the cigarette, and then drew his finger across his throat and showed Dew and Forbes his wrists which were criss-crossed with wide scars. 'I'm not ashamed I tried but now I just take one day at a time.'

'Well, help us now and we can pull strings; you could start getting your head back together as a Category B, or even a Category C. An open prison is even possible. There are murderers in open prisons.' Dew leaned back in his chair and smiled.

'Yes,' Powell snarled, 'men who have killed their wives, not criminals . . . men who are full of remorse, murderers like that, but me, I hacked to death a couple of villains who tried to stiff me . . . hacked 'em good . . . while they were alive, watching their own limbs being chopped off bit by bit and, yeah, I did it . . . but remorse . . . I don't know the meaning of the word.'

'OK,' Forbes held eye contact with Powell, 'no open prison but Cat B or C, that's possible, as is an early release once you've served your thirty.'

'I could be interested,' Powell also sat back in his chair, 'but I won't grass anybody up and I won't give evidence in court. I don't care what you offer, those two things I do not do.'

'Fair enough,' Dew nodded in agreement, 'but let's see how far we get. If you point us in the right direction and if we get a result, we'll put in a good word.'

'Fair enough, as you say,' Powell smiled, 'fair enough.'

'Twenty-seven years ago . . .'

'The good old days . . .' Powell glanced dreamily at the ceiling, '. . . only other people went down then. I had money . . . I had property and I had the Richards lining up to eat out of my hand, then it all went south, all of it. No Richards in here, just the younger boys in the showers. All my assets frozen, the law attempted to seize them, my brief put in a challenge so they're frozen . . . still . . . after twenty-five years. Law can't get at them for the public good but neither can I. The only people benefiting are the fat barristers in their silk shirts.'

'Pirie, Peabody and you.'

'We got busted; the law rounded us up one night. They were watching us then they lost one of their own boys and thought we had him. That was a nice little earner we had going, then they closed us down, or so they thought. We just started up again, different locations, and not where they could get close enough to watch us, we learned that lesson. Good old Phil Ott, how is he?'

'Retired,' Dew said. 'We saw him yesterday.'

'Where?'

'Norfolk,' Dew replied. Forbes remained expressionless.

Powell smiled and tapped the side of his nose. 'You mean Devon, or anywhere except Norfolk.'

'Maybe,' Dew smiled, 'can't tell you.'

'No matter, Phil Ott was just doing his job. When I get out I won't be looking for him, no scores to settle there.'

'Good. That's good to hear.'

'Yes, so we were growing high-strength cannabis – now it's called "skunk", in those days it hadn't got a name. It was us who had developed the means to grow it in the UK rather than import it. We, me and Peabody and Pirie . . . but uncomfortable in those houses . . . the inside of a sauna feels like a walk in the park on a frosty day by comparison. That's why ethnics made good "farmers", used to the heat, you see. Then Phil Ott raided but we had covered our tracks. They couldn't link us to the farms and anyway he was looking for a lost copper. He arrested some low-key workers and closed down the farms but that didn't hurt us. We started other farms and were soon in business again. Oh, the money, I mean big, big money. We kept the farms in remote locations and put our own guards round them. We could afford the manpower. We were in a good way of business for a few years.'

'So what do you know about the copper who vanished?'

'Nothing.' Powell's expression was serious. 'Gospel. Nothing. Nothing. Nothing. I mean, stands to reason, do you think we wanted to get raided? We didn't know the cops were watching us so closely. That's true. That came as a surprise but we knew that if we did abduct one it would bring the law crashing down on us, which is what happened.'

'Where are Pirie and Peabody now?'

'Still out there.'

'Still producing home grown skunk?'

'Well, that would be like you telling me that Phil Ott really does live in Norfolk,' Powell smiled. 'They are doing OK, but back then we had no reason to murder a copper and every reason not to.'

'How do you know he was murdered?'

'He didn't surface. Stands to reason he was topped. Someone topped him, but it wasn't anybody from our team. We avoided cocaine and heroin because of the long stretches that go with them and to murder a cop on duty would attract just that sort of long sentence we didn't want.'

'So who would benefit from the officer's death?'

Powell shrugged and smoked the cigarette down to the butt. 'Someone who wanted the police operation to fail and let the likes of me and Pirie and Peabody carry on raking it in. Someone like that.'

'The police were taking bribes?' Forbes sat forward.

'No names, no pack drill. All I can say is that I wasn't part of that, we divvied up the responsibilities. I was in charge of transport, anything that had to be moved, I saw to that. Fertilizer in, food for the "farmer", moving crop out, I saw to that, also transporting it to the street dealers.'

'So we talk to Pirie?'

'Or Peabody, but they won't talk back. They are not inside. You have nothing to hold over those two and they're not going to admit bribing the cops to stay away.'

'We'll see,' Forbes growled.

'I'll leave that to you. Oh, how are the girls?'

'The girls?'

'The female officers that used to come to the Stork Club. The girls who pretended to be secretaries looking for a merchant banker to pull them off the shelf. The crew clocked them as cops straight away, made bedding them so much more fun, so they said.'

Mead Way, Croydon, SE London, interwar bungalows, a few semi-detached houses but in the main a road lined with bungalows on either side, some detached, some in pairs, many with an 'L' shaped ground plan, all with generous garden space. In one such neatly kept bungalow, a detached one, in the evening, a man and a woman sat in stony silence; the family dog had taken refuge under a chair that stood in the corner of the room. In another room the radio played defiantly. It was the woman who eventually broke the silence.

'It's too harsh!'

'It is harsh,' the man growled. 'It's supposed to be harsh.'

'But for the whole of the school holidays . . . that's six weeks.'

'She can go into the back garden for fresh air. She can go

out with you during the day but not out on her own again until September.'

The woman paused and then said, 'Are you sure you should not have joined the prison service?'

'Look.' The man flung that day's copy of the *Daily Telegraph* on to the carpet. 'I work in A-Ten. I like the job, I have the appetite for it but it means my conduct *and* the conduct of my family has to be perfect . . . faultless . . . beyond reproach. I am not just a police officer, I am part of a police force within the police force and I often find myself hated by the other police officers. I have separated many policemen and a few policewomen from their pensions but I do what I do and I do it with all my vigour, all my enthusiasm.' Garrick Forbes paused and leaned over to his left to scoop up the newspaper. 'Every police force in the western world is the same, or it has the same, a force within a force. In the USA it's called Internal Affairs, in Canada it's the same except in Quebec where it's called Affairs Internes, in the Czech Republic it's called the Anti-Corruption Squad, in Australia it's called the Crime and Corruption Committee and in Sweden it's called Rickenheten met Korruption and all officers who work in such a unit . . . well . . . their conduct and the conduct of their families has to be impeccable. She is fifteen years old, she came home rolling down the Way last night shouting and vomiting and singing at the top of her voice, soaked in vodka and whatever else went down her stupid throat. If we hadn't called the ambulance, if she had collapsed before she reached home . . . she's lucky to be alive and it was only nine thirty p.m., everybody was up and awake, our neighbours and our neighbours' children. We are going to have to go away for a few days as a means of apologizing to them. We'll do that a.s.a.p., busy at work right now but a.s.a.p. . . . the shame . . . the indignity on top of nearly losing her. So that's it. She is not allowed out beyond the gate by herself until the new school term starts in September. So it's harsh and unfair, but so is life.' Garrick Forbes stood. 'I'm taking the dog for a walk.' At the mention of the word 'walk' the spaniel slithered out from under the chair but did so in a subdued, rather than excited manner; family arguments had always had that effect on him.

\*   \*   \*

The man sat in the driver's seat of his car. The youth sat beside him. The canvas hood was up despite the sun beating down and inviting the pleasures of open-top motoring.

'That's the mark there.' The man discretely indicated ahead and to their left. 'See him, the man sitting on the wall in front of that house? That's his house, that's where you wait for him.'

'Yes, I see him.' Gaylord Midnight stroked the barrel of the revolver he cradled gently in his hands. 'This is sweet.'

'Can you do it?'

'Yes.' Gaylord Midnight spoke matter-of-factly. 'Yes, I can do it. Nobody give you diss with this in your hand, nobody man . . . like nobody.'

'Nobody will ever diss you again if you do this.'

'No?'

'No. S'a fact. For this you get street cred and bling.'

'Yeah,' Gaylord Midnight's eyes brightened, 'cred and bling.'

'Yes. They told me you were the man when I asked in the street.'

'Yeah . . . I'm the man.' Gaylord Midnight continued to stroke the smooth surface of the well-oiled firearm. 'The man.'


The couple strolled arm in arm along the pavement of Whipps Cross Road. The woman pointed to her right and said, 'That's not the Epping Forest where they found the body?'

Harry Vicary smiled. 'No, no, that's just a small part of the original forest that has been swallowed up by London's urban sprawl. The body was found in the main part of the forest up in Hertfordshire, next to a camping site. No one is going to put up their tents or park their vans there. So . . .' he paused as a low-flying KLM 747 passed overhead on its final approach to Heathrow, drowning any conversation. When the roar of the plane's engines had subsided Vicary continued, 'Well, a lovely evening but getting a little chilly now. Are you thirsty?'

'Yes,' Kathleen Tate, hotel receptionist, replied. 'I am quite thirsty. Where is there?'

'The pub.' Vicary nodded to a building that stood on the street corner.

'You're joking!' Kathleen Tate stopped walking. 'We can't go in there!'

'Why not? I wouldn't go in by myself but two of us, to watch each other, soda water and lime each? I won't be tempted. My job's on the line as it is, promotion prospects are poor, if not altogether blown.'

'Blown?' She glanced at him.

'Yes, I haven't told you but the Met has allowed me a six month probation period. I have to prove I am fully dried out, it's on my record. So if I do get promotion it won't be for a likely time. Have you lost much?'

'I'll tell you in the pub; soda and lime for you and an orange juice for me and nothing else.'

'Packet of nuts, maybe?' Vicary smiled. 'I am sure we are allowed that.'

Archibald Dew placed his knife and fork on the plate and smiled at his wife who sat opposite him. 'Thank you, I enjoyed that meal.'

'Good.' Miriam Dew returned the smile. 'Shall we have coffee in the garden, it's still warm and light enough?'

'Yes, that would be pleasant. Tell me, what's a Richard?'

'A Richard?'

'Yes, I interviewed a felon in Wormwood Scrubs today. He said the "Richards were lining up to eat out of his hand." Didn't want to show my ignorance, especially since Garrick Forbes seemed to know what he was referring to.'

Miriam Dew smiled. 'I haven't heard that expression for a very long time.' She reached forward and gathered the used plates and serving dishes towards her.

'Well he was an old lag, been in there, well, since about when our Olivia was born.'

'Well, it's rhyming slang.'

'I guessed, but what does it mean?'

'Young women. A Richard is a young woman, a "Richard the third", a "bird" and it does not get my approval.'

John Shaftoe sat in front of a pint of IPA and grinned across the circular table at his wife who sat in front of a large schooner of port and who grinned back at him. The pub was pleasantly full, not too crowded, a gentle hum of conversation interrupted by the thud of darts into the cork board in the time-honoured rhythm, thud, thud, thud, then a distinct pause, thud, thud, thud, pause, thud, thud, thud. Outside the frosted-glass window red double-decker buses and black taxis hummed by. Both the Shaftoes were dressed in tee shirts, blue jeans and sports shoes and blended successfully with their surroundings, completing the process by 'talking common', though no one could overhear them.

'I heard about thee before I met thee.' Linda Shaftoe sipped her port.

'You never told us.'

'Not by name. I were on the top deck of a bus in Barnsley with a lass called Becky Forthrop and she told me about these weekends where you get to meet quality people. She said, "Not like the fitters and the electricians we meet, quality people, doctors and lawyers and that. They're looking for girls," she said, "and all you have to be is pretty and you're pretty enough", and I said, "Do you think so?" and she said "Yes", and then we got off at the next stop.'

'Really? I remember you coming on that weekend, you were so nervous.'

'I was shaking like a leaf. Me, little more than a shelf stacker, and me dad a railway station porter, and all these guys with posh accents and flash motors but all were really nice, never took advantage. All the girls slept in the same room and felt so safe. Each man had his own room. Then folk began to partner up on those long walks. All you could do was talk to each other. It took thee and me until Sunday afternoon.'

'Aye, but it was a four-day weekend.'

'To think I used to fly off to those Mediterranean hotspots looking for a fella and then met a boy from the next town 'cos of a chance remark on the top deck of a bus in Barnsley. A local lad made good. And Becky married a plumber after all. When I told me parents you were a doctor they were over the moon. My mum started doing handstands.'

'Only a pathologist, I told you, sort of third division doctors.'

'Hey,' she slid her hand across the table and rested it on

his, 'if you come off the estate I came off and pull an "ologist", any sort of "ologist", then that's a major score in any parents' eyes. Our dad didn't know what a pathologist was but he was chuffed that his daughter was going out with one, "Our Linda with an 'ologist'."'

John Shaftoe rested his elbow on the table and cupped his jaw in the palm of his hand. 'So I am only wanted because of my occupation?'

'You know I don't mean that,' she smiled warmly. 'Another pint?'

# FIVE

Archibald Dew put the newspaper down on the top of his desk. He looked first at Vicary and then at Forbes.

'Has to be.' Forbes spoke in a flat, matter-of-fact manner. 'I mean, how many Freddie Wolfes are there recently retired from the Metropolitan Police, same name as on Philip Ott's Operation Fennel team? And that murder, shot in the head at close range . . . that was a hit. He was targeted for a reason; he wasn't randomly selected by a crazed gunman in sleepy Rickmansworth who then goes and commits suicide by cop a few hours later. They have to be linked.'

'Pity we have to find out by reading the first edition of the *Evening Standard*.' Dew patted the newspaper.

'No reason for anyone to contact us, boss, we are not flagged up as being interested in either person, just Jim Coventry.'

'For now,' Forbes growled.

'Right, I am going to split the team. We can do that because we are only picking brains, we are not even taking statements. Mr Forbes . . .'

'Sir?'

'I want you to drive to Wales. Call on Owen Davies, find out what he remembers about Operation Fennel.'

'Sir.'

'Harry.'

'Sir?'

'Jump on the plane to Edinburgh, talk to Julia Crabtree. She might be willing to say something she wasn't willing to say twenty-seven years ago. Personnel will furnish you with their addresses. Better phone them first.'

'Very good, sir,' Harry Vicary replied eagerly as both he and Garrick Forbes stood.

'I'll . . . I'll pull some strings, get rapid confirmation that the gun this fella was waving about in order to make the police shoot him was in fact the one used to murder Freddie Wolfe.'

'They'll be linked.'

'I know,' Dew smiled, 'but we still need confirmation.'

'Two murders, one suspicious death, cops resigning from the force, seemingly out of fear, and a con like Trevor Powell telling us to look for rogue cops.' Forbes put on his summer hat. 'There will be a link.'

'You're right, of course,' Dew leaned back in his chair, 'but let's not rush our fences. So think, if, and it's a big "if", if Wolfe was crooked why would someone have him shot?'

'To stop him talking,' Vicary offered.

Dew smiled and pointed at Vicary. 'Exactly. So watch your backs, gentlemen. Watch them, carefully.'

Harry Vicary took the tube to Heathrow Airport and boarded the first available British Airways shuttle to Edinburgh. There were few passengers on the flight and the cabin crew had no difficulty serving refreshments to all before the plane began its descent into Edinburgh airport. It was in complete contrast to the last time he had flown to Scotland when every seat was taken and the cabin crew could only smile sheepishly at the passengers in the rear seats who could not be served complimentary coffee, the cabin crew having to secure the trolley and assume landing positions before the plane began its approach to Glasgow airport. Vicary had never feared flying but, at the end of each flight, as the ground got closer and clearer, he always developed a nagging worry that the flight crew had forgotten to lower the undercarriage. On that occasion he was once again reassured when the plane touched the ground with a gentle bump, followed by the rumble of wheels upon concrete. At the airport he selected a postcard showing a view of Edinburgh's Royal Mile. He wrote a brief message on the reverse and addressed it to Kathleen and posted it. That done, he walked to the taxi rank and took a cab to Julia Crabtree's address in Warriston, EH3.

The taxi driver proved to be a man of few words, probably, thought Vicary, either because his fare was English or a serving police officer, or both. It was, though, preferable to a taxi driver who once entertained him on a journey across London about the best ways to solve the energy crisis, and win the war in Afghanistan, and deal with the Al Queda threat and what he would do to an Islamic terrorist if he ever had one in his cab. Of the two, Vicary's preference was to be driven by a driver who drove in surly silence.

Julia Crabtree's address in Howard Place proved itself to be on the edge of the 'New Town' of Edinburgh, a prestigious area of solid grey stone tenement and terraced housing on wide streets, and really, thought Vicary, the last word in urban elegance, far preferable in his view to Regency Bath.

Vicary paid the driver for the journey through the small gap in the glass which separated driving position and the passenger compartment, and only then did the driver, trusting soul that he was, unlock the passenger door to allow Vicary to exit the vehicle. Vicary stood on the pavement and noted with interest that the house he stood in front of had a blue plaque on the wall announcing the building to have been the birth place of Robert Louis Stevenson on 13th November 1850. He turned and noted a line of shops opposite him, three antiquarian book dealers and a very useful mini market, with flats above them. He walked a few yards up the road along the row of townhouses built in a solid terrace, with front doors atop a flight of stone steps and set back behind small gardens from the pavement, until he reached number forty-seven and turned into the short path, scuffed his shoes up each step and pulled what appeared to be the original early nineteenth-century bell. He heard a loud jangle echo within the house which caused a large-sounding dog to bark, equally loudly.

The heavy wooden door seemed to Vicary to swing open easily and revealed a slender woman in her fifties, with short blonde hair, cheesecloth shirt, ankle length cotton skirt and moccasins upon her feet. She wore neither jewellery nor make-up and smiled a ready smile whilst holding an eager St Bernard back by its heavy collar. 'Mr Vicary? I'm Julia Watmore née Crabtree.'

'Yes.' He extended his left hand to allow the dog to take his scent whilst extending his right to shake Julia Watmore's hand.

'Don't mind the dog; he's a big softie . . . not dangerous.'

'Good,' Vicary smiled.

'Do come in.' She pulled the St Bernard back and stepped aside.

Vicary climbed one more step and walked out of the sun into the welcoming cool of the cavernous entrance hall, with a curved staircase leading up to the first floor. Julia Watmore closed the door and let the dog go, true to her description of him as a 'big softie' the animal reached up and placed two massive paws on Vicary's chest and attempted to lick his face whilst wagging its tail vigorously. 'Come through to the kitchen.' Julia Watmore turned and walked with such a lightness of step that she could, thought Vicary, be fairly described as 'gliding' across the floor.

'You haven't asked for my ID.' Vicary gently pushed the dog aside and followed her into the kitchen which revealed itself to be a large room complete with Aga, and had two twelve foot high sash windows that afforded a view on to a well-maintained rear garden in which was a model railway track that writhed in and out of shrubs. At the foot of the garden was a wall in which a door was set. To the left of the door was a gazebo.

'Don't need to,' Julia Watmore smiled, 'it's stamped upon your forehead. Once you've been in the force you can recognize a police officer. We can't hide from our own. My husband's a little boy,' she added, following his gaze.

'Little boy?'

'The model railway in the garden. I confess I think Herbert had more fun building it than he has playing with it, levelling the track with a spirit level, inch by inch and inventing names for the stations like, "Gazebo Halt" and "Kitchen Parkway", "Lawn Central". He sent the train round a few times and then seemed to lose interest.'

'Ah . . .' Vicary replied warmly.

'Do take a seat.' Julia Watmore indicated the chairs round the long rectangular kitchen table.

'Thank you.' Vicary sat down.

'Herbert's a lawyer.'

'Very good.'

'Specializes in Criminal Law and strangely that is the one

thing we do not seem to talk about.' She placed a kettle on the hot plate of the Aga and prepared a teapot. 'Sugar? I presume you'd like a cup of tea?'

'Yes, please . . . and no . . . just milk, thank you.'

'So.' She spoke in a soft but distinct London accent while pouring milk into two mugs. 'You were not very clear on the phone this morning. Something I was involved in?'

'Operation Fennel.' Vicary watched as Julia Watmore's head and shoulders bowed at the mention of the name. She recovered quickly and placed the two mugs on the table.

'Jim Coventry and Jacqueline Boot,' Vicary added as he realized that the mention of Operation Fennel had reached Julia Watmore. 'Phil Ott and his lieutenants, Detective Sergeants Parsloe, Neve, Wolfe, Last . . . The Stork Club.'

'Don't!' She slammed the palm of her hand down on the table. 'Don't! Don't!' She turned to face the window and folded her arms. 'Those names haunt me. I knew it would all come back to haunt me no matter how far from London I moved. I should have known that nowhere on the planet is out of reach of the Long Arm of the Law and the longer arm of your life's regrets.'

'Are you telling me that you have had some criminal involvement, because if so, I have to caution you?'

'No,' she held up her hand, 'no, nothing like that. I have nothing to hide. I heard about Freddie Wolfe being shot last night, it was on the news this morning.' She pointed to a massive veneer-covered radio of what seemed to Vicary to be 1950's vintage. 'It had to be the same Freddie Wolfe that I remember from Operation Fennel.'

'It was.'

'And the man went on to commit suicide by cop. He had heart disease or some other terminal condition . . . and well advanced.'

'Had he?'

Julia Watmore nodded but kept her lips firmly together. 'Yes, he had, you'll find that out. It was one of Pirie's hallmarks. That shooting and the suicide has Pirie's fingerprints all over it. Find a dying petty crook who has not made any money in his life, offer him more money than he can dream of to shoot someone so he'll have something to leave to his

family, hand him the gun and show him the target. What has
the dying petty crook got to lose? If you know you are going
to die in two or three weeks, what fear do you have of a life
sentence? You won't even be alive for your trial. You'll
murder someone and still be buried in sanctified ground
because you have not been found guilty of the crime.' She
turned to Vicary. 'Now that is what I call immunity from
prosecution. And that's all I am going to say.'

'I've come a long way . . .' Vicary protested.

She took the kettle from the hotplate of the Aga and poured
the boiling water into the teapot.

'That's all I am going to say in here, in this house, my
home. I don't want this house contaminated. We'll have tea
then we'll take the wretched dog for a walk. Talk outside.'

Archibald Dew listened closely as the tale unfolded.

'We have him on CCTV from the moment he emerged
from Bethnal Green Tube Station.' The sergeant of the
Tactical Response Unit was, Dew found, a serious-minded
individual, which he thought highly appropriate. Killing
people, whether crazed gunmen, terrorists or an unlawfully
liberated Japanese hunting dog is not a job to be taken
lightly, and any officer exhibiting a flippancy of attitude
would fall at the first fence of the selection process.
'Anyway, he hung around a bit and then enters the pub . . .
this is just after eleven a.m. and the pub has opened for
the day's business. So he walks into the pub and pulls a
gun from his bag . . .'

'He had used it to kill the retired officer up in
Rickmansworth yesterday evening?' Dew asked.

'Yes, sir . . . we made a rapid match. We don't know at
which point he entered the underground system. London
Transport won't be able to give us the CCTV tape from
within the train until tomorrow; then we'll have to trawl
through it . . . painstaking job.'

'Yes.'

'But we have him on our street cameras as he emerged
from Bethnal Green Tube Station at eleven fifteen this
forenoon. He goes into a pub and according to eye witnesses
he says, "This is a hold-up", or something of that nature and

he's caught on the pub's CCTV. He was a sickly, wasted-looking guy and a couple of punters in the pub laugh and the barman just tells him to get out, they just don't take him seriously. So it was then that he pulls the gun and starts shooting up the pub, the light shades . . . the bottles on the spirit rack . . . So the barman and the punters dive for cover and the guy just continues to shoot up the pub, beer glasses explode and beer flies everywhere.'

'Doesn't shoot anybody?'

'No . . . just glass, he clearly liked the sound of breaking glass. Then he leaves the pub, hangs around Cambridge Heath Road and then turns into Bethnal Green Road, walking up the road carrying the gun in his right hand. So by this time the pub has dialled three nines and our control is beginning to get inundated with people phoning in from their mobiles reporting a man with a gun.'

'Understandable.'

'Yes. He walks under the railway bridge and stops at the corner of Ainsley Street, the pavement widens out there. By this time the first car is on the scene and confirms reports of a man with a gun and the officers request TRU attendance.'

'All right.'

'The man stays where he is . . . just looking around, not going anywhere. The police close off the road but onlookers are beginning to gather and are using their mobile phones to film the situation.'

Dew groaned, 'So it will be on the evening news today?'

''Fraid so, but we are not bothered, we did everything by the book.'

'Good.'

'It took us twenty minutes to get there . . . four TRU officers in two cars. Once on foot, we approach until we are about twenty feet away, four officers, line abreast, have our weapons trained on him at all times, tell him to put the gun down, but he keeps hold of it, keeps it pointing down towards the ground but he is not letting go. We can't shoot unless we believe that we or some other person is in imminent danger . . .'

'And all being filmed?'

'Yes. We also have our own video of the incident. I don't know how long we were like that, only a few minutes, then the guy starts to smile.'

'Smile?'

'Yes, but more with his eyes than with his mouth, that expression you sometimes see when someone has a trick up their sleeve, when someone knows something you don't know.'

'The-cat-that-got-the-cream look?'

'Yes, that's it. I like that expression, "the cat that got the cream". So it's a stand-off. He's not letting go of the gun but not being threatening with it. He looks around, up at the sky, and then says something like, "OK, let's do it." We all agreed he said something, but differ in what we think we heard him say.'

'Understand.'

'I am sure I heard him say, "OK, let's do it", but whatever he said, it was just then that he pointed his gun at the police. Four of us shot him, two rounds each. We examined the weapon, a twenty-two automatic. The magazine was empty; once he shot Mr Wolfe he'd then used all the remaining rounds to shoot up the pub. In the bag we found a note. It's been logged into evidence but it said, "Never thought I'd thank the police for anything, but thanks for this!" It was suicide by cop.'

'He had no intention of taking life?'

'None, not after he'd shot the retired officer last night.'

'Where did you take the body?'

'The London Hospital, it happened right on their doorstep.'

Garrick Forbes and Owen Davies walked across the steeply inclined grass-covered hillside, both men wearing lightweight waterproofs as protection against the occasional burst of drizzle. Davies' Border Collie walked contentedly behind the two men. To their right the hillside rose until it was jagged against the blue but cloud-laden sky, whilst to their left the hillside fell away to the cluster of grey-tiled roofs that was the village of Abercorrwg.

'This is dry,' Davies spoke warmly. 'Here,' he said, pronouncing 'here' as 'yur', 'there is light rain or heavy rain.

It never stops raining unless it's about to start raining but the ground is never dry, the ground is always soggy, see,' pronouncing 'soggy' as 'sog-eee'.

Forbes, who had never before set foot in Wales, thrilled to the musicality of the accent.

'Sorry I didn't wait for you in the house, but the Mrs, she knows nothing of this, see. It's a part of my life I never talk about and wish to forget, see.'

'Fair enough.'

'I am reluctant to give evidence. I am happy here, settled, see, witness protection has no appeal. I have a successful farm as hill farms go, my children are settled in school and my marriage is happy. So . . . no . . . no . . . no . . . no statements or evidence. I am not giving this up to go and live in a mad city in a witness protection scheme. Understand?'

'Yes.'

'I can point you in the right direction but that's all I am going to do.'

'All right.'

'Fair play then, so what can I tell you about Operation Fennel?' pronouncing Fennel as Fen-nel.

'Everything you know.'

'Which isn't much. You say the file has gone missing now?'

'Yes.'

'There's sinister for you.' Davies was a large, red-faced man.

'As you say . . .'

The two men approached a stile set in a hedgerow. Davies deferentially stood back and let Forbes climb the stile before he did. The two men fell into step side by side at the far side of the stile. Rainfall stopped but only for two or three minutes.

'I see what you mean,' Forbes turned his rain-streaked face to Davies, 'and this is summer?'

'Summer in Wales, anyway.' Davies strode on strongly, clearly having powerfully developed leg muscles. 'Well, I knew Jim Coventry, not well, oppos, see, but not like good mates.'

'OK.'

'We were watching a house in East Anglia, watching the comings, watching the goings, gathering evidence. Jim was a shrewd boy, he said to me one night, "You know how it is if two people are together for a long time, walking, sitting in a car or just watching a house, they'll start to talk?"'

'Yes, I've been there.'

'And some confession or home truth will come out?'

'Yes.'

The conversation halted abruptly as a silver military aircraft rocketed down the vale leaving an ear-splitting roar in its wake.

'Damn things.' Davies watched the plane twist and turn as it negotiated the valley. 'I suppose the Realm has to be defended but I don't see them practising contour flying over the monied areas south of London, but Welsh hill farmers don't matter, apparently. Those things make horses foal and cows calve before they're ready, terrifies the sheep. It's the only thing that spoils the peace of the vale, low-flying jets, but there won't be another one today. Expensive, see, they make my Land Rover seem economical.'

'I can believe it.' Forbes watched the jet twist round the side of the hill, some miles away by then and it was quickly lost from sight.

'Still, I'd prefer to be here where you can breathe and see the stars at night. Where do you live in London?'

'Leytonstone Way.'

'Don't remember that part.'

'So, Jim Coventry said something when you were watching a house one night?'

'Yes, Jim said that Phil Ott wasn't in control of the operation.'

'What did he mean by that?'

'That the middle ranks were pulling the strings and calling the shots.'

'The middle ranks?'

'The Detective Sergeants, Parsloe, Neve, Last and Freddie Wolfe, the fellow who was murdered last night. It made the national news. I nearly fell out of my chair when I heard that on the BBC news this morning, then you phoned. If they can murder one of their own, no one is safe. It means that Jim Coventry was right, Parsloe and the other DS's were taking kickbacks.'

'Bribes?'

Davies nodded. 'There was big money in cannabis; the sort of cannabis Pirie's gang was growing in their "farms", so called. The market was huge, overheads low and risks minimum. No smuggling tons of the stuff through customs, see?'

'Yes, I see.'

'So it was softly, softly, catchee monkey time. Bit by bit we were closing in on Pirie, Peabody and Powell.'

'The three "P's"?'

'Yes, that's what we called them. Then one night Jim Coventry said, "You know there isn't the three 'P's', there's four, DS Parsloe's bent . . . he's crooked."'

'Proof? Evidence?'

'None. None then anyway, but Jim said he'd seen Parsloe up the West End driving a Jaguar.'

'Could be any number of reasons why he was driving a Jaguar through the West End, it didn't mean it was his car.'

'Yes, that's what I said but there's more, they were close to each other, in a narrow street, and they had eye contact and the look of anger in Parsloe's face, that look which said, "You should not have seen this." Jim said he felt he was in danger. Then he said something else that then made sense. That was that of all the cops in the team it was only Parsloe, Neve, Last and Wolfe who never griped about money. There was no sign of wealth about them, they didn't drive top of the range cars and wear Cartier watches, nothing like that, but they were the only ones that never complained that the Met didn't pay enough to enable its officers to live in London. Everybody else used to complain when they opened their pay advice slips.'

'But not those four?'

'No, not those four. Jim was right. I hadn't noticed it but he was right. They never complained about not having enough money. They seemed very content with their income.'

'Interesting.'

'It was along Old Compton Street in Soho that Parsloe was driving the Jaguar when Jim saw him.'

'Soho?'

'Yes, narrow streets redolent with the gentle scent of organized crime and the sex industry. Jim had a mate visiting from the Shires, heard about Soho but had never been so Jim took him there. Didn't go into any of the clubs, they were just walking the streets, soaking up the seediness of the place, when Parsloe came gliding slowly past in his Jaguar, or a Jaguar, and he and Jim had eye contact for about three seconds, so Jim said, and which in those circumstances is a long time.'

'I'll say.'

'Long enough for Jim to pick up the "You should not have seen this" look flash across Parsloe's eyes.'

'Did he report his suspicions?'

'I believe he was going to do so, and that might have been his downfall . . . the delay, see, but you know how it is, reporting someone like that is a big step, especially if you think you might be mistaken. Then there's a further delay because you have to come to believe what you think is happening. It's so enormous it's more comfortable to ignore it. Then you have to fight against the notion that you are grassing up a fellow police officer. Then roll all that into one and you have the reason why he hesitated. The next night he was back on duty and watching this house and all of us were in pairs except Jim Coventry. Jim was on his own. Not unknown but it was unusual, especially for Phil Ott because he always looked after his team, didn't like putting them at risk.'

'Who decided Jim should be on his own that night?'

'Freddie Wolfe,' Davies glanced at Forbes, 'he who met his maker last night. Gunned down by the man who went on to commit suicide by cop this morning, so the midday news reported. Freddie Wolfe was allocating positions that night. Phil Ott often delegated that duty.' Davies paused and said, 'Then, for me at least, Jacqueline Boot's death a few weeks earlier became a bit suspicious, and hill farming in Wales began to have an appeal . . . so I handed in my notice. Probably saved my life by doing so.'

'So, off the record, what do you think happened?'

'Parsloe killed two birds with one stone. He stopped Jim

going to A-Ten by having him abducted and murdered. He used Pirie's heavies for that, or hired his own. He and the other Detective Sergeants were alibied up. When Phil Ott heard about Jim's abduction he had to blow his cover to try to find Jim so the whole operation went down the tubes. We closed one or two "farms" and netted a few little fish but the big fish swam away, started new "farms" elsewhere, and Parsloe, Neve, Last and Wolfe continued to receive bribes. Now Wolfe has been murdered . . . So what happened there?'

'Which is a question we need answering.'

Davies stopped at a fork in the pathway. 'Well maybe he was going to blow the whistle, who knows? After all, he did set up a young man to be murdered. You'd have to be a seriously hard man not to let that eat away at you and Freddie Wolfe . . .' Davies shook his head. 'Was there ever a man who did not live up to his name? I always thought him soft for a cop. Freddie bunny rabbit would be a name more in keeping with his nature, as I remember him. Well . . .' Davies extended his hand, 'it was nice to meet you, Garrick, but in the kindest possible way, I never want to see you again. Not ever.'

Forbes shook hands with Davies. 'I know what you mean. Thanks.'

'That's your path by here, follow it, it will take you back to the village and your car. Drive safe, now.'

Dew sat in front of John Shaftoe's desk in his office in the London Hospital.

'Died instantly.' John Shaftoe scanned the report he had written following the post-mortem he had just completed. 'Classic "dead before he hit the ground" number. Eight bullets tightly grouped, in the chest, his heart exploded, but he was a walking corpse anyway. Nothing left of his lungs, secondary cancers in his stomach and pancreas, and also cirrhosis of the liver. He must have been in some discomfort and breathing with great difficulty. The blood tests will doubtless show heavy traces of morphine but that would only have taken the edge off the pain. He could have turned the gun on himself, but it was only a twenty-two. One shot might not have been fatal. I dare say he thought that by getting the police to shoot

him he would be certain of the result he wanted. Better statement too; go out with a blaze of glory with many mobile
phones recording the action. He was definitely not a man
for an inbetween-the-sheets sort of death, surrounded by
weeping relatives, soaking up all the attention. Good for him
I say . . . I mean in a sense . . .'

'Yes, I know what you mean; being shot has its attraction
as a form of death, quick, clean, painless. There are certainly
worse ways to go.'

'Indeed. No evidence of pain in this case.'

'You can have evidence of pain?' Dew was genuinely
surprised.

'Oh, yes, it can be frozen on the face of the deceased but
this fella had a look of peace about him, he looked to be at
rest. I performed a post-mortem on another fella once who
had forced the police to shoot him, also terminally ill, also
with a look of contentment about his face, he left a cheque
on him made payable to the police benevolent fund for a
few thousand pounds and a note inviting the officers who
shot him to have a drink on him, attaching a hundred quid
in tens and twenties to the note. Whether they did or not, I
never knew. Do you know anything about him?'

'Nothing as yet.' Dew adjusted his position in the hard,
upright chair. 'He also left a note which indicated some prior
contact with the police. "Never thought I'd thank the police,
but thanks for this" . . . or something like that. So his fingerprints will be on record.'

'But believed to have been the man who shot the retired
police officer last night?'

'Yes, believed to be.'

'Some story there.' Shaftoe inclined his head and raised
his right eyebrow.

'Yes.' Dew stood and screwed on his panama. 'As you say,
some story there.'

Julia Watmore née Crabtree took Harry Vicary along the road
in which she lived, with the St Bernard walking patiently
beside her, not pulling on the leash in the slightest. At the
end of the row of townhouses they turned left and walked
along a similar row of such homes, one, noted Vicary, also

having a blue plaque attached to it beside the door, announcing that Franz Schubert had once lived there. At the end of the road which proved itself to be a cul-de-sac for vehicles, Watmore and Vicary joined a narrow footpath that rose up to a wider more elevated pathway and which was occupied by other dog walkers and joggers and elderly people walking in the summer afternoon.

'This pathway used to be a railway line.' Julia Watmore bent down and slipped the St Bernard off the leash.

Vicary and Watmore walked in silence, Vicary allowing her to lead the way and allowing her to speak only when she felt ready. She led him to an overgrown Victorian cemetery of vast tombstones and mature trees in full foliage.

'This is Edinburgh's Highgate Cemetery,' she announced, 'though unlike Highgate, it's still in use. It's what you might call a "living graveyard" in that they still plant coffins here, though not in this part. This part is a very "dead" cemetery. The best time to visit is on an autumn or a winter's afternoon, then it is powerfully atmospheric.'

'I can imagine.' Vicary's eye was caught by numerous bulging white plastic bags hanging from the branches of shrubs.

'They're very good.' Watmore followed Vicary's gaze. 'They pick up after themselves after their night-time liaisons.'

'Who does?'

'The people of the night who come here in great numbers . . . usually of the male sex . . . but other weirdos also.'

'I see.'

'Yes, a pretty boy can find himself to be very popular in Warriston Cemetery during the hours of darkness. Some druggies too, though you don't seem to see needles lying about, but as dawn approaches they pick up after themselves and put their beer cans and cider bottles in plastic bags and hang them from branches for the council refuse men to collect. It is the alternative community policing itself. It's as though they have worked out that if they don't clean up behind them then the authorities will crack down, close the cemetery at night and ask the police to patrol it. It seems to be working; the Gays and the Druids and the Wiccans and the Goths get to use their weird playground during the night as long as they don't damage or litter.'

'Fair enough.' Vicary watched the St Bernard lumber forlornly after a grey squirrel.

'Also children,' Julia Watmore said after a minute or two of silence.

'Children?'

'Yes, another of Pirie's tricks was to use children. Probably still is. Children below the age of criminal responsibility if he can get 'em, so they'll get a lenient sentence for the most savage act. A few years in Juvenile Detention, then paroled for the sort of crime that an adult would get life imprisonment for.'

'Oh . . .' Vicary groaned.

'Yes . . . using dying men and women and young children, Pirie had a lot of his enemies iced that way. He, of course, was nowhere to be seen, often provenly sunning himself at his Spanish villa. So Operation Fennel . . . well . . . you know what the target was.'

'Cannabis "farms", producing strong stuff.'

'That's it. Cutting edge technology back then.'

'Commonplace now.'

'Yes, but you know we, that is the Detective Constables, myself, Jackie Boot, Jim Coventry, Owen Davies and others, we had the impression that the operation was being compromised.'

'Compromised? How?'

'Well, when we had good reason to believe that Pirie, Powell and Peabody . . . the big fish we were after, were going to be where we could link them to the production and sale of cannabis, they just were not there. Happened a few times, as though they were being tipped off.'

'Any ideas?'

'Parsloe.'

'The Detective Sergeant?'

'Yes. Trying to get hold of his personality is like trying to nail jelly to the wall . . . slippery. I tell you; my impression at the time was that Parsloe was a cop because he wasn't a villain. The other three DS's too, but mainly Parsloe. And it seems clearer now twenty-seven years later.'

'Did you see anything?'

'Oh, no, didn't expect to. You're not going to be there

when Parsloe stops at a phone box and makes a quick phone call but that's all it takes. And we didn't have any phone taps in place.'

'Of course.'

'Me and Jackie worked the Stork Club where Pirie and his mates drank. It isn't there now, not as a wine bar anyway, it's now a shoe shop near the King's Road in Chelsea. At least it was the last time I was down there. I have reached the age in life where I find myself looking back as much as looking forwards. I have taken to walking my roots and visiting other significant places of my life. I do that once a year and I visited the Stork Club so I could leave it, but this time leave it on my terms. But I found it was a shoe shop.'

'You didn't leave it on your terms before, clearly?'

'No. And I still feel contaminated. Phil Ott asked me and Jackie to go along and observe, so we did, and to chat. Phil Ott said chat if you can. We saw the big men, the three "P's" as we called them but never any police officers, that would be just too brazen of any corrupt officer. Anyway, the rule was "get out if you feel uncomfortable or in danger". It's easy for Phil Ott to say that, it covered him but it's not so easy when you're in there on the ground. Me and Jackie were very vulnerable . . . and you're dealing with East End blaggers, not educated stock market brokers. Play hard to get too long and you'll get a slap . . . and I don't mean a slap, I mean a slap . . . a put-you-in-hospital sort of slap. That sort of slap. And we couldn't ever say we were police officers . . . that would have been suicidal.'

'You deserved a medal.' Vicary glanced to his left as he and Julia Watmore walked by a huge nineteenth-century tombstone which gave the name of the deceased, her date of birth and her date of death followed by the terse inscription, 'She died at Edinburgh'. There did not, thought Vicary, seem to have been a great deal of passion in the final years of that lady's marriage.

'Well it was inevitable we'd do horizontal duty, just couldn't get out. Never got close to Pirie or the other two.'

'Powell and Peabody?'

'Yes. We got no nearer than the gang members. One of them took a shine to me, a big, heavy geezer called Barr . . . in his late twenties then. He was a used car dealer in Clapham, that was his front at the time.'

'Barr?'

'Big Cyril Barr . . . and he was big, weighed a ton, didn't know how to take his bodyweight on his elbows, damn near crushed the life out of me.'

Vicary groaned.

'But he was a big softie really; like my dog, he didn't seem to be cut out for crooking. It was as though he was in the gang because it was trendy to be in. He had done a few daft things in his youth and had done time inside, so he was "all right" in Pirie's eyes but he was really only a gofer. It might be worth leaning on him if he's still around, if he's still with us.'

'I'll pass that up.'

'He'll be in the system, but it was because of him that we got to know of Pirie's policy of using dying adults or very young boys as one-off hit men. Big Cyril told me that and I told Phil Ott, so we got something but it was a poor return for the investment.'

'What they paid you wasn't enough.'

'I found that out.' She forced a smile. 'That I found out the hard way.'

'When did you get out?'

'When I realized that I wasn't going to get any information, when I realized I wasn't safe and when I realized I was never going to get anywhere near the three "P's" and when I heard about Jackie Boot drowning. No accident that.'

'You think?'

'I know. They must have known we were cops . . . and Jackie also found herself doing horizontal duty. We saw the smoke but never got near the fire. After Jackie drowned in the river, I went to see Phil Ott and handed my notice in. He was very good but I am still convinced that if I hadn't resigned, I would be a floater like Jackie or would have disappeared like Jim Coventry. I'll never know how close I came . . . it haunts me . . . terribly so.'

'It would do.'

'But I am glad you're looking into the matter. So why the interest after all these years?'

'Well, we haven't made it public, but Jim Coventry's body has now been found, buried in Epping Forest.'

'Oh . . .' Julia Watmore leaned forward and buried her face in her hands, weeping uncontrollably, and could not be comforted.

# SIX

Dew, Vicary and Forbes sat in front of Commander Gentle's desk. The silence had lasted for fully twenty seconds until Gentle said, 'This is going to be very, very bad for the Metropolitan Police. Very bad indeed.' He spoke softly. 'Very bad, but it will all have to come out . . . murdered police officers . . . corruption . . . even after nearly thirty years, it will still look bad.'

'No, sir.' Garrick Forbes leaned forward, resting his elbows on his knees and spoke with noticeable determination. 'It will be very good for the Metropolitan Police Force, very good indeed.'

'The act of cleansing, you mean?'

'Yes, sir,' Forbes smiled. 'That's exactly what I mean. It is for this that I volunteered for A-Ten, the rooting out of corruption. Do that and what remains is good, strong and healthy and clean. When the public see that we can and will police ourselves then their confidence in the police force will be solid.'

'All right, I can see the advantage, perhaps good will come from this. So when do you propose to issue a press release about the discovery of Jim Coventry's corpse?'

'I'll take advice on that, sir,' Dew replied, 'see what the other officers think. I don't want to alert the corrupt officers too early. Speaking for myself, I'd rather hold back on that for a while, keep it up our sleeve.'

'I would agree with that,' Vicary said. 'I think it's sensible.'

'Me too.' Forbes glanced at Dew.

'Very well.' Gentle sat back in his chair and glanced out of the window of his office. 'I'll leave that decision with you. Looks like you'll be keeping it secret for a few days but on the other hand it may be that the cat is out of the bag anyway. Freddie Wolfe was murdered for a reason and if he is the sort of man that Owen Davies recalls, he might have been having a crisis of conscience and about to talk . . .'

'We just don't know, sir.'

'Very well, keep it quiet for the time being. So what are your next moves?'

'Well, sir,' Dew also sat forward, 'I would suggest we talk to Mrs Wolfe, Freddie Wolfe's widow. Can't be an interview as such, so I can do that alone.'

'All right.'

'I'd like Mr Forbes and Mr Vicary to interview Mrs Spicer, widow of the felon who shot Freddie Wolfe.'

'Yes.'

'Have to do that under caution, so that will have to be a two hander.'

'Of course.'

'Can't close down on Parsloe and Last and Neve until I have sufficient on them.'

'They'll likely be circling the wagons.'

'I am aware of that, sir, but we need more than we have at the moment. Confess I rather like the sound of Cyril Barr, the secondhand car dealer who knew policewoman Crabtree and did so in the most unpleasant sense.'

'Very well.'

'I'd like to organize a surveillance on Parsloe, Last and Neve. If we let them know they're being watched it might put them off their stroke, might unbalance them.'

'You can do that?'

'Yes, sir.'

'If you are going to do that you might as well announce the discovery of Jim Coventry's body.'

'No, sir, we mustn't let them know what we know.' Forbes was insistent. 'This case is more the realm of A-Ten now, sir.'

'I don't want to be relieved of this case,' Dew growled.

Gentle held up his hand. 'Things stay as they are, but DS Forbes is correct, Archie, this is edging more and more into an A-Ten pigeon. It may be that you and DS Vicary will have to bale out at some point.'

Dew sat back in his chair and folded his arms.

'But at the moment it's still your investigation.'

It was the size of the house which first impressed Dew. It also caused him to worry. Chestnut Avenue, Rickmansworth,

Herts, was not, he thought, Detective Sergeant (retired) of
the Metropolitan Police territory. Here were large, very large
houses, large in any man's language, rambling interwar-built
properties with double garages and large front lawns on tree-
lined roads. Here was money: big money.

Dew halted his car, which he saw seemed to be the least
prestigious in the road, outside the Wolfe household. He
exited it, leaving one window lowered by an inch or so to
allow the interior to 'breathe' in the heat. He locked the
vehicle, out of habit rather than any need for security in that
street, and walked up the concrete driveway of the house,
negotiating a passage between a Range Rover and the neatly
cut front lawn. He pressed the doorbell and heard the soft
chime of the bell resonate in the interior. The heavy-looking
and richly varnished door was opened rapidly by a confident-looking young man in his mid to late twenties. The man
had a serious expression, thought Dew, which, in the circumstances, was wholly appropriate and was also dressed in
sombre clothing and was again fully appropriate for a household in mourning.

'Is Mrs Wolfe at home?' Dew asked when the young man
was clearly going to remain staring at him without speaking.

'Yes.'

'DCI Dew of Scotland Yard.' Dew showed the young man
his identity card.

'I will ask.' He shut the door slowly but firmly.

Dew turned and looked about him. It was, as he had
first noticed, an area of wealth. The houses were large, the
sort inhabited by stockbrokers and successful solicitors,
he guessed, with BMW's and top of the range Audis in
the driveway. Each home was detached, clearly nothing as
vulgar and lower middleclass as a semi-detached house in
this part of Rickmansworth, each property being separate
from the adjacent property by a mature hedgerow, and, as
he looked, not one living soul to be seen. Though each
home would have its occupant, if only a maid or a daily
help. The houses, thought Dew, did not seem to be sufficiently large to be butlered homes, but he doubted that
each could not be managed without some form of domestic
help.

The door reopened with a gentle click and was swung wide by the serious-minded young man. 'Mrs Wolfe is in the garden. If you'll follow me, please?'

Dew stepped into the cool of the shade of a cavernous-looking entrance hall of dark stained panelling and carpet of dark red. The hallway smelled of the fresh cut flowers that stood in a vase on a table at the side of the hall. The youth shut the door behind Dew and then led him down a long corridor with rooms off, to a clearly lavishly equipped kitchen, to the scullery beyond the kitchen and to the rear door and the garden. The garden, Dew noted, was a little wider than the width of the house but extended deeply beyond it. Probably, he guessed, it was three times longer than it was wide. It was surrounded by tall, close-planted trees and seemed to him to be, like Philip Ott's house in Norfolk, unable to be overlooked. A swimming pool surrounded by wooden reclining chairs stood off to the right. On one such chair a woman lay, dressed in an all-enveloping blue towelling robe; she also wore sunglasses and light-weight sandals. The young man led Dew to the swimming pool and to the resting woman. 'Mr Dew of New Scotland Yard,' he announced.

The woman levered herself up into a sitting position, keeping her legs together on one side of the recliner. 'Mr Dew . . .' she held out a hand, 'I am Helen Wolfe.' She took off her sunglasses with the other.

'Archibald Dew.' Dew shook her hand.

'Do take a pew, please. Such a hot day, would you care for something to drink?'

'Not for me, thank you.'

'I'll be just inside if you need me, Mrs Wolfe.' The young man turned and walked slowly back across the lawn to the house.

'Thank you, Ralph,' Helen Wolfe called after him and then turned to Dew. 'That's my son-in-law. He is a very serious-minded young man.'

'I had just that impression.'

'He's an accountant with a large firm in the city. He provides well for my daughter and they seem very content, which is all I can wish for . . . but . . . will he call me "Helen"?

Not a chance it seems. He is just happier with formal address, dare say it's the neat, logical mind of the accountant at work.' She replaced her sunglasses and laid back on the recliner. 'This will be about Freddie . . .'

'Yes.'

'I am sorry if I don't play the grieving widow dressed all in black but . . . well . . . just "but" . . .'

'No matter. And yes, it is about your late husband.'

'I have been visited by the Hertfordshire Police but couldn't tell them anything. So the Yard is interested also . . . I am still in a state of shock, nothing seems real, which is probably why my dress is inappropriate for a recent widow.'

'I could call back later, in a few days.'

'No . . . no . . . I'll focus.' She put her hands at either side of her sunglasses in a manner suggestive of horses' blinkers. 'I used to be in the force, Policewoman Mallon. I know the importance of the first few hours following any murder in the police investigation. So, come on, Mallon, focus . . . focus . . . focus.'

'Thank you.'

'Though I don't know what I can tell you.'

Birdsong filled the air. The sound of water splashing and teenagers' laughter floated over the hedgerows from a distant property.

'No witnesses, I understand?'

'None, no one heard anything either. The man . . . or woman must have had a silenced weapon. We don't have CCTV in this road. Freddie was found by a motorist, the beam of his headlights caught my husband's body lying on the pavement. Some other cars might also have seen him and driven past thinking him to be drunk . . . we'll never know . . . but one motorist did stop and raised the alarm and that was very soon after he was shot. The police said his body still had some residual heat.'

'I see . . . tell me, is that an East End accent I detect?'

'Plaistow.'

'Ah . . .'

'A world away from Rickmansworth but this is where Freddie wanted to live when he retired. So dutiful wife I, ever dutiful wife, followed my husband wherever he went. So here we are in sunny WD3 or rather here I am now, but it was better than Upton where we lived until Freddie retired and which was better than Plaistow.'

'Did you win the football pools?' Dew asked with a note of humour.

'Nope . . . nor did we win the lottery. What happened was that Freddie inherited a fortune and took early retirement. He retired at fifty, about five years ago, and we bought this house as it is. The pool was already here, useful for a few weeks of the year but a waste of space for the most part. Have you ever seen a swimming pool in a snowstorm? I'd rather have shrubbery here but at the moment it is quite pleasant, something soothing about still water, I find, especially at a time like this.'

'Yes, I am sorry . . .'

'Well, I am a widow at forty-five. I did expect to become a widow at some point as all married women must but not quite this early. It's a bit soon. I dare say I'll feel cheated but at the moment I can't seem to feel anything.'

'Do you have any plans?'

Helen Wolfe shook her head. 'No emotions . . . no plans. Any plans I did have were wrapped up in Freddie's life, can't think for myself at the moment.'

'Yes, I am sorry, that was a little insensitive.' Dew watched a lone magpie alight upon the lawn some distance away and recalling childhood superstitions said to himself, 'Good morning, Mr Magpie'.

'Are you married, Mr Dew?'

'Yes . . . one daughter.'

'Is she married?'

'No . . .' Dew lowered his head. 'She's unwell.'

'Oh . . . serious?'

'Serious enough, she's in a psychiatric hospital.'

'Oh . . . I am sorry . . . so . . . two wounded soldiers we, eh?'

'Dare say you could say that but I am really here to ask about your late husband.'

'Yes.'

'Could you tell me what sort of man he was?'

'Oh, I don't know how to answer that.'

'Well . . . ambitious? Career orientated?'

'Freddie, a careerist?' Helen Wolfe smiled. 'Hardly, more of a home boy really. For Freddie family came first, the job was a means of providing, not an end in itself.'

'Drug Squad, I believe?'

'Yes, he was motivated there, he seemed to believe in what he was doing, having seen the human wreckage caused by drug abuse. He did have a lot of job satisfaction in that sense but it was still family first and foremost for Freddie.'

'I see, lucky he.'

'Yes, we have a family friend who works for an insurance company and he got a bit tight, a bit three sheets to the wind once over dinner and said, "Don't you just 'ate your job, don't you just 'ate it something rotten," and Freddie said "No, actually I quite enjoy it." Not every man could say that, not every man can.'

'So doubly lucky to be able to take early retirement. It all seemed to have fallen into his lap.'

'Yes, the money came as a surprise tinged with sadness. His brother Julian died and left him a seven-figure fortune.'

'Seven figures!'

'Yes. We attended the funeral in Portsmouth. His brother was older than Freddie. He was an art dealer and he also apparently played the stock market. Not a man of great visual income, small house, a Volkswagen . . . one art gallery . . . no family. Anyway, a few days after the funeral Freddie attended the reading of the will and found out his brother was worth millions, more by stocks and shares rather than selling art. Freddie came home and said his brother had been worth five million pounds and we have got two of them. It was then that Freddie took early retirement. We sold our modest little semi in Upton and moved to Rickmansworth.'

'I see.' Dew glanced up at a wide blue sky as a bead of sweat ran down his brow.

'Freddie was close to his older brother. He still has another brother though, although they do not seem to be as close. I don't know what the other brother did with his inheritance.'

'So . . . latterly, what was Freddie like, in himself?'

'Looking for a motive for someone to murder him?'

'Yes, yes, I am. He seems to have been a definite target.'

'Well it's strange that you should ask that, he did seem to have changed.'

'In what way?'

'He seemed to be withdrawn, not talking, poking at his food rather than tucking into it . . . preoccupied . . . even feeling guilty about something, drinking more than usual, as if he was running away from something in his past . . . and yes, I did ask and no, he wouldn't tell me what was on his mind. I did hear him mumbling, "Shouldn't have done it, shouldn't have done it", when he didn't think I was in earshot. He also once said, "Time to improve the silence".'

'Improve upon the silence?'

'Yes, I remember once in our early days he used the phrase, "Improving the silence", but I never asked what he meant. And then he used the phrase or a variation of it just before he was murdered. I am afraid I don't know what he meant by it.'

'I see,' Dew said again, 'that's a puzzle.' He paused. 'Do you have any papers in respect of your brother-in-law's death?'

'A few.'

'It's just that something has occurred to me.'

'I do hope he will be left in peace, both Freddie and his brother died before their time. Like I said, only one of the brothers is still alive, the Reverend Wolfe.'

'Reverend? An Anglican priest?'

'Yes, he is the vicar of St Lawrence's Church in Elm Park, lucky man.'

'Lucky?' Dew smiled.

'East London. You asked if I had plans, well I haven't but having said that I can't see myself staying here, we never really felt at home here. Oh . . . something else Freddie said when he was in his cups just a week or two ago, "Father will be turning in his grave", but he didn't explain what he meant.'

'His father was an influence in his life?'

'Isn't he always? Freddie's father was also a clergyman. Freddie grew up in a vicarage, one of three sons of the

Reverend Wolfe who had a parish in the Midlands, so he had that background and he always had a strong sense of morality.'

'Interesting. Do you know the name of your deceased brother-in-law's solicitors?'

'Yes. I can't remember the name but it will be in the papers I have.' Helen Wolfe sat up, gracefully so. 'I'll go in with you. What was the name . . .? Rearden . . . Rearden and somebody in Plymouth.' She stood. 'Come on, I'll find a sheet of headed notepaper from them for you.'

One and a half hours later, Archibald Dew was sitting at his desk in his office. The phone on his desk began to warble. He waited for a second or two and then picked it up, 'DCI Dew.'

'Julian Rearden speaking of Rearden, Pryce and Co.'

'Yes. Thank you for phoning back, Mr Rearden.'

'We have to be sure to whom we speak. I am aware of the old joke about the difference between a police officer and a lawyer.'

'That a lawyer will still persecute you when you're dead?'

Rearden laughed, 'Yes, that's the one but the reverse also holds true. A lawyer will still protect you when you're dead. So I don't see how I can help you. I cannot furnish details of my clients' business, even deceased clients, in the absence of a Court Order compelling me to do so.'

'Understood, but I may not need details.'

'All right . . . see how far we get.'

'Well the question is, did your late client, Mr Julian Wolfe, bequeath a fortune to his surviving brother Frederic?'

'Define a fortune . . . one man's ceiling being another man's floor.'

'Two million pounds.'

Rearden gasped. 'Not in the will I drew up. Julian Wolfe wasn't a rich man. He just left small three-figure sums to his surviving relatives. Dare say it's safe to tell you that.'

'Thank you, sir.' Dew spoke solemnly. 'It's all I need to know.'

Vicary halted the car by the kerb and he and Forbes got out of the vehicle in Leppoc Road, Clapham, and walked along the pavement towards the last known address of Big Cyril Barr.

'Can I ask you a question?' Vicary glanced along the line of late-Victorian terraces that was Leppoc Road. He was familiar with the type of house and was fond of them with their 'L' shaped floor plan, and generously proportioned rooms, often with equally generous gardens. He thought they made excellent family homes.

'If you like,' Forbes fell into step with Vicary, 'though I reserve the right not to answer. Depending.'

'Fair enough. So, have you ever been a soldier?'

Forbes smiled. 'A lot of people ask me that. It's the way I walk, I think.'

'It is. You have a military gait, very soldier-like.'

'The answer's "no" but it is in the genes. My father and grandfather both served for extended periods in the Grenadier Guards, career soldiers. Both paraded before the Sovereign on Horse Guards Parade during the Trooping of the Colour ceremony . . . all that number. My father was Provost Sergeant, the most hated man in the regiment and he loved it. There was a lot of pressure on me to enlist, expectation even, so it was a bit difficult for the old man when I didn't but the police was good enough. Not quite HM Forces but good enough. Do you have a military background?'

'No.' Vicary, with a policeman's eye noted a parked car with an out-of-date road tax disc but was content to leave the discovery of same to the next constable who patrolled Leppoc Road. 'No, my father was a railwayman. He was very particular about timekeeping but wasn't a tyrant. Nice bloke really. Delighted when I joined the force.'

'Lucky you.' Forbes stopped at the address and walked up to the door and pressed the bell. It rang loudly with a harsh tone that would have annoyed him if he lived in the property.

The door was opened quickly upon the pressing of the bell. The woman on the threshold was fresh-faced, devoid of any form of cosmetics, short hair, mid forties. 'Yes?' She said confidently.

'Police.'

'I know. I can tell.'

'We are looking for Mr Cyril Barr. Is he at home?'

'I'll see.' She turned and shut the door behind her.

Vicary held out his hand and stopped the door catching on the lock. 'It's serious, although we only want information. But he's got form; we can return with a warrant and start tearing up the floorboards.'

'So just tell him we want to see him,' Forbes added with a smile.

The woman flushed with anger and walked strongly away down the lengthy hallway of the house. Moments later, Cyril Barr ambled down the hallway to greet the officers. He was as Julia Watmore had described him and Vicary winced at the thought of her, when she, as WPC Crabtree, was crushed beneath his bulk because 'He didn't know how to take his weight on his elbows'. Barr stepped out of the house and on to the steps. 'The Bill?' He asked.

'Yes, DS Vicary and DS Forbes from New Scotland Yard.'

'The Yard!'

'Yes. Are you Cyril Barr?'

'Yes.'

'You're not employed?'

Barr shook his head. 'Sold up. Retired. I'd made enough. No point in working if you can see your way clear.'

'Understand that.'

'So . . . what do you want?'

'Advice. Information.'

Barr looked questioningly at the two officers. 'You're from the Yard, not the local nick, so it's not about the other business?'

'No, we're going back nearly thirty years.'

Barr took a deep breath. 'Things have moved on a lot in that time.'

'The past is resurfacing. Remember Pirie, Powell and Peabody? You were one of their gofers?'

Barr gasped, 'Dangerous boys.'

'We just need information, Cyril.'

'All right . . . look, I don't want you in the house, Gloria . . .' he lifted a finger to indicate behind him, 'she . . . well, I'll explain. Let's go somewhere. You know where the common is from here?'

'Yes, we drove past it.'

'Let me grab some clothes . . . shoes, and I'll see you there, boating lake by Rockery Road. It will be easier to walk from here. I'll be ten minutes behind you.'

'Hope so,' Vicary smiled, 'because . . . well, you know the score.'

'I know the score. I'll be there.'

Twenty minutes later the three men walked abreast with Barr in the centre, round the perimeter of the boating lake on Clapham Common. There were few other people on the common despite the summer weather, it being midweek.

'So, you need information about Pirie and Peabody and Powell. They're retired now . . . in Spain . . . except for Powell, he's in the Scrubs.'

'And you're retired also?'

'As much as I can be, they just won't let you settle and put your past behind you.'

'Who?'

'You . . . the cops, the Bill.'

'You remember the Stork Club?'

'Oh, yes.' Barr's eyes brightened up.

'And a young woman called Julia?'

'Yes, and her friend Jackie, the policewomen.'

'You knew they were policewomen?'

'Yes, trying to get near Pirie, it was so obvious. They went to the Stork Club dressed up to the nines and in the club were all these posh public school educated toffs . . . called Fabian and Charles and Dominic, smooth manners and smooth voices, paying with credit cards. Just the sort of man a girl wants to slide a ring on her finger. Lawyers they were, stockbrokers, merchant bankers, blokes like that, and when they tried to chat up Julia and Jackie they got nowhere . . . but us lot, East Enders, paying in cash, really uncouth . . . I mean, no culture at all, blokes like me and Eddie the Tooth Fairy . . . He had this knack of helping people remember things or making them part with money they owed by applying a crowbar to their teeth. I mean real skilful and artful and gentle-like . . .'

'I can imagine.'

'And Charlie Clay, hair all over his body, breath what

smelled like a sewer . . . and we get everywhere with those
two girls. We pulled them on Pirie's orders, keep them
under control. Let them see Pirie and Powell and Peabody
from time to time but never when any turn is going down,
just in the club having a meet. Normally they wouldn't let
us in a club like that but the owner was on Pirie's books
. . . protection money. That was a little side interest Pirie
had in the day. I can tell you that now because the Stork
Club has closed down and Pirie's retired to Spain but
they're still not men to be crossed. So, no statements about
them.' He paused. 'I mean Powell, he's doing a very long
stretch.'

'We know.'

'He took a machete to this young geezer. This young geezer
gave this chick a slap. You know how it is, she was being a
bit bad news and so the geezer put her right. Wasn't much
and nobody in their manor would have thought twice about
it. It was nothing you don't see in any Bethnal Green boozer
on a Saturday night. Only problem, see, was that this chick
happened to be Powell's granddaughter.'

'Ah . . .'

'So Powell is not a happy man and a few days later this
young geezer is without arms or legs . . . just four little stumps
. . . and the rest of him is in the river. So not men to cross.
Anyway, Pirie sold up, gave Peabody and Powell their fair
wedge.'

'Sold up?'

'To the Vietnamese. They run the skunk farms now. No
violent takeover. They sold the whole operation like a legit
businessman sells his business for his retirement money. No
paperwork but a good wedge is given by the Vietnamese to
Pirie. Powell helped there; he's got Vietnamese blood and
has Vietnamese relatives, and oriental middle names on his
birth certificate.'

'I see,' Vicary glanced round the expanse of green that
was Clapham Common, 'interesting.'

'I haven't been asked for any favours and I was beginning
to think it was all behind me . . . then I met Gloria.'

'Wife?'

'Wife to be.'

'She's into the notion of people changing. She takes Sunday School classes . . . and she's accepted me on the basis that I am an ex-blagger but reformed.'

'OK.'

'So I have told her that there's nothing in the pipeline.'

'But?'

'But the local Bill have been leaning on me for something.'

'Really?'

'Yes, turns out some boy was caught with some blow, a small amount but enough to make a charge of possession with intent to supply stick. Now he is muchly worried and also works in the Civil Service.'

'Oh . . . silly boy.'

'So he is now looking at prison time and the loss of his comfy job with its inflation-proof pension at the end of it. So he is giving information to the Bill in return for charges against him being dropped . . . and this information could put me in the slammer instead of him and this is after me telling Gloria that there is nothing in the pipeline. I could do three years but Gloria won't be there when I come out and this is causing me grief. Mucho, mucho grief.'

'So what are they wanting you for?'

'Handling.'

'It's not much of a crime . . .'

'Well, handling thirty or forty stolen Rolls Royces.'

'Ah . . .'

'You see, I might have used my garage to assist in the export of flash motors to Russia or the Middle East. A boy might have nicked one from up the West End, driven it to my yard here in Clapham, where I might have resprayed it and put false plates on from a wrecked car which had not been reported as wrecked.'

'So the plates were still valid.'

'Right. And then someone else may have come along and collected it and taken it away on the back of a lorry under a tarpaulin to Felixstowe docks where another geezer might have slid it into a container to be shipped to another geezer in some foreign land where ownership papers are not required prior to sale.'

'I see . . . and this was when?'

'About five years ago, if it happened. Right now the local Bill are a little bit short of proof but only a little bit.'

'OK. So, tell me, supposing we could pull strings and make this little,' Vicary glanced skyward, 'this little escapade of yours go away . . . is their anything else in your past likely to surface that could make things difficult for you and Gloria?'

Barr glanced hopefully at Vicary. 'Well, there's always things in a blagger's past, commit nine crimes and get done for the tenth . . . but no investigation, not that I am aware of.'

'Anybody hurt in this business you had?'

'Just the insurance companies.'

'All right. We don't want to nail Pirie and Peabody, they can stay in Spain.'

Barr looked questioningly at Vicary and then turned to his right and glanced equally questioningly at Forbes. 'Who then?'

'DS Vicary works for the Murder Squad,' Forbes said calmly, 'but I work for A-Ten.'

'A-Ten . . .' Barr stopped walking. 'You're wanting to nail the corrupt coppers, the ones Pirie was paying off?'

'Yes, Detective Sergeants Parsloe, Neve, Last and Wolfe.'

'Wolfe was shot a few nights ago.'

'Yes,' Barr started walking again, 'all over the news. I wondered if it was the same Mr Wolfe.'

'It was.'

'Pirie wouldn't have had a hand in that, nor Peabody but it was Pirie's technique to use a dying man, someone picked that up from Pirie, someone learned that dodge from him.'

'You think so?'

'I know so.' Barr looked down at the ground as they continued to walk round the boating lake upon which a radio-controlled model warship was twisting and turning. 'So how will this work? What do I have to do to make the bent Rollers investigation go away? I don't want to lose Gloria. I'm settled for the first time ever and I have come to like it.'

'A statement and evidence in court, we'll need that.'

'But nothing against Pirie or Peabody or Powell? If I give evidence against them a dying old blagger will walk up to me in the street with a sawn-off under his coat . . .'

'We'll keep them out of it. We want the bent coppers. One's dead, that leaves Parsloe, Last and Neve. We want them, Cyril.'

'Yes, I can understand that.'

'So what do you know about the murder of Jim Coventry and the drowning of Jackie Boot?'

Barr turned to Vicary. 'Nothing. Nothing at all. I remember Jackie Boot drowning but never knew anyone called Jim Coventry. Who was he?'

'A police constable,' Forbes growled, 'just twenty-seven years old . . . about thirty years ago.'

'So, now?'

'Now, now he'd be happy in retirement, with a lovely full index-linked police pension, enjoying his grandchildren in the autumn of his life with another twenty years good living still ahead of him. It makes Jackie Boot's drowning very iffy, Cyril. Very iffy indeed.'

'Don't know nothing about either. Honest. I was just a gofer and a delivery boy but I tell you one thing, Pirie and Peabody and Powell would not have offed a copper, that really would be out of order.'

'We agree, which is why we want to talk to Parsloe, Last and Neve.'

'Well I don't know nothing about them being involved in icing anyone. They took money, lots of it . . . I was the bag man.'

'And you'll give a statement to that effect?'

'Yes, but no mention of Pirie, I won't say who the money was from.'

'That's not necessary, so long as you gave them large sums of money.'

'Which I did. This will make the noise about the stolen Rollers die down . . . like silenced?'

'Yes.'

'I'll need that guaranteed.'

'We'll see what we can do . . . we can talk to people. If we can link them to the murder of two cops, then what's a few bent wheels? Strings can be pulled.'

'So tell us what you know,' Forbes stared straight ahead, 'off the record for now.'

'Well there were five bent coppers, not four.'

'Five!'

'Yes . . . five . . . there was the four you mentioned and then one other. I never knew his name.'

'Description.'

'Tall and thin as I recall. And he came late in the game.'

'How did it go down?'

'Once a month, I took a carrier bag full of money, hard cash, used notes, fives, tens and twenties . . . usually fives and tens. Nearly thirty years ago five pounds was . . . well . . . bigger than it is now.'

'I'll say,' Vicary smiled, 'but go on.'

'The drop was always the same, really casual. It was well north of the smoke . . . no CCTV in those days. We always did it on a Sunday evening. I'd be given this holdall, stuffed with money, then I'd drive it out to the first motorway service station on the M1. Not many cars in the car park after dark on Sunday. I'd park my car in the furthest corner from the petrol pumps and shops and another car would park beside me. I always had to arrive first and always use the same vehicle. Then I'd hand the money over, sometimes to Parsloe, sometimes to Last, sometimes to Wolfe, sometimes to Neve and occasionally to the fifth geezer.'

'The tall, lanky one?'

'Yes. Wolfe was the weakest,' Barr announced. 'I always felt that. There was always this sense you had that he was uncomfortable, that someone had a gun to his head. The other four were cool as cucumbers but Wolfe was a . . . dunno . . . just hadn't the bottle for it but did it anyway. Neve, too, was shaky but not as shaky as Wolfe.'

'All right, we'll have words, pull strings, see what we can work out, then we'll take a written statement.'

'In front of a brief with a written guarantee that the investigation about those stolen Rollers will disappear forever? I mean that's the only way you'll get what you want from me – if I get what I want from you . . . and no mention of Pirie's crew.'

'We'll be in touch,' Vicary replied. 'Just leave it with us.'

'Watch your backs, gents.' Barr turned to go. 'If Parsloe's offing people . . . because Pirie wouldn't have offed Mr Wolfe

... if Parsloe is offing people, or having them offed after learning from Pirie how it's done, then watch your backs. I'll be watching mine.'

'Thanks but we'll be all right.'

Barr paused. 'You could try British Telecom.'

'British Telecom?'

'Barry Tew, he got called British Telecom because of his initials, sometimes just "Tellycom" or "Telly". He was a low-grade player in Pirie's team, just like me. He was Jacqueline Boot's fella, just as I was Julia Crabtree's fella. We kept the policewomen occupied as a means of controlling them, like I said, letting them see a little bit but not too much, just enough to let them think they were getting somewhere.'

'Barry Tew?'

'He's got plenty of form. Also known as "Mole" because of the way he could shift soil. I haven't seen him in years but he might be able to tell you something about Jackie's drowning, being as he was her escort and all ... but watch your backs.'

Driving back towards central London Vicary said, 'We are going to need more than his statement.'

'I know,' Forbes slowed the car and halted for a red traffic light, 'but it's a good start. In fact it's a very good start, a very good start indeed. But he's right, we need to watch ourselves. Time to draw firearms.'

'I smelled immoral money.' The Reverend Sydney Wolfe sat in his study in the vicarage of St Lawrence's, Elm Park. It was a newly built building adjacent to the newly built church. 'Simple as that.' Dew found the man to have a comforting, reassuring presence and liked his soft speaking voice. He was, Dew found, a very easy man to talk to. 'It was when I went to view his huge house in Rickmansworth that his wife Helen told me that they had bought it with the money bequeathed to them by our late brother. I didn't say anything and left soon after and have never returned. The shoe began to pinch overmuch at that point.' The Reverend Wolfe was a heavily set man with a shining, bald head. A double chin hung heavily over his clerical collar. 'I have treasure of my own. I do not need Mammon. So Frederic is now also

deceased. Gangland-style shooting they say. Well that probably does confirm my suspicion that he was involved in
crime, unless you really can buy a seven bedroom house in
Rickmansworth for three hundred pounds, which is what our
brother left us in his will.'

'Tell me something, sir, if you can, just before his death
your brother seemed to be a troubled man.'

'Did he?'

'So his wife told me.'

'I see.'

'And one of the things he was heard to mumble to himself
was "time to improve the silence", something like that.'

'Ah . . .' the Reverend Wolfe smiled, 'I can shed a little
light there. It was one of our father's admonitions. Father
cared not for idle chatter in his home. He did not mind
debate, or discussion or negotiation . . . it wasn't so repres-
sive . . . but he often would say, "Do not speak, unless by
doing so, you improve upon the silence." I think if Freddie
was saying that when in a troubled state of mind, it meant
that he was struggling with a terrible secret and was looking
for a way to tell someone, to disclose it, as we might say.
He must have made a huge error in his life and it was
weighing heavily upon his conscience. I will pray for his
soul, but I am so pleased that father is not alive to see
this.'

Parsloe, Neve and Last sat around a small, circular table in
the Feathers and spoke in hushed but confident tones.

'If they were building a case they'd be more discreet.'
Parsloe lifted his beer to his lips. 'They're making it obvious
we're being watched, they're hoping to trip us up because
they know they have no case. So stay cool. Stay focused and
the nasty men will all go away soon.'

'And we're watching them as well. That they do not know.'
Last also sipped his beer. 'Two of them had a chat with the
big fat bag man this morning, walking round the boating
pond on Clapham Common.'

'Big Cyril?' Neve gasped.

'That's the one. I know he looks like a heart attack
waiting to happen,' Parsloe drummed his fingers on the

table top, 'trouble is we can't wait for it to happen. He could damage us.'

'I'll give that a bit of a think,' Last offered, 'come up with an idea or two.'

'Good,' Parsloe smiled. 'Got a phone call from the boss this morning, he's worried about Dew, wants his home address.'

'He lives in Seven Kings, I believe,' Neve offered. 'It's a first step.'

'Yes,' Parsloe sneered, 'he's a p.b.h.'

'P.b.h?' Neve smiled.

'Poor but honest. Like my wife's family. First time I was introduced to them, little house in Essex on the edge of the marshes, her father actually said to me, "We're poor but honest, just simple folk," so throughout my marriage my in-laws have been the p.b.h.'s,' he grinned. 'But the wife never heard . . .'

'Of course.'

'But Dew's a p.b.h. cop and he drives a lovely little Skoda, the registration number of which we know. A job for a couple of street turks wanting to make the right connection.'

'I know just the lads,' Last said. 'Good lads, too.'

'All right, give them a wedge and tell them to get up to Seven Kings and start walking the streets looking for a green Skoda. Give them the registration number. If they come back with an address, give them another wedge. Confirm it with the Voters Roll. If it checks out as the home of Dew, let me know, I'll phone the boss. Don't know what he intends to do.'

'Don't want this to become a habit.' Vicary held the cigarette out above his head as Beethoven's Choral Symphony played quietly on the hi-fi. 'Once visited a house full of dried-out alcoholics just passing cigarettes between themselves . . . quite the smokiest room I have ever been in.'

'You mean they had just replaced one addiction with another?' Kathleen Tate lay beside him, naked as he was, under a single cotton sheet. She glanced out of the window at yet another vast, scarlet sunset that settled over London.

'Yes, exactly, that's exactly what they each had done.'

'Well, we won't do that then.' She reached up and took the cigarette from him and stubbed it in the ashtray upon the bedside table which stood on Harry Vicary's side of the bed. 'No more mention of cigarettes . . . or booze . . . remember, strength comes from silent places.'

# SEVEN

Archibald Reginald Henry Dew was killed by a single bullet to the chest. The bullet entered his aorta and lodged there. The single shot echoed in the canyon of terraced housing, being Pembroke Road, Seven Kings, and Tom Fintry, a long-time neighbour of Dew's, heard the crack of the gunshot from within his front bedroom in which he was standing. Fintry had served for fifteen years in the army and recognized the sound for what it was. He looked out of the window of his bedroom to see Archie Dew collapse on to the pavement outside his house. He also saw a youth running from the scene in clear panic. Fintry dashed down the stairs, grabbed his car keys and mobile phone. He lifted his landline phone off the hook and dialled three nines and then ran from his house to where he had parked his car, knowing that the three nines call would bring police rapidly to the scene. He drove his car after the fleeing youth, noticing his clothing, white sports shoes, blue jeans, grey hooded top . . . closing on him but not overtaking him, as he fumbled for his mobile phone and managed to dial three nines again, though this time he spoke and told the police control what he had witnessed and where he was at that moment. 'Pursuing the gunman . . . a "hoodie".' He fought to keep his voice calm. 'Running down Meads Lane towards Aldborough Road South.'

By this time the air was full of the sound of approaching police klaxons and the youth in panic threw the gun into a front garden as he passed it. Fintry noted the location where the gun had been discarded and continued following the youth. On Aldborough Road South a police vehicle finally caught up with him and drove alongside. Fintry pointed to the fleeing youth and mouthed, 'It's him', and slowed to let the police vehicle complete the chase. Fintry turned his car around and drove back to the house with the overgrown front garden into which the gun had been thrown and for the third time in as many minutes he dialled three nines. When two constables arrived at the scene he indicated the garden and said, 'It's in there somewhere. The gun is in there.' Then feeling suddenly agitated, and too shaken to drive, he walked back to Pembroke Road, continuing to tremble uncontrollably.

The youth who had shot Archibald Dew was Afro-Caribbean. He wore his hair in a huge mop. He sat sullenly in the police interview room with his hands thrust deeply into his jacket pockets. He had given his name as Gaylord Midnight. He was eleven years old.

Vicary and Forbes viewed Gaylord Midnight through the one-way mirror as they waited for an 'Appropriate Adult' to arrive at the police station, so that the interview could be conducted in accordance with the Police and Criminal Evidence Act 1985.

'Makes it harder and it makes it easier,' Vicary spoke softly.

'What do you mean?' Forbes glanced sideways at Vicary.

'Well . . . easier to break him, he'll be easy to crack. I don't care how hard he thinks he is, he's still just eleven years old, so easier in that sense, but harder in the sense that there just won't be any justice for Archie. I mean, what sort of sentence is an eleven-year-old going to get, even if he murdered a police officer? I mean deliberately targeted a police officer? He seemed to know where Archie lived; he seemed to be loitering, waiting for him to come home. Whole life tariff if he was an adult, but eleven years old? In this climate, when it's all down to early rehabilitation, what's he going to get? Five years in a holiday camp which is what passes for youth custody.' Vicary paused, controlling his anger. 'I mean, tell me, who was this fellow Parsloe and who learned from him to make hit men out of dying men and eleven-year-olds? Julia Watmore was right, that is immunity from prosecution . . . an eleven-year-old will never be seen as fully accountable. Never.'

'We should have warned him,' Forbes said quietly. 'Cyril Barr was right. We should have warned Archie to watch his back too . . . a simple phone call, that's all it would have taken . . .'

'I never thought . . .' Vicary clenched his fist and banged

it on the wall beside the one-way mirror. 'We could have had a couple of constables outside his house. If nothing else, the constables would have moved the boy on. They might even have lifted him and found the shooter.'

'It's going to haunt me that we didn't do that. Why didn't we phone him and organize protection?'

'Dunno.' Vicary turned and sank back against the wall. 'Dunno, dunno . . . dunno . . . but this has racked things up. We take the initiative now, pull Neve. Cyril Barr said that after Fred Wolfe, Neve was the weakest one.'

'The Spicer family, the family of the guy who shot Fred Wolfe, we talk to them . . . and Tew, Barry Tew, we talk to him. We can hold the lad pretty well indefinitely. He's been charged with murder, he's not going anywhere in a hurry.'

'Is that a shooter?'

Forbes pulled his jacket over his chest and buttoned it. 'Yes, yes it is. You are not supposed to see that but yes, it's a gun.'

'British police don't carry guns.' The boy was about eighteen years old, Forbes guessed.

'But occasionally, we have to,' Forbes explained.

'You shot my dad,' the boy replied still in the strange, deadpan expression, as if in shock.

'Yes.' Vicary sat beside Forbes. 'We are sorry about Mr Spicer.'

'S' all right,' the boy smiled. 'He wanted it that way.'

It was, thought both officers, an impressively mature response for an eighteen-year-old. He, like his mother and brothers, wore black mourning bands.

'You must know by now that he murdered somebody just before he was shot?'

'We know that now,' Mrs Spicer replied, 'but he was like that, he always said, "What you don't know you can't tell the Old Bill."'

'You could be implicated.'

'Oh?'

'The money he sent.'

'What money?' Mrs Spicer glanced around the room.

'Anybody got money from your dad you're not telling me about?'

The Spicer boys shook their heads. 'No, ma . . .' each said, 'honest.'

'See,' Mrs Spicer said proudly, 'no money and my boys is good boys, they won't tell no lies. They've been brought up to be truthful, especially to the Bill.' She extended her arms. 'Search the place, it's not big, it won't take you long.'

Vicary held up his palm. 'No indeed, we won't find it here, but you know the man your husband killed . . .' Vicary's attention was drawn to a framed photograph on the mantel-piece above the gas fire, of a thin, wispy-haired man standing between two young boys with the sea in the background. He wore a red shirt and white trousers and he was captured smiling joyfully at the camera.

'Yes, that's him, that's my Ernest. He was a good man, never amounted to much in life but unlike most men that never amount to much he wasn't a monster to his family. He did like to go to Clacton each year. That's him with the two eldest at Clacton. He was a cancer personality . . . wrapped up in himself. He'd brood and sit fuming about something instead of losing his temper. Wrapped up in himself, cancer personality, so when he did get the news . . . well it came as no surprise to me.'

'Still, we're sorry.'

'The thing you should know is that the man he murdered was a corrupt police officer.'

'Is that right?' Mrs Spicer sat up.

'Yes, so any information about who paid your late husband to off him won't get you into trouble with the mob, you won't be grassing up anybody who can do you hurt . . . just another corrupt copper.'

An interested silence descended upon the room.

'You're talking about a reward?' The oldest of the Spicer boys asked.

'Yes, possibly. We could even also make any investiga-tion that's happening right now go away . . . no promises . . . but . . .'

'We don't expect something for nothing,' Forbes inter-rupted, 'put it like that.'

'Clear as crystal,' said the Spicer boy. 'Clear as a bell.'

'Depends on what you can tell us. Sing like a canary and you'll earn your birdseed. Point us in the right direction and you'll get something and all in proportion. A lot of good information means a lot of good reward.'

'Where can we reach you?' Mrs Spicer asked. 'Have you got a business card or something?'

In any man's language Barry, 'British Telecom', or 'Tele', or 'Mole' Tew would have cut a pathetic figure. It was an observation shared equally and privately by both Forbes and Vicary. Tew sat propped up on a single bed resting the weight of his body in the corner of the walls of the room. He wore a short towelling bathrobe which exposed his hirsute arms, legs and chest. His right arm ended in a stump. He was fully bearded and his hair hung in straggles from the side and the back of his head down to his shoulders, he being bald elsewhere. He sat with both legs folded up under his body in what Vicary thought was an apologetic and an effeminate manner. Soft pornography 'top shelf' magazines were strewn about the floor. The windows were closed despite the heat and the curtains were almost wholly drawn across the window, leaving only a six inch gap to admit daylight. The room was, unsurprisingly, very stuffy. Both officers found breathing difficult. The odour of unwashed body hung heavy. Forbes answered for both officers when he declined Tew's invitation by saying, 'No thanks, we'll stand.'

'So what happened, Barry?' Vicary held up his right arm.

'Got caught skimming, didn't I.' Tew had a soft East London accent. He seemed to Vicary to be more like a hairy pet than a lifelong villain.

'Silly.'

Tew shrugged. 'You don't need to tell me but I owed money to a crew who were going to shave me with a blowtorch if I didn't pay . . . rock and a hard place time. I meant to pay Pirie back but didn't get the chance.'

'How much did you skim?'

'A few hundred.'

'Come on, Barry, I said how much?'

'Ten large.'

'Ouch.'

'That was ten large about twenty years ago.'

'So, ten, fifteen times that in today's money?'

'So he set Powell on me, Powell and his goons. You heard what Powell did to that geezer what slapped his grand-daughter?'

'We know.'

'So you keep in touch with the crew?'

'Irish Tony calls round from time to time. Brixton's a long way to come from Whitechapel but he does the journey once or twice a year . . . he's a good bloke . . . so yes, I hear.'

'So what happened?'

'They took me to a warehouse, didn't they, bounced a ten pound sledge off my legs a few times, cut off my right paw because Pirie told them to. He said that that's what they do to thieves in Iran, cut their paws off. Then they nailed my feet to the floor and left me for three days and then . . . then . . . they dialled the ambulance, told them where to find me. Nice of them really, I mean considerate-like. I mean, I'd worked for Pirie for ten years by then, never more than a gofer . . . a bit of an enforcer sometimes but I gave him good service . . . you know . . . and then he goes and he does this to me for borrowing ten K. You know how much Pirie is worth. Borrowing ten thousand pounds from Pirie is like borrowing ten thousand pounds from the Bank of England.'

'Dare say that isn't the point, Barry, not from Pirie's angle.'

'Aye, but I enjoyed being in the team even if it was only as a gofer . . . hours are good, pay is good.'

'So, tell us about Jackie Boot.'

'Jackie Boot . . . Jack Boot . . . there was a joke in there, in that name, somewhere but nobody could find it. Sweet girl. She drowned. Poor chick'

'Or was drowned,' Vicary replied.

'Perhaps she got to know something she wasn't supposed to know,' Forbes added.

Tew glanced at Forbes and then at Vicary. 'So what do you know?'

'Enough,' Forbes answered, 'but also not enough either.'

'Silly.' Tew glanced at the pile of magazines on the floor. 'She was like them, you know, like the girls in the magazines

and Phil Ott sent them to the Stork Club to get picked up by
me and the likes of me. I mean me, pulling a girl like that?
Of course they were the Old Bill. Even if Ott did tell them
to get out if they felt threatened, once they're in the back of
a car going east there's not a lot they can do, especially if
they've already had a bit of a slap.'

'You did that?'

'Yes, so did Big Cyril Barr. Pirie told us to control them,
let them get in but only so far, just so long as they think
they're getting somewhere and me and Barr were told to take
whatever we could get.'

'And did you?'

'Of course, we were boys in our twenties and two women
who look like that . . .' again he nodded to the magazines,
'. . . and they fall into your lap. I never had a girl before then
and not many after, so Jackie was the star of my sex life.'

Vicary swallowed hard. Forbes asked, 'How did she die?'

'Drowned, like you said.'

'Yes . . . but specifically . . . details.'

'I wasn't there.'

'Look, Barry, to level with you,' Vicary spoke calmly, his
eyes still adjusting to the gloom, 'we are not after Pirie or
Peabody or Powell.'

'No?' Tew sounded relieved.

'Powell's in the Scrubs and that's as near as we are going
to get, we accept that, and the other two are in Spain. They're
too fly to have anything pinned on them.'

'Fly!' Tew snorted. 'They're like a barrel load of monkeys.
They cover their tracks all right.' He took a metal foil
containing food from the bed and laid it on the bookcase
beside him. 'Meals on Wheels,' he explained. 'I get them
delivered each weekday. On the weekends I live out of tins.
Two old ladies in a little green van deliver them. By the time
I get it, it's cold. They don't like visiting me . . . in and out
at the rush, but it's food.'

'We are interested in coppers, Barry.'

'Coppers?'

'Bent coppers.'

'You serious?'

Forbes unbuttoned his jacket and opened it to reveal the

revolver in its holster. 'Yes . . . serious. One of ours was murdered this morning, so we're getting a little short-tempered. So tell us something we don't know.'

'I heard about that this morning on the radio.'

'Yes, Mr Dew.'

'Never knew him.'

'We did and we liked him,' Vicary snorted.

'A lot.' Forbes buttoned his jacket. 'We liked him a lot.'

'I knew Wolfe.'

'And . . .?'

'Parsloe and Last and Neve.'

'Any others?'

Tew shook his head.

'Barr said there were five bent cops, those four and a tall, lanky one.'

'Well, he'd know, he was the bag man. You sure you're not after Pirie . . . or Peabody?'

'No. They know how to cover themselves like you just said. We take what we can get; low-hanging fruit for us . . . bent coppers. Mr Dew was shot by an eleven-year-old boy. Mean anything to you?'

'That's a trick used by Pirie, someone learned that from Pirie. Don't just use someone else as a hit man, use someone the law can't easily touch.'

'And Fred Wolfe was shot by a dying man.'

'That's the same Pirie trick. Use the very young or the dying but nobody inbetween. Someone learned that from Pirie as well.'

'Someone like Piers Parsloe?'

Tew shrugged.

'Help us, Barry. Help yourself.'

'Look . . .' Tew gasped with pain. Neither officer thought he was anything but wholly serious. 'If you are trying to frighten me or get to Pirie in some way . . .'

'He's in Spain!'

'He could be in the middle of the Kalahari desert and still reach out to South West Two if a skull required cracking or a leg was needing breaking, even if just a couple of teeth needed a bit of rapid dentistry, that's Pirie. I am not safe from Pirie.'

'We are not interested in him,' Vicary spoke slowly.

'Sure?'

'Yes, very sure.'

'His yacht's still on the Medway.'

'His yacht?'

'A powerboat type yacht, not one with sails. Jackie Boot was launched from it.' Tew spoke softly.

'What is the boat's name?'

'*Chaffinch.*'

'*Chaffinch?*'

'Yes, on account of the fact that it's yellow in colour.'

'Tell us about the yacht, the *Chaffinch.*'

'I was never allowed near it. I wasn't on Pirie's entertainment committee. If ever I got invited to go on the *Chaffinch*, it would be for my going away party.'

'Going away party?'

'Yes. Pirie used to entertain on the boat but also he'd use it for a going away party. Anyone who needed to go away had an old car engine chained to them, their stomach punctured with a carving knife so the body gasses would escape and over the side they'd go, at night, east of Sheerness as near mid-channel as could be got. Pirie got rid of a lot of people like that but he was always somewhere else of course, establishing his cast-iron alibi.'

'And Jackie?'

'Well, she went over the side because she was on to the bent cops not because she was on to Pirie . . . and Jackie had to drown so it would seem like an accident. The geezers that dumped her knew what they were doing. Took her right out, but just as the tide was turning to come back in and knowing it would bring her body with it, by which time she would have drowned or frozen to death. Either way she would not be telling anybody what she found out.'

'And you know this?'

'It's what was said. I had no part of it, but I was in the gang and the gofers gossip, word spreads. You know how it is. I've often thought that that is how Jackie and the other WPC . . . Julia . . . Cyril's chick, how they found out about the bent coppers. Those two girls were kept with the gofers, and gofers talk. They must have heard about Parsloe and the other cops from the gofers. Julia got out . . . saved her life . . . Jackie just wasn't quick enough.'

'Jim Coventry?'

'Don't know anything about him, the cop that disappeared, but I can tell you I was bunged a good wedge by Parsloe, he was the leader of the bent coppers, to dig a hole. I could shift soil, that's why they called me "Mole", not just because of this . . .' he ran his fingers down his hair-covered right forearm, '. . . but because of the way I could burrow. All done in one night. Covered it with branches and then drove away.'

'And Parsloe gave you money to do that?'

'Yes.'

'You'll sign a statement?'

'Possibly.'

'On what?'

'On who else is saying what. I don't want to be prime witness because that makes me prime target. I don't have much of a life but I value it and I'd like to keep it as long as I can.'

'We can understand that.'

'Tell you something else as well.'

'Oh?'

'Pirie wasn't just bribing those bent coppers.'

'No?'

'He was blackmailing them,' Tew said with a smile.

'He was? How?'

'Photographs.' Tew smiled. 'Those cops, they got to like the good life and Pirie had a house, sold it since, but a big house in its own grounds . . . you know the type, Surrey or Kent, entertained people at his garden parties. You know, trays of champagne being served by skinny girls, naked of course, walking about on tiptoe.'

'Of course, and Parsloe, Last, Neve and Wolfe were there?'

'Yes, those four but not the fifth one you spoke of.'

'And they were photographed at the party with Pirie in sight?'

'Yes, that I was part of. Pirie had his men, lots of 'em hiding in the trees overlooking the lawn, huge elephant guns of telescopic lenses, clicking away. After a few parties like that Parsloe and his mates were well hooked but they still got paid anyway. Then after a few years Pirie sold out to the Vietnamese and retired but by then a fortune had been made and shared by all, except the gofers. It was about then that I got silly.' Tew held up the stump of his right arm. 'Tell you what, you get the photographs, then I'll make a statement because then my statement will be just icing on the cake . . . and only, *only*, if there are no charges brought against Pirie or Peabody.'

'OK,' Vicary nodded. 'You're on.'

Gaylord Midnight slouched in his chair seeming unconcerned with the situation, as if it was an annoyance and a nuisance, akin to a fly buzzing angrily on a windowpane. It was, thought Vicary, as though he seemed to resent the inconvenience of being detained. The 'Appropriate Adult', chosen at random from a list of fully vetted volunteers for the role, was a middle-aged woman who appeared to both Vicary and Forbes to be well-meaning but timid and worryingly out of her depth when it came to monitoring the interview of an eleven-year-old murderer. The room in which the interview took place was painted in two-tone brown; it had a hard-wearing Hessian carpet, a table and four chairs, all highly polished. A tape recorder was set in the wall, the red recording light glowed brightly, the twin cassettes spun silently.

'We have a witness and we have the gun, the murder weapon on which are your fingerprints. These match the fingerprints found on the Stanley knife, the knife used to wound that infant in his pram . . . six months old and he needed twenty stitches,' Forbes growled. 'You're going down for life, Gaylord. Solid case.'

'Out in five, man.' Gaylord Midnight jabbed the air with his right hand, with only his first and little fingers extended, the middle two fingers being held back in a fist-like manner. 'Out in five.' Then he thrust his hand back into his jacket pocket.

'You think?'

'Yeah, I think. I'll be eighteen by then, out on the streets, slain a cop. Nobody give me diss, no man, no one.'

'So you're going to plead guilty?'

'Yeah.' He shrugged his shoulders. 'I want to go down. I want to do time . . . real time. I need to do time to get serious respect. I'll be in the gym, work on my pecs and my abs, push the weights. So be cool man.'

Forbes took photographs from a brown paper envelope and laid them on the table in front of Gaylord Midnight who glanced at them and said, 'What's this, man?'

'Recognize any of these men?' Forbes asked, the photographs being large black and white prints of Parsloe, Neve and Last.

'No.' Gaylord Midnight looked away to his left.

'Prefer you to take a careful look.'

'I looked already.'

'You see, Gaylord, someone put you up to this, someone gave you a gun and that person pointed out the man you were to shoot. And we think that person was one of these three men.'

'Na!'

'You know, Gaylord, you might be right about being out in five years but only with full co-operation. If you withhold information about a murder, especially the murder of a police officer . . . well . . . you'll be staying inside for a very long time indeed. Life could mean life.'

Gaylord Midnight glared at Forbes. Then he glanced at Vicary who raised his eyebrows and nodded as if to say, 'That's right'.

'So why don't you take another look at the photographs?'

'Don't need to, he's not there. Chow! It wasn't any of them, chow!'

'So tell us about the man who set you up to murder Mr Dew.'

'Old guy . . . really old, like dying soon old.'

'So how old is that?' Forbes pressed, realizing that to a boy of Gaylord Midnight's age anyone over the age of forty is elderly.

'Dunno . . . old, old.'

'So what sort of car did he drive?'

'Dunno . . . that was old as well.'

'Colour?'

'Dunno.'

'You didn't notice the colour?'

'It was dark.'

'Just dark?'

'It was night already.'

'Night-time?'

'Yes . . . you know when the day goes black already.'

'Don't get smart, Gaylord, you're still in deep water.'

'Chow!' He glared at Forbes. 'But nobody diss me now . . . already.'

'Diss me?' The 'Appropriate Adult' appealed to Forbes and Vicary.

'Diss me.' Forbes explained, 'It means disrespect me, give me diss . . . give me disrespect.'

'I see,' the woman smiled. 'I have to understand every-thing, it's the rules.'

'Of course,' Forbes returned the smile.

'So the car . . . estate . . . four door . . . what?'

'Two seater.'

'A sports car?'

Gaylord Midnight shrugged. 'Yes, a sports car.'

'So an old geezer in a dark-coloured sports car. Was it a modern car?'

'No, old as well.'

'So what did the old geezer offer?'

'Money . . . money . . . and all the street cred a boy could want.' Again he jabbed the air with two fingers extended and two in a fist-like manner.

'He sounds like he knew you.'

'I have a record, little record.'

'Possession of a controlled substance at your age is not a little record, nor is going equipped, nor is greivous bodily harm.'

'It is little by comparison to murder. I iced a cop. *That is a record*.' Gaylord Midnight looked at Forbes with cold eyes. So cold that Forbes felt a chill run down his spine. The police, he felt, were going to know this boy again. If he wasn't cooled in a gangland fight, he'll be back behind bars doing a life stretch before he was thirty. Forbes felt more frightened for him than of him. He was the sort of boy who is going to find out that street cred evaporates rapidly, and that he can be 'dissed', usually finding out both truths when he is on his knees holding his stomach, feeling his life's blood oozing warmly through his fingers while all his friends are running away upon hearing and seeing the approaching blues and twos. That, felt Forbes, would be the end of Gaylord Midnight and in the not-too-distant future.

Outside in the cell corridor Vicary and Forbes and the 'Appropriate Adult' who had been supplied by the Social Services Department, stood in a circle.

'Parents?' Vicary asked.

'Unknown father . . . mother went to Jamaica and dumped him on his "auntie" who is no relative, just a friend. She can't control him, just feeds him when he comes home. What can we do? He's finished before he's started.'

'Rather wished that you hadn't come here.' Idris Neve seemed to Vicary and Forbes to be nervous, worried, agitated.

'We can do it at the station if you'd prefer,' Vicary offered, 'or we can do it here.'

'But we're going to do it.' Forbes remained stone-faced. He fixed Neve with a hostile glare.

'Is this formal?' Neve asked. He was a round-faced, well-set man.

'No, just a chat, we are asking for your co-operation.'

The three men sat in Idris Neve's house in Hamilton Road, High Wycombe. The lounge was, Vicary thought, well furnished with conservative tastes and offered a view out over the large rear garden, in which at that moment Mrs Fiona Neve was contentedly, it seemed, pruning the rose bushes, wearing a yellow dress and a matching sunhat. Neve sank further back into his chair. 'A chat . . .' he echoed. He looked far from comfortable. 'I know that you have had me under surveillance.'

'Yes,' Forbes replied coldly. 'We haven't been discreet; it was our way of letting you know that we are interested in you. That is to say in the way that police officers are interested in people.'

'How long have you been drawing your pension, Idris?'

'Not long . . . a few months.'

'You retired as a Detective Sergeant?' Forbes pressed.

'Yes.'

'Not bad.' Vicary glanced round the room. 'You did well for yourself in life. Does your wife work?'

'Staff nurse at the hospital.'

'Rewarding, fulfilling sort of job,' Forbes replied, 'but hardly well paid.'

'Meaning?'

'Meaning that I am a Detective Sergeant and I live in a bungalow in Croydon.'

'I too am a Detective Sergeant,' Vicary added, 'and I live in a conversion in Leytonstone. You must be the only Detective Sergeant in this road. What do your neighbours do?'

'We don't talk to each other.'

'People who live in these sorts of houses don't often talk to their neighbours,' Forbes observed, 'but they are executives with multi-nationals, high-powered city solicitors, and you have managed the same lifestyle on a Detective Sergeant's salary.'

'And a staff nurse's salary,' Vicary added. 'Don't forget Mrs Neve's contribution.'

'Well my wife also works,' Forbes spoke softly, 'and we still only live in a bungalow in sunny Croydon.'

'What are you driving at?' Neve spoke with a soft Welsh accent.

'Bribery of police officers, corruption, blackmail. Murder,' Forbes replied coldly. It was, he thought, because of officers like Idris Neve that he had joined A-Ten. He was closing on his quarry, he scented a kill.

'Be careful what you say.'

'Don't be so touchy, Idris,' Vicary smiled. 'This is just a chat, remember. Nice cosy fireside chat, but having said that . . .'

'Things are very serious,' Forbes growled. 'You will have heard about Archie Dew being murdered.'

'Yes, it was all over the news. Bad show that.'

'He was our boss,' Vicary said calmly, 'my boss, anyway. Garrick Forbes here is with A-Ten. I am Murder Squad. Joint working you see, but Archie Dew was in control. We take it a bit personally that our boss was murdered on his own doorstep.'

'You shouldn't be on the case.'

'But we are. A lot of time invested. You will have heard of Freddie Wolfe being shot, also pretty well on his own doorstep?'

'Yes.'

'He was a colleague of yours.'

'Operation Fennel,' Forbes said. 'Rings bells?'

Neve sighed. 'I was part of it, a long time ago.'

'Twenty-seven years ago.'

'It all started for us just a few days ago when a body was found buried in Epping Forest, as bodies often are found there . . . buried or not . . . the villains' graveyard, so called.'

Neve remained silent.

'Turned out to be the body of a young Detective Constable who by all accounts had a very promising future. So we found out about Operation Fennel. We were hampered because all the records of it have disappeared.'

'Funny that,' Forbes sneered, 'but it makes A-Ten very interested, very interested indeed.'

'And we went on to find out about Woman Police Constable Jacqueline Boot who drowned. Did she fall or was she pushed? Went swimming in the Channel in her wine bar kit. We talked to other officers who were also part of Operation Fennel and who probably saved their own lives by retiring. Remember Julia Crabtree and Owen Davies? They remember you. They went in looking for information about Pirie, Peabody and Powell, came out having found out about Parsloe, Last, Neve and Wolfe. They saw things and heard things and two of them disappeared, the other two got the message and quit the force and moved a long way from London.'

Idris Neve sat still, stone-faced, but his attention was clearly riveted.

'But when Jim Coventry disappeared, Phil Ott was forced to blow his cover to try to rescue his man, but he didn't find his man because the villains hadn't got him. Jim Coventry was murdered by the bent coppers to prevent him blowing the whistle on them, wasn't he, Idris?'

Idris Neve's face drained of colour.

'And Jackie Boot was pushed. No accident there, was there?'

'I don't know anything about Jackie's death. That was down to Pirie, he took her out on his boat, so I heard.'

'Probably after some discussion with Parsloe.'

Idris Neve fell silent.

'We just need to find the photographs.'

'Photographs?' Neve's voice cracked.

'The photographs of you and Parsloe and Wolfe and Last being entertained at Pirie's garden parties. So Pirie had you both ways, accepting bribes and blackmailed you into co-operation. That's how things went on for years and years until Pirie sold out to the Vietnamese and retired to Spain. He got away with it, no flies on him.' Vicary paused. 'But you, Idris, it explains why you never went after promotion . . . no need, money coming in to buy a house like this upon your early retirement.'

'You see what we believe, Idris, is that Freddie Wolfe had a crisis of conscience, guilt was eating him up inside like a maggot inside an apple and he was going to come clean. He even lied to his wife about his source of wealth . . . what that must have done to the sanctity of his marriage. Told her he had inherited it from his deceased brother and she believed him.' Forbes drove on. 'So how did you explain your wealth to your wife?' He nodded towards the window beyond which Mrs Neve was by then weeding the herbaceous border.

Neve remained silent.

'Once we find the photographs that will be sufficient to arrest you, then you'll have to explain to us where the big money came from. You know the rules, if you can't prove the money was earned, or won legally, your assets will be seized. You will swap this for a prison cell and your wife will swap it for a single person's council flat.'

'Unless she was in on it,' Forbes pointed out. 'If she knew you were on the take and willingly spent the money, she's on her way to the slammer as well.'

'You can't go anywhere, can you?' Vicary spoke quietly. 'Can't run, can't hide, just waiting for the seven o'clock knock.'

'Time to come clean,' Forbes said. 'You see we are doing you a favour. An old blagger who knew you were bent told us that of the four remaining bent coppers, you, Last, Parsloe and the one we have still to identify, you were the least comfortable, after Wolfe. That is, you didn't like what was going on.'

'Freddie Wolfe was doing himself a huge favour; he was going to turn Queen's evidence. You could do the same. The first one of the remaining four to start singing will do himself a huge favour. The last ferry is about to leave, Idris, it's got just one seat remaining. The first one to jump aboard has that seat, will it be you?'

'You can't prove anything.' Neve's voice was shaking.

'Not yet, but we've come a long way in a few days and we are not slowing down any.'

'And remember,' Vicary added, 'we know about the fifth man . . . tall, lanky guy, runs a classic sports car. No name yet but we'll find him. We'll wrap all of you up one way or another. Help yourself, Idris.'

'Take a leaf out of Freddie Wolfe's book.' Vicary stood. 'Time to sing before we make you squeal.'

'Don't get up, Idris.' Forbes also stood. 'We'll let ourselves out.'

Walking down the driveway of Idris Neve's home, back to where they had parked their car at the verge of Hamilton Road, Vicary said, 'Tall, lanky old guy, with a dark-coloured old-fashioned two-seater car . . .'

'I know.' Forbes fished for the car keys in his jacket pocket. 'I have been thinking the same but we'll wait until we are on firmer ground . . . agreed?'

'Yes.' Vicary stopped at the passenger side of the car. 'Yes, safer that way and at this rate it won't be more than a few days . . . but why did he have Archie killed? Why did he have to do that?'

'Panic.' Forbes waited at the kerb until a silver Mercedes Benz glided past. 'We panicked him, Harry. We panicked him without realizing what we did. We panicked him.'

The funeral, by the size of the attendance at the chapel at the North London crematorium, revealed the deceased to be a man of small family and few friends. It seemed to Vicary as he glanced round the cool, stark interior of the building that more police officers were in attendance than friends or relatives. Garrick Forbes nudged him. 'Who's the girl?' he hissed.

'Daughter,' Vicary whispered.

'He never mentioned her.'

'She's ill.'

'Oh?'

'Yeah, tragedy really, I'll tell you outside. Don't know how his wife will cope now.'

Vicary and Forbes fell silent as the priest stood up at the lectern, switched on the microphone and said, 'We are gathered here today to remember our brother, Archibald Dew . . .'

'You know when I was a nipper I always fancied being a cop.' Cyril Barr sat in the rear seat of the unmarked police car. Vicary and Forbes had rendezvoused with him outside Upminster Bridge Tube Station at Barr's insistence. 'You can,' he had insisted, 'always tell if you're being followed on the tube train.'

'Interesting,' Vicary said.

'Yes, well one silly error and one cow of a female magistrate who thought a spell inside would be "good" for me, even as a first offender, and that sent me down the wrong path for life.'

'That's often the way of it,' Forbes growled. 'So what have you got for us?'

'Did some digging, didn't I?'

'Did you?'

'Yes, and the yacht, Pirie's boat the *Chaffinch* is well gone.'

'Sunk?'

'Sold.' Barr glanced nervously around him. 'New owners. Won't be anything at all on her now that will be of interest to you boys but I was set to thinking. Pirie will want to keep those photographs, especially the negatives, and I set to wondering where he'd keep them because he won't have taken them to Spain.'

'He won't?'

'No . . . believe me . . . I know Pirie, he'll want to keep himself well distanced from anything that could link him to corrupt police officers, makes him less of a target.'

'OK, so where do you think?'

'Well not his house in Surrey, for the same reason.'

'He kept hold of that?'

'Yes. He spends the summers in Surrey usually, but he's in Spain this summer.'

'OK, so where?' Forbes pressed irritably. 'This is a long drive from Scotland Yard, Cyril.'

'Well, I remembered he had this lock-up. He keeps his Roller there and a few other items he doesn't want close to him.'

'They can be linked if he is renting the lock-up.'

'Nah . . .' Barr shook his head. 'He rents under an assumed name, pays cash in advance, like a year in advance and the Roller is his but is unregistered, lovely car, 1969 Silver Shadow, two-tone grey under a dust sheet. I reckon if the pics are anywhere, they'll be there.'

'Good enough. Where is the lock-up?'

'Tottenham, near White Hart Lane football ground.'

'Tottenham!'

'I told you, Pirie likes to keep things at arm's length.'

'Where exactly?'

'I'll have to show you, don't know the address. I'll visit and then draw you a map.'

'OK.'

'But for this I need something. I need that case against me dropped.'

Vicary and Forbes glanced at each other. Forbes said, 'If the pics are there then I reckon we can pretty well guarantee it.'

Barr breathed a sign of relief.

'So when do we get details of Pirie's lock-up?'

'I'll go there tomorrow, just take a stroll past to see if it's still there. Remember we are going back a few years now, buildings get demolished.'

'If you want the investigation on you dropped we must have the photographs.'

'I know. We both want the lock-up to still be there and still rented by Pirie. I'll be in touch.' He opened the rear door of the car. 'Thanks, gentlemen, this is like a lifeline for me, for me it is a second chance.'

\*    \*    \*

'It's Mrs Spicer.' The voice on the phone was hushed, almost a whisper.

'Yes, Mrs Spicer.' Vicary sat forward.

'My eldest has just been arrested . . . he was always the wild one'

'I am sorry to hear that.'

'I was thinking about what you said. My other two don't know I am making this call . . .'

'Yes?'

'But my husband told me he was doing what he did for a bent copper called Parsloe.'

'Parsloe?'

'Yes.'

'Will you make a statement to that effect? It's only hearsay really but it can still help our case.'

'Yes. Will it help my boy?'

'Can't hurt, can't hurt at all. What's he been arrested for?'

'Armed robbery.' The woman seemed close to tears. 'He only got himself a shooter and walked into the post office, didn't he. He was going to make a deposit but tried to make a withdrawal instead. He got greedy . . . just like his dad told him not to.'

Vicary's heart sank. All he could say was, 'No promises.'

Garrick Forbes folded the newspaper and put it on the coffee table. 'I am not relenting, I said grounded until the new term and I meant that, grounded until the new school year.'

'Garrick . . .' his wife pleaded. 'She'll grow up to hate you, do you want that?'

Forbes stood. 'I'm taking the dog for a walk. My father was right . . . he was right . . . children must know they've been punished. They must know . . . they must know.'

'Garrick,' his wife gasped. 'I am so sorry. Why didn't you tell me, we could have talked about it?' But by then she was sitting alone in an empty room.

'I just have a bad feeling,' Vicary sipped his drink, 'just a worrying feeling that is gnawing away at my insides that all is not well.'

Kathleen raised her glass of orange juice to her lips and

sipped from it. 'If he doesn't come up with the goods . . . what then?'

'The case is pretty well out of the window. All of it . . . it all hinges on the photographs that Cyril Barr said he could acquire for us and that was nearly three days ago.' He drained his glass and went to the bar and ordered another soda water and lime. As he waited to be served, he glanced casually out of the pub's window at the white building on the opposite side of the road, which gleamed with eye-straining brilliance in the sun. When he returned to the table, walking through a gentle hum of conversation, which he and Kathleen had claimed for themselves, he sat and said, 'It's just not like him to be so silent. I hardly know him at all but when I did meet him he came across as being eager to help, to do something for the others involved as much as for himself. He seemed to want to do something for the undercover officers who lost their lives.'

'Motivated?'

'Yes,' Vicary smiled, 'that's the very word. He was powerfully motivated. Now he's as quiet as the grave.'

'Does it put you in danger?'

Vicary shrugged. 'Well, we pose a threat to cornered animals, even without the photographs because they know that we know, but I can't see them moving against me and Garrick Forbes, they wouldn't be so . . .'

'Merciless?'

'Well, I was going to say "stupid" . . . but yes, as you say . . . merciless.'

# EIGHT

John Shaftoe sat back in his chair. 'You look upset, Mr Vicary. Are you?'

'Yes, I dare say I am a little.' Vicary glanced out of Shaftoe's office window at the Whitechapel skyline, that strange blend of the old and the new which was in keeping with the rest of London, with so much being demolished and replaced. 'He was doing us a favour you see, so that we would do a favour for him in return . . . and . . . I never met him before but he didn't seem to me to be a criminal, I mean not in terms of his mindset.'

'I know what you mean.'

'He just seemed to have been an easily led sort of geezer who made a wrong turn early on in his life, the sort of turn you can't reverse. When I met him he seemed to have got himself well clear of criminality, in a relationship he valued and was hit by an old offence from out of the blue, a handling charge from a crime of some years earlier. It threatened to destroy his relationship and drag him back into the underworld, so called.'

'Handling?'

'Stolen goods.'

'Ah . . .'

'Cars in his case, expensive ones.' Vicary again glanced out of the window over the rooftops of Jack the Ripper territory. 'Just his silly nature, you see, the criminals put upon his good nature.'

'Pity.'

'Yes, a great shame. His warm personality had just not been quashed despite living his life among thieves and vagabonds. So what happened to him? What happened to Cyril Barr?'

'Fractured skull but he was deceased before he was set on fire . . . no carbon deposits in the trachea, means he wasn't breathing.'

'That's a relief.'

'Yes. The interested police officer is one . . .' John Shaftoe consulted his notes, '. . . John Fisco, Detective Sergeant of Tottenham Police Station.'

'Fisco?'

'Yes. Mr Barr was found tied to a metal chair, no evidence of clothing on his body. I attended the scene. It was a lock-up.'

'Was the Rolls Royce there?'

'No, no car at all but there were remains of a large dust sheet, the sort that you would cover a car with.'

'I see.'

'And the lock-up seems to have been ransacked. Some old bits of furniture that had had all the drawers pulled out and the doors opened. They were full of smoke and soot deposits so they had been searched before the fire was started, but the fire officer could tell you more.'

'OK, but it's Cyril Barr? ID has been confirmed?'

'Yes, we checked his dental records, as unique as finger-prints, as you know.'

'He'd been kept against his will for some time before he was despatched.'

'Really?' Vicary glanced at Shaftoe with a concerned expression.

'Yes . . . bloated tongue, still evident despite the thermal damage . . . empty stomach . . . for up to two or three days I'd say.' Shaftoe paused. 'This has caused difficulty for you, I think? Over and above your sadness at this death . . . there seems to be other issues?'

'You're very observant and very sensitive.' Vicary smiled at Shaftoe. 'Yes, he was going to provide evidence which would have clinched the case for us . . . sufficient to obtain convictions of four individuals wanted in connection with the murder of at least one police officer and possibly a second officer, also by linking them to organized crime.'

'Linking them?' Shaftoe raised his left eyebrow. 'The indi-viduals were not criminals themselves?'

'Well, yes and no . . .' Vicary stood. He forced a smile. 'They were police officers. Bent. About as bent as you can get, but they were police officers.'

\*　　\*　　\*

Roderick Himes held the phone hard against his ear and cupped his hand around the mouthpiece to shield the phone from the noise of the street market. 'I've got something you need,' he spoke loudly. 'Cyril Barr told me to phone you if something ever happened to him. I heard the news about Cyril getting torched.'

Vicary leaned forward and reached for a pen; he raised his hand to attract Garrick Forbes' attention. 'Tell me what you have and who you are.'

'No names, not yet. I have some photographs . . .'

'Of what?'

'Dunno, doesn't look much to me, some folks on the lawn outside a big house, a lot of really fit young women without any clothes on carrying trays of drink, looks like.'

'OK.' Vicary pointed to the phone he was holding and mouthed 'interesting'. Then he asked, 'Where are you?'

'Public phone box top end of Walthamstow High Street, near the post office. Cyril said you could do me a favour.'

'You want charges dropped?'

'How did you know?'

'Just a guess, it's what a lot of folk seem to be wanting, including Cyril Barr,' Vicary sighed.

'I can't be seen handing this envelope to you.'

'So drop it off at any police station for the attention of DS Vicary, New Scotland Yard.'

'No, I want to hand it to you so I can ask for that favour otherwise anyone can claim they turned it in.'

'Fair enough.'

'But Cyril said that geezers were after him because of these photographs, they'll be looking for me because they know I was a pal of Cyril's. I have the photographs and the negatives . . .'

'So let's meet somewhere.'

'OK, I know a place but do I get a favour in return?'

'Depends.'

'On what?'

'On the favour you want.'

'I knocked over a jewellers in Brighton.'

'Anyone hurt?'

'No, it was a clean job.'

'That's all?'

'That's all.'

'Well . . . yes . . . if the photographs are what I think they are then, yes, we can work something out, so long as no one was injured.'

'So we'll meet?'

'Yes . . . where? When?'

'Soon, it has to be soon.'

'All right. Where?'

'Do you know Potters Bar? North of London?'

'Yes . . . yes, I know it, not well but yes, I know Potters Bar.'

'All right . . . well from Potters Bar drive out to a village called Northaw.'

'Northaw?'

'Yes.'

'Got it.' Vicary wrote the name of the village on his notepad. 'I think I know Northaw, is it on the road to Cuffley from Potters Bar?'

'Yes, that's it. Well at Northaw village there is a wood . . .'

'Northaw Great Wood? Yes I do know Northaw and the Great Wood. Haven't been there for years but, yes, I know where you are.' Vicary spoke calmly in an attempt to soothe the youth, whose voice was racing and panting with excitement.

'So you know where the car park is at the entrance to the wood?'

'I'll find it.'

'OK, well I'll see you in the car park. We'll be safe there. It isn't out of the way but it's out of the way enough, no danger of me being seen by those geezers that did it for Cyril . . . they are heavy geezers, really serious boys but Potters Bar to them is like . . . well, they don't like leaving London, don't like it at all. It will be safe there and I won't be followed, not the way I ride.'

'All right, seems fair.' Vicary gave a 'thumbs up' sign to Forbes.

'And you'll do me that favour? That's what I really need. No one was hurt . . . you can check.'

'We will . . . don't worry . . . but if you're telling the truth about that and if you come up with the goods and the photographs are what we need, then we can work something out.'

'Thanks . . . I don't want to go down again. So what time? Have to be soon, while I have these photos I'm a gonner . . . I'm dead . . . I need to get rid of them quick.'

'All right, don't panic.'

'Easy for you to say, nobody is going to pour petrol over you and light a match but I know what happened to Cyril . . . it's all over the manor . . .'

'Calm down,' Vicary spoke soothingly. 'Just try to stay calm.'

'I'll try. Say three p.m. . . .'

'That's less than an hour.'

'Yes . . . but . . . if I can't get them to you like yesterday, I'm going to burn them. I told you, while I've got them I'm a dead man . . . Roman candled . . . you know the number . . . get the picture?'

'All right, we'll be there . . . three p.m.'

'We?' Himes paused. There was, thought Vicary, a note of alarm in the youth's voice.

'Myself and a colleague.'

'Just two?'

'Yes.'

Himes paused once more. 'Well, all right . . . but no more than two. People talk, even coppers, and if there are more than two of you I just won't show myself. I'll go into the wood and burn the photographs. I'd rather go down for the jewellery job than get Roman candled. I just can't risk these geezers finding out and all it will take is for one copper to shoot his mouth off . . . because I have to give you my real name if I want the favour, if I want the charges dropped. I can't give no false name . . . so they'll know who gave you the photographs.'

'All right . . . three p.m.'

'Yes. I can get up there on my bike. What car do I look for?'

'Blue Ford. Blue Ford Mondeo. Two guys.'

'OK.' Himes put the phone down and turned to Tom Last. 'Did I do all right, Mr Last?'

'You did well,' Last smiled. He took his mobile phone

from his pocket and dialled a number. He held it to his ear
and when it was answered he said, 'It's a go, three p.m.
Northaw Great Wood.'

'But he went out four hours ago.' Phyllis Ott tried to remain
calm, yet also tried to impress on the police officer who
answered the phone of her worries. 'He went to walk on the
salt marsh and the sands at Burnham Overy; it was high tide
an hour ago. He hasn't returned. I am so worried. He left
the house looking troubled, something was on his mind. Isn't
there something you can do?'

Vicary turned the car into the car park at the entrance to
Northaw Great Wood. There were a few cars parked there,
a Jaguar, a BMW, a silver Mercedes Benz and a yellow
Honda motorcycle.
    'That'll be his bike,' Vicary remarked, pointing to the
yellow Honda. 'You know, the funny thing is that when he
said "his bike" I thought he meant a pedal cycle, it just
sounded that way.'
    'Yes. There's something familiar about that Merc . . .'
    'You think so?'
    'Yes, nothing to set it apart from other silver Mercedes
Benz of which there are many in London, but I just have the
sense that I have seen it before somewhere . . . can't place it,
but recently . . . in the last few days anyway. Nobody around,
do you think we should have brought some back-up?'
    Vicary glanced about him and relished the foliage and
the birdsong. 'No, I think we'll be all right. I mean, look
at the cars . . . a dozen or so. You see the Great Wood is quite
a popular place. There are people about, it really is very
public here, joggers, dog walkers, bird watchers, folk just
out for a stroll. The boy was right, this is out of the way
enough to be safe but it's not an isolated or a remote location. There is safety here and he was as nervous as anyone
I've ever heard. He is genuinely scared of Parsloe and Last
and Neve and that puts us under time pressure. If we didn't
turn up he was going to burn the photographs and they are
everything. We owe it to Jim Coventry and Jackie Boot. If
he sees too many coppers he won't show himself.'

'Suppose . . . just a bit quiet though and we haven't brought our guns, we're unarmed. I don't like this.' Forbes looked nervously from side to side but saw only thick vegetation and heard only birdsong.

At that moment a youth stepped on to the car park area from behind a stile which led to footpaths through the Great Wood. He was tall, slender, wore motorcyclist leathers and waved a large manilla envelope above his head and then retreated into the foliage.

Vicary and Forbes glanced at each other and then without speaking, left the car and walked towards the wooden stile and followed the youth. The wood was thick with rhododendron shrubs, so much so that Vicary thought 'rhododendron plantation' might be a more apt name for that area of the Great Wood. He did sense that that Great Wood might be an ancient name and suspected that the Great Wood might have once been part of Epping Forest. Within the stands of rhododendron bushes the visibility, while clear, was limited to a few feet in any direction. So dense was the vegetation that Forbes was about to say, 'Where on earth did he go?' when the youth's voice said, 'In here.' The sound came from the officers' right and they turned, followed it, pushing aside the branches of bushes until they found themselves in a large natural amphitheatre, an area of short grass, about twenty feet in diameter, surrounded by bushes about ten feet in height. Above the bushes was the tree canopy and, above that, blue sky. The youth stood at the far side of the amphitheatre, staring at them, clutching the envelope in one hand and his bright-red crash helmet in the other. He held up the envelope. 'So do I get my deal?'

'If the photographs are what you say they are.' Vicary remained still but he sensed Forbes' apprehension, so much so that a small voice inside his head seemed to say, 'Turn and run' but for some reason he remained where he was.

'See for yourself.' The youth skimmed the envelope through the air so that it landed close to the centre of the clearing.

Forbes and Vicary stepped forward together and stood over the envelope. Vicary stooped to pick it up. He opened it. It contained nothing but a copy of a tabloid newspaper. He felt colour drain from his face as he and Forbes glanced about them anxiously.

'Had to give the envelope some weight or it wouldn't look inviting.' The voice came from behind them. The officers turned as a smartly dressed, well-built man emerged from the bushes.

'Tom Last?' Vicary asked.

'No, that's me.' A second man emerged from the shrubs and stood beside the first. 'Last, but not least.' He held a gun, a small automatic but quite lethal at that close range. A plastic bottle had been taped over the barrel. It would look quite comical, thought Vicary, were it not so sinister. He too was tall, casually but smartly dressed.

'I am Piers Parsloe,' the first man added with a sneer.

'Did I do OK, Mr Last?' The youth was excited.

'You did very well, Roddy,' Last replied. 'Come and stand over here, it's dangerous where you are standing.'

'We meet again.' Idris Neve also emerged from the thick stand of rhododendron bushes. 'Sorry it's in such circumstances.' He too held an automatic pistol, also with an empty plastic bottle taped over the barrel.

'The pauper's silencer once again,' Vicary observed, 'surprised that you think you need one.'

'Can't be too careful, we don't exactly have the Great Wood to ourselves, although at the moment it's quite empty,' Neve explained.

'Simple and effective,' Last said. 'As I observed very recently.'

'You haven't got a gun, Mr Parsloe?' Forbes growled. 'Other people do your dirty work for you, do they? And also for you, Mr Last?'

'Just turn around, gentlemen. It will be easier for you, you won't feel anything.'

Forbes and Vicary slowly, and with resignation, turned round.

'Sorry,' Vicary said looking up at the blue sky, 'I should have listened to you.'

Forbes smiled. 'No worries, we'll talk about it later.'

'Can I do it, Mr Last?' Roderick Himes' voice was heard by Forbes and Vicary to be high-pitched, excited.

'Sure you're ready for it, Roddy?' Last asked. 'You'll be doing well for yourself if you are.'

'Yes . . . I'm ready.'

The silencer did indeed prove to be simple and effective. The first two shots made a barely audible 'phutt', 'phutt', sound, insufficient in volume even to quieten the birdsong. The third shot made a distinct 'crack' sound and was followed by a high-pitched scream.

Forbes and Vicary glanced at each other, and then realizing that neither had been shot, turned round. Last lay on the ground, quite still. He had been shot, twice, in the side of his head, just above the right ear. Himes lay on the ground, bent double clutching his stomach, containing screams behind gritted teeth. Parsloe stood still; he had turned and was facing Neve. Colour drained from his face.

'What are you doing?' Parsloe screamed at Neve, his arms wildly gesticulating. 'What are you doing? Kill them . . . not us. Kill them.' Parsloe pointed to Vicary and Forbes. Neve slowly shook his head. He held the gun steadily, calmly pointing it at Parsloe. 'We have to rescue something from this, Piers, there's been enough killing, quite enough . . . quite sufficient. I never got into this with any intention of being party to murder, let alone the murder of two young police officers. We killed two officers who had everything ahead of them; we are not going to kill two more.'

'Quiet! Quiet!' Parsloe raised his voice. 'Kill them! Kill them!'

Neve continued to smile, 'Keep your voice down, Piers, there's plenty of people in the woods, that's why we agreed to use silencers. No . . . I got to thinking . . . Freddie Wolfe was right, he was doing the right thing, just doing it too late.'

'Christ's sake, Idris . . .' Parsloe hissed, 'we can rescue this, there's still time. Shoot them! Shoot them! Now . . . the pair of them.' He advanced towards Neve, arm outstretched. 'Give me the gun . . . give it to me . . . I'll do it.'

'Stop!' Neve raised the gun and levelled it at Parsloe's forehead.

Himes continued to writhe on the ground, continued to contain screams behind gritted teeth.

'Come any closer and you'll join him,' Neve nodded to

Himes. 'Bullet in the stomach. Very painful, very, very painful, lethal within two hours.'

Parsloe stood still. 'We had it, we had it all . . . we still have if you ice them now, these two.' He pointed towards Vicary and Forbes. 'Ice them! Now!'

'No.' Neve shook his head. 'No . . . it's over, Piers. It always was a non-starter but once in . . . once in we couldn't get out . . . none of us. It's just that you and Tom Last,' Neve pointed to the body of Tom Last, 'you and Tom were a little more eager to stay in than were me and Freddie . . . and Freddie was the least eager of all.'

'You're mad,' Parsloe hissed in an agitated manner. 'Mad. Mad. Mad. Insane.'

'Probably,' Neve answered quietly in a relaxed tone of voice. 'Probably, I am.'

'So what's ahead of us if you don't kill these two? I'll tell you. Life in prison, life without the possibility of parole at our age. I can't believe you can be so stupid.' Parsloe suddenly ran towards Neve, arms outstretched. Neve stood his ground and squeezed the trigger, a single bullet sent Parsloe tumbling to the ground like Himes, also clutching his stomach, also containing screams behind clenched teeth. Idris Neve then, quite calmly, pointed the gun at Parsloe's head and squeezed the trigger twice more . . . and Piers Parsloe lay still.

'Nine rounds in the clip.' Neve held up the gun. 'Just a twenty-two but it does the job if you aim the bullets in the right place.' He unwound the tape which held the remains of the plastic bottle to the barrel of the gun. 'He would . . . neither of them would have survived prison, dropping from the lifestyle they enjoy to life in the Vulnerable Prisoners' Unit. I did them a favour and this way they get to be buried in sanctified ground. Imagine that, those two getting lowered as a bell is tolling.' Neve knelt and plucked a blade of grass from the ground and examined it. 'It's . . . it's quite true, there is beauty in a blade of grass but visible only to a dying man,' he smiled. 'Quite true.' He paused. 'It all went wrong right from the beginning really, those keen young officers volunteering for undercover work, inserted to find out about Pirie and his mob but instead they found out about . . . well . . . about me and Freddie Wolfe and those two there . . .' He pointed the gun at the bodies of Last and Parsloe.

'Makes no sense, Idris,' Vicary appealed. 'Phil Ott was running Operation Fennel; by inserting undercover officers he was digging a hole for himself . . . he was making a rod for his own back . . . he was hoist by his own petard.'

'No . . . no . . .' Neve smiled, 'Phil Ott was on the up and up when he inserted James Coventry and Jackie Boot and the others . . . the others who escaped when they saw how the ball was bouncing. Phil Ott, he had a big gambling problem, he was well in debt, threatening his marriage and his career in the police . . . he was a desperate man. He had his price and Parsloe brokered the deal. Pirie paid off his debts and then gave him a regular wedge . . . by then he was on our team. But two undercover officers had been dead for a number of years by then.'

'So that house in Norfolk,' Forbes sighed, 'it was bought with bent money after all?'

'Probably . . . as all our houses were.'

'So what happened to James Coventry?'

'We arranged for him to be alone and he was overpowered by thugs we hired from Pirie. Ex-army boys, do anything for money. Trussed him up and drowned him in the swimming pool of the villa we were also watching as part of Operation Fennel, while "Mole" Tew dug his grave in the forest. Jim Coventry just saw something he shouldn't.'

'Piers Parsloe in a flash car in Soho?'

'Yes, but that was sufficient.'

'And Jackie Boot? Did she fall or was she pushed?'

'Pushed, of course. We borrowed Pirie's boat for that, he was abroad at the time, but we wanted her body to be found, couldn't have two young officers vanishing.'

'We thought that was the case.'

'Cyril Barr?' Forbes asked.

'That was messy. We were following you, you see, knew everybody you talked to. Barr pushed it, took too much of an interest in Pirie's lock-up so we persuaded him to tell us why. Gave it all up in the end, told us about the photographs . . . we found them and destroyed them, negatives, the lot. Tom Last was cultivating him.' Neve pointed the gun at

Roderick Himes who was still screaming through gritted
teeth whilst holding his stomach. 'Told him to phone you,
kid on he was a friend of Cyril Barr's . . . and you're here.'

'Why didn't you let them go through with it? Nobody
could have proved anything.'

'Time to do the right thing.' Idris Neve calmly separated
the gun from the plastic bottle. 'My wife and family will be
all right, she knew nothing about the graft. I told her the
same cock-and-bull story that Freddie Wolfe told his wife.
I inherited it from a distant relative, laundered enough to see
her out in comfort. Freddie did the same, so did Parsloe and
Last. Whether she keeps it or not is a matter for her conscience
. . . same for the other wives.'

'Archie Dew?'

'You have to ask Phil Ott, that really was not our doing.'
Neve slowly but calmly brought the pistol up to his mouth.

'Don't do anything stupid, Idris,' Vicary appealed. 'You've
done well for yourself; you can negotiate something for
yourself.'

'I am implicated in . . .' he paused, '. . . I'm in too deep
to negotiate anything. No, this isn't stupid, it's just very, very
sensible.'

Mrs Forbes stood with her daughter in her daughter's bedroom
in Mead Way, Croydon. 'Something has happened,' she said,
'something which caused him to relent. I don't know what it
is or was. Your father is a very private person and after twenty
years of marriage I am still discovering things about him, so
I will probably never find out what caused his change of mind
but you can start going out with your friends again. But do
be careful. Do watch the alcohol intake . . . another episode
like the last one and . . . well, I doubt you'll get a second
chance. Now go and find him and thank him.'

'Seven murders?' The woman, dressed in a long coat and
fur hat, slid her arm inside the man's arm and glanced out
across the Thames estuary, grey and wind battered.

'Yes, seven all told; Jim Coventry, Jacqueline Boot, Archie
Dew, Freddie Wolfe . . . Cyril Barr . . . Last and Pirie . . . one
suicide by cop and two self-inflicted suicides – ten deaths. And

the only conviction was against Roderick Himes for threatening behaviour, reduced from unlawful possession of a firearm with intent to endanger life. He's a hard case, we'll hear of him again.' Vicary shivered despite the sheepskin coat he wore. 'But you know what irks me is the attitude of the wives.'

'The wives?'

'Or the widows I should probably say, Mrs Parsloe, Mrs Last, Mrs Wolfe, Mrs Neve and Mrs Ott, all five of them kept the money and the property their husbands left to them in their wills.'

'They did?'

'Yes, every penny, every brick and every square foot of land. Everything. Not one of them volunteered to return even a token sum to the Exchequer.'

'Heavens. But I thought you could recover proceeds of crime?'

'We can,' Vicary cast his eye across the grey waters of the estuary, 'but only from convicted persons. The wives committed no crime, not that we know of, and the money was thoroughly laundered. It's impossible to tell how much each man received.' He paused. 'You know we called on Mrs Parsloe shortly after her husband's funeral, found her taking up a new pair of jeans and wanting to talk only about her planned holiday to Scotland. She just would not be drawn on the issue of any immoral money she might have inherited . . . she's relocated to Scotland now anyway.'

'She must have enjoyed her holiday up there.' The woman squeezed his arm.

'She must have, her forwarding address is in one of the most prestigious areas of Edinburgh, but the point is that she has now placed herself under Scottish legislation, makes it more difficult for English law to reach her . . . not impossible, just an extra obstacle for us, but as I said, there is no evidence of any provable wrongdoing anyway, just the suggestion of amorality. The other women are content, it seems, to carry on living in the very desirable residences that their husbands could not possibly have been able to afford to buy on their modest police officer's salary.'

'As you say . . . amorality . . . if only if it was to keep a silence instead of voicing suspicions.'

'Well, that is police work, you get to know about one tenth of what actually happens.'

'But questions were answered. Puzzles solved. Closure achieved.'

'Yes, Mr and Mrs Coventry found out what had happened to Jim, they got a body to bury and now have a grave to visit and I discovered a place for us to visit . . . delightful spot.'

'Oh?'

'North Norfolk, lovely part of England, used to be famous only as near to the birthplace and home of Lord Nelson of Trafalgar. Getting quite posh now but still a pleasant place to visit . . . next full weekend off, yes?'

'Yes,' Kathleen squeezed his arm, 'but right now Herne Bay is perfect. Even in winter.'

'Well . . .' Harry Vicary returned the squeeze, 'room service will have finished their job by now. Shall we return to the hotel, Mrs Vicary?'

'Yes . . . husband of mine. Let's do that.'